By the same author

The Bait

Policewoman
  A young woman's initiation into the realities of justice

The Witness

An Inner Sanctum Mystery
by DOROTHY UHNAK

SIMON AND SCHUSTER

New York

PUBLISHED BY SIMON AND SCHUSTER

ROCKEFELLER CENTER, 630 FIFTH AVENUE

NEW YORK, NEW YORK 10020

FIRST PRINTING

SBN 671-20192-1

LIBRARY OF CONGRESS CATALOG CARD NUMBER: 69-14286

DESIGNED BY RICHARD C. KARWOSKI

MANUFACTURED IN THE UNITED STATES OF AMERICA

BY H. WOLFF, NEW YORK

To my mother and father, with love:
another promise kept

*The
Witness*

ONE:

Christie Opara opened her eyes and her body stiffened with the fear that she had overslept. She rolled onto her stomach and slid her fingers under the pillow. They curled around the small metal alarm clock and Christie held her breath until she saw the time: it was six-thirty. She had time, but not enough to lie back and close her eyes for just an extra minute. That was what had happened at six o'clock when the alarm shattered her sleep, and the minute had extended to half an hour. Moving mechanically, Christie got out of bed, placed the clock next to the radio on her dresser, turned on the radio and switched the air conditioner to high.

The commentator was reporting various disasters around the world, starting with international events: wars, skirmishes, their losses, our losses; national scene: politics, strikes, an air crash in the Midwest; moving closer to home: report on New York State lottery winners; and then circling in on New York City. By the time he finished describing some racial clashes on the East Side and some anticipated picketing by some group or other, Christie had her bed made, her pajamas folded and put away. She wanted to know what the weather was going to be; that was what was important to her. Two quick commercials and then, finally, the cheerful voice advised that it would probably break 100 again for the fourth day in a row. Christie snapped the radio off. Great. Just great.

9

She resisted the urge to let the shower run ice-cold over her. A tepid shower was better, although its effects wouldn't really last long. A heat wave. On what was to have been the first week of her vacation, they were in the middle of a heat wave. Christie rubbed the towel over her body. Damn Reardon. He had no right to switch her vacation around.

Christie flung the closet door open and searched indecisively among her dresses. Usually she had everything picked out before she went to bed: underwear, stockings, dress, shoes, pocketbook. But she hadn't gotten to bed until after two. That was Reardon's fault too. In a way. If she had gone out to Sag Harbor with Nora and Mickey, she wouldn't have been out last night with Gene O'Brien. Christie pulled a yellow cotton dress out of the closet, her mind on Gene. Her underclothes felt sticky against her still-damp body. She needed some time away from Gene. She needed some perspective on the whole thing.

Gene, at thirty, was a captain in the Police Department. Christie had first known him when he was Mike Opara's partner, working in plainclothes. They had both made the sergeant's list; Mike had been killed by a young narcotics addict and Gene hadn't. Gene, a bachelor intent on his carefully planned career, had gone on studying, taking the tests, getting the promotions. He hadn't come around as Mike's friend, looking after Mike's widow. In fact, Christie hadn't seen Gene O'Brien until last Christmas at a P.D. Emerald Society party and they were surprised to see each other. He had followed her career in the Department through unofficial channels and, of course, through the newspaper publicity that had accompanied her rise to first-grade detective, but they had just never run into each other.

The sight of Gene O'Brien had momentarily opened old wounds, but Christie had learned not to live in the past. She told him of her present: of her son Mickey, six years old and the living image of his dead father; of wonderful Nora, Mike's widowed mother, who lived with them. She hadn't told him about her job: just that she was assigned to the

D.A.'s Special Investigations Squad, and that said as much as he should know or she would reveal. These last months Christie had seen Gene frequently, casually at first; then gradually their relationship had assumed an intensity which Christie was not quite sure she wanted.

Christie slipped the dress over her head and began to zip up the back. She caught a glimpse of herself in the mirror and stopped. Damn. She stepped out of the dress, slipped it back on the hanger. That would be a great dress for a tail job. Christie forced herself to plan. She needed something quiet and inconspicuous. She selected a lightweight blue denim shift, then dug in a drawer for some scarves. A bright-red print and a solid navy. Alternated, they could change her appearance enough.

Christie carried the transistor down to the kitchen. The silence of the house depressed her. She made some toast and instant coffee after first reaching for some eggs and deciding against them. Nora spoiled her: bacon and eggs, fresh coffee, toast all ready. Nora insisted she wasn't trying to add to Christie's slight frame; she was merely setting a good example for her grandson. Christie licked beads of moisture from her upper lip. At least Mickey and Nora were out at the beach cottage. Christie's brother Christopher had the usual mob out there: his wife and their four boys, a few cousins, Nora, Mickey. There was always room. She glanced at her watch. Her timing was good.

The seven-o'clock news was a rehash of the earlier stories of continuing gloom, doom and despair, and Christie didn't listen. As she rinsed the cup and plate, she began putting the blame exactly where it belonged.

On Reardon. Casey Reardon. He had waited until Friday to inform her that instead of leaving for vacation, she had to postpone her plans for a week. The assignment didn't make sense. And she wasn't too sure of the legality of it, either. Christie dried the dishes and put them away and her mind lingered on that aspect of her assignment. It would seem to her that it wasn't exactly legal for the Supervising Assistant

District Attorney of New York County to assign a first-grade detective to tail his own daughter. The People of the City of New York might resent paying first-grade money to someone for following a college girl from Jamaica Estates to Columbia University for five days. Was someone trying to abduct the girl? Had Reardon received threatening phone calls or letters? If he had, he certainly hadn't told Christie Opara.

In fact, all Mr. Reardon had told Christie was that one of his twin daughters, Barbara, was taking a few summer courses at Columbia and the courses would end the first week in August. Something had come up, Reardon had said vaguely, and he wanted Christie to see that the girl got to the University and back home. Period. The expression on Reardon's face had stopped Christie's questions cold. He had waved his hand abruptly, then said, "I guess I don't have to tell you that this is strictly between us—strictly confidential." At least she had had the final word: "You were right the first time, Mr. Reardon. You *don't* have to tell me."

Christie picked up a pair of torn sneakers and wondered if they were to be thrown out or if they were a favorite pair that Mickey had forgotten to take. She would ask him when she called tonight.

Reardon's assignment not only annoyed her; it unnerved her as well. What if Reardon's daughter was planning to elope with some boy? Christie smiled at the thought. Maybe she'd be a witness at some hurried City Hall ceremony. After all, Reardon hadn't instructed her. All he had said was "Use your judgment if anything comes up." Christie slipped sunglasses and tissues into her pocketbook and checked the vital contents: detective shield, .38-caliber Smith & Wesson revolver, makeup case, comb, scarves and keys.

She clicked the radio off in the middle of the 7:30 news. She couldn't care less about demonstrations and racial violence this morning. Her main concern was the weather and it was hot.

TWO:

The similarity between the two men was startling. In height, build, darkness of skin, lightness of eye, they could easily be mistaken one for the other. They were both twenty-three years old with high cheekbones, aquiline noses, thin lips, hair cropped to the contours of their skulls. Each was dressed in a white cotton knit shirt, which indicated the lean hardness of somewhat thin shoulders, and clean starched chinos, which emphasized the narrowness of hips.

The dreariness of the small furnished room was filled with an intensity that seemed to bounce off the walls and furnishings, touching everything except Rafe Wheeler. He lay stretched the length of the lumpy mattress, his arms over his head, his eyes half closed in concentration on a small piece of plaster that was hanging by a tiny edge in the middle of an old ceiling pattern. His eyes shifted without blinking or widening to Eddie Champion.

"Hey, man, can't you just light somewhere? I mean, you been going like this all night. We don't have long to wait now."

Champion whirled from the small window through which he could see nothing but a garbage-laden back alley. He yanked the stained window shade down and it snapped sharply and spun around the roller. "God damn," he said, and pulled it back into place. His hands seemed alive with the need to hold onto something and he jerked a cigarette from his shirt pocket, put it between his lips, patted his trousers for matches, then tossed the cigarette in annoyance onto the small table.

"You just lie there," he said accusingly to Rafe Wheeler. "You just lie there like nothing." His eyes narrowed against the dimness of the room and his hands worked along the intricate pattern of the footboard, grasping and sliding. His voice was low and hoarse. "What gets to you, man? I been wondering about you. I been wondering plenty about you."

Rafe sat up, pulling himself into a cross-legged position. His face was calm and relaxed. "You just go right on wondering, Champ."

"I mean it, Rafe. I seen you. Sleeping like a baby all night. Now, that's just not natural. Considering."

Rafe smiled. "Why, you just like to go to pieces, Champ. I never expected that of you. I surely didn't."

Champion's body stiffened from his neck down to his feet. He felt his toes curl against the soles of his shoes, and his fingers tightened. "Listen, you cool bastard . . ."

A hardness crossed Rafe's face but it was the only tensing visible. His posture was still easy, loose. "We *supposed* to keep it cool, remember? Maybe you keeping it all to yourself making it harder on you. But"—he moved his hand in the air "you tell me what you want to. Any way you want it, Champ. Maybe take some pressure off you, you tell me now what's going to be."

Champion stood absolutely still, a flicker of suspicion pulling at his mouth. "Tell you when we get there. Soon enough. Tell you when I tell you, and you better be ready. I'm in charge of this operation and we do it *my* way."

"Be ready. For whatever."

Champion kneaded his fingers, hunched his shoulders, stretched his arms. He seemed to be trying to escape from his body. He rubbed his neck, and a long, ugly, wordless sound came from between his parted lips. He stalked to the window, pushed the shade aside, glared down into the alley. He looked at his wristwatch. "Seven-thirty. You got seven-thirty?"

Without moving, Rafe confirmed the time. "Seven-thirty. We got two more hours."

Two more hours; the weight of time hit Champion. It was the heat of the room, the smallness of the place and that son of a bitch so untouched by it all. "The hell. Going out for some coffee."

"I'll make us some fresh instant on the hot plate. Relax."

"Forget it. Sick of that crap. Need some real coffee and some air. I be back in fifteen minutes."

Rafe eased himself back onto the bed, stretched his body. "Suit yourself. Bring back a cool breeze, will you, baby?" He winked and smiled.

Champion stood for a moment, regarding him thoughtfully; then he shrugged. "Okay, man, I'll just do that."

Rafe Wheeler did not move for six minutes: six full minutes by his watch. There was no point in looking out the window; Champion wouldn't be in the alley. He slipped his loafers off and walked silently to the door, opened it slightly, his body positioned so that his shadow wouldn't be cast into the hallway. He listened for a moment without breathing, his teeth pressed tightly together, then eased himself out of the room. It was a break he hadn't dared hope for and it had been Champion's own idea. That made it even better.

He removed the receiver from the wall phone and dropped a dime in the slot, shocked by the loud clang as the coin made contact. It was unnerving how loud an ordinary dial tone could sound. He dialed quickly, his slender brown finger impatiently picking out the next number before the dial returned from the previous spin. The phone rang twice and was interrupted midway through the third ring by a terse "Yeah?"

"It's me," Rafe said. His whisper was loud in his own ear.

"What's up?"

"Going to be a shooting this morning. At the construction

15

site. He still don't trust me enough to say who or why. But it's going to be a real bad one. He's got a gun. None of us is supposed to but I know he's got a gun. He don't know I saw it and—"

"Yeah? Go on, kid. Anything wrong? Rafe?"

Rafe stood with the receiver pressed against his ear, his voice frozen in his throat. He could hear words calling out to him from the earpiece and the rising concern in that normally quiet, steady, controlled voice.

Champion had moved from the shadowed darkness behind the staircase and he was smiling and his voice was pleasant. "I *knew* it. God damn, but I just *knew* it."

Rafe said nothing. There was nothing to say, and even if there had been, he was physically unable to make a sound.

"Don't even tell the man goodbye," Champion instructed softly. "Just hang up."

Rafe heard the voice as though it were inside of his head, calling out to him even after it was cut off abruptly when he replaced the receiver. As though hypnotized, he moved backwards into the room in response to the wordless but definite gestures of his roommate, who leaned against the door, shutting and locking it behind him.

He had two sharp, distinct impressions. The first was that Eddie Champion was relaxed for the first time in days, his hand absolutely steady and certain as he pressed the nozzle of the .38 revolver against Rafe's forehead. The second impression—the last Rafe Wheeler was ever to have—was that just before he squeezed the trigger, Champion's eyes seemed to have turned the strangest color: almost yellow.

THREE:

Casey Reardon scowled over an article in *The New York Times*, making quick, uneven slashes with his pen under certain sentences, bracketing a paragraph to indicate that the article would bear closer reading later in the day. He reached absently for his cup, not noticing it was empty. He looked up, raising his chin slightly, indicating the cup.

Katherine Reardon took the cup from her husband's hand, carried it into the kitchen, and filled it with strong black coffee, adding one level spoonful of sugar and just a drop of milk. She caught a glimpse of herself, reflected in the gleaming window of the wall oven, adjusted a loose lock of dark hair, licked her lips. She intoned a silent prayer that Casey would forget about this second cup of coffee and leave for the office, but reentering the dining room, she realized it was too late.

Her daughter Barbara hadn't listened to her advice; she never did. Katherine should have expected it. Casey didn't look up from his newspaper; he reached automatically for the cup which he knew would be placed at hand. Katherine tried to motion Barbara into the kitchen but the girl stood at her place and loudly greeted her father.

"Good morning. Nice weather for a change, isn't it?"

Not looking up, Casey answered, "Good morning."

Still standing, the girl spoke in an unnaturally bright voice. "Good day for the day's event, wouldn't you say?"

Casey raised his face, an expression of annoyance freezing his features. Slowly, he surveyed his daughter.

Katherine brought the pot of coffee to the table, poured some for Barbara. "Sit down and eat something, Barbara."

"What the hell are you got up for?"

Sitting now, stirring the coffee, buttering a piece of toast with nervous jabs, the girl said softly, "You know what for."

Casey clicked the ball-point open-closed, open-closed. "No. Tell me."

"*You know*," the girl insisted.

"I would say, judging from the evidence at hand, that you were going on a picnic or a field trip or maybe to rob a gas station. Dungarees, turtleneck"—he ducked his head down under the table—"and sneakers."

"You know," Barbara said, her voice wavering.

Casey's voice hardened, his pale eyes seeming to fill with color. "No. I don't know. Because, it seems to me—now, I may be wrong. God knows, I'm often wrong. At least in this house. But it seems to me we had a conversation about, oh, about two nights ago. Relative to your nonappearance at any rallies, strikes, protests, rabble-rousings, lynchings, book burnings, et cetera. It also seems to me that we discussed the entire matter quite thoroughly and came to some conclusions."

Her eyes dropped to the cup and she played her spoon over the surface of the coffee.

"Look up at me when I talk to you!"

She jerked her head up and the spoon leaped convulsively across the table, but her eyes met his steadily if with effort. Christ, those round eyes: Casey felt a surge of admiration and respect, of love and anger. Those familiar eyes, trying to stare him down. "Go ahead, I'm listening."

He could see the quick blinking, the dry swallow, the resolve that she would speak without letting her voice give her away. "All right, Dad. I am going to the Lincoln construction site this morning. We are going to protest the prejudice, narrowness, unfairness, cruelty, unfairness . . . rottenness of the hiring practices of the building trades." She bit her lip, aware that her voice had risen. "And," she said softly now, "we are going to sit down, lie down, stop the trucks and the bigots from building that federally sponsored project!"

Casey nodded curtly and ran his finger over his bottom lip. "Uh-huh. That's what you're going to do?"

"Yes."

He glanced at his wife; she nervously fingered the collar of her robe. Her lips trembled and her voice was too loud. "Casey, I've talked to her. You know I've talked to her. She won't listen to me."

He covered his forehead with his hand, addressing his daughter. "Are you going to get arrested too? Going to lie down on the street and have the policemen—you know, the big burly fascist brutes—drag you away? Did they teach you how to relax your body, how to let yourself go limp so that your—what? hundred and ten pounds?—will seem like a hundred and ninety?" His voice became harsh and mocking. "And did they tell you what to say when they drag you past the TV men and the newspapermen? Do you have it by rote, or what—you gonna play it by ear?"

Her face paled and he knew the shame she experienced at being unable to control the long tears that streamed down her smooth cheeks, but she ignored them by refusing to wipe them away.

"And did they tell you," he said brittlely, "how to handle things in five years, ten years, from now, when you are in the middle of a career or married to some nice guy who's looking to get ahead in life and a routine check of his background— your background—shows, in *red ink,* that Barbara Reardon, when she was just a confused little college girl of eighteen, got mixed up with a bunch of hippies and got herself locked up and dumped in a tank with an assortment of prostitutes and boosters and junkies? And maybe that she did thirty days as protest? Huh?"

She smeared the tears across her face with the back of her hand, as his voice became softer but at the same time crueler.

"Oh, I know; the future doesn't matter. You don't want any kind of future that isn't *your* kind of future. Right? Christ, you little dumbbell. If there was anything I thought I could count on it was your intelligence: that your brains could put a check on your emotionalism."

There was a stark, empty silence now; he picked up the cup and drained the coffee, then slammed the cup back onto the saucer. He looked up suddenly, confronted by his other daughter, Ellen, firstborn of his eighteen-year-old twins. "Well, the Sleeping Beauty has decided to favor us with her presence. And what the hell are you made up for—the Grand Ball?"

Ellen glanced uncertainly at her mother, then at her sister. Not able to measure the conflict, unprepared for her father's attack, she said, "We're having the college fashion show today at Lord and Taylor's, Dad. I told you about it. I'm one of the commentators."

Casey slapped his hand on the table. "Jesus Christ," he intoned. "Jumping Jesus Christ. One hippie and one clothes horse and both out of the same egg! It's funny. I mean, in a way, it's really funny, only maybe I don't have a sense of humor."

Barbara, her paleness flushed by anger, shot out at him. "Oh, you have a sense of humor all right, Dad. A good, sharp, biting sense of humor! Maybe what you lack is a *sense of justice!*"

Katherine, her voice shrill, her eyes on Casey, said, "Barbara, don't you dare talk like that to your father!"

Casey waved his hand impatiently at his wife. "No, let her go ahead and say what she thinks. I think that's very interesting, Barbara, I really do. I see, I get it now. *You* have a sense of justice. *You* understand what it's all about. *Not me.* I've spent the last sixteen years of my life in courtrooms and investigating rooms and in every corner and alley of this city, so how could *I* possibly have any sense of justice? I'm warped. Yes, I see: I'm not pure and innocent, seeing things as clearly as you."

The quiet mockery of his voice was his most effective weapon with Barbara. Knowing how desperately she wanted to be taken seriously, knowing the urgency of her feelings, he could reduce her to spouting the slogans she now began reciting impassionedly.

"Justice? In the courtroom? *Equal* justice, Dad? For poor and rich? For black and white? For Puerto Ricans? For the articulate and the inarticulate? And—justice for all? Where, Dad, where?"

He leaned back easily, his elbows resting on the arms of his chair, his hands dangling loosely. Not answering her, he could defeat her. She continued until she realized her voice betrayed her; trembling, it merely mouthed words that suddenly seemed to have no meaning, that did not convey her feelings. Stopping in the middle of a sentence, she pressed her hand over her mouth and leaped to her feet, knocking over her chair. Katherine gasped; Ellen looked up, her eyes wide. Casey didn't move or blink. In one final burst, Barbara whispered, "You don't prosecute in your courtrooms; *you persecute!*"

"Good exit line," Casey muttered at the empty place where his daughter had been. He motioned at the chair. "Ellen, be a good girl; pick up your sister's chair." He folded his newspaper carefully, clicked his pen and placed it in his jacket pocket.

"May I be excused," Ellen murmured softly, leaving before anyone answered her.

Katherine took a small sip of her coffee, waiting.

Casey whistled between his teeth, shook his head. "Breakfast at the Reardons'. This is going to be quite a day. We're off and running."

He headed for the telephone on the desk and Katherine called out softly, "Casey? Casey, what about Barbara?"

He stopped dialing, replaced the receiver and turned to face his wife. Katherine Reardon was smaller than her daughters, a fragile, pretty, slender woman. She turned her hands palms up and shook her head.

"I don't understand her, Casey. I just don't understand her. *Why* does she want to get *involved* in these things? Why can't she just . . . just . . ."

Reardon inhaled slowly. Her bewilderment was genuine. Her daughters, particularly Barbara, were a mystery to her. They always had been. What was it he had told her the day they were born, the day she apologized for giving birth to two girls? "You raise the girls, Kath, I'll raise the boys." But there hadn't been any boys for the simple, or complicated, reason that there hadn't been any Katherine. He had accepted that a very long time ago, not easily, but with a tense finality. She looked so forlorn, so completely at a loss, standing there before him. Casey reached out, pushed a stray lock of black hair from her forehead then dropped his hand abruptly in response to the familiar tightening of her lips.

"Don't worry about it. *I'll* talk to her, okay?" She nodded, hesitantly. "It'll be all right, Katherine. *I'll* take care of it." The way I always have. The unspoken words hung between them for a minute, then his wife, reassured, smiled.

"It's just a stage she's going through. I can't seem to keep up with all these 'stages,' Casey, that's all."

He turned his back and spoke so softly and quickly into the telephone that she couldn't hear him. Nor would she have been interested if she had heard him. After all, Casey's job was Casey's responsibility.

Barbara Reardon sat hunched on the window seat of her room, staring vacantly out the window without seeing the garden or the leafy branches of the tree that tapped against the pane with every small breeze. Her arms were wrapped around her knees, her chin rested on her locked hands. She heard her father's step, the light, springy tread on the stairs, the sharp click of his shoes on the uncarpeted section of the hallway, then the three sharp raps on her door.

Rubbing her hands over her face, she called out, "Come in."

Casey motioned for her to stay where she was. He stood looking out the window, his eyes almost orange in the sunlight. He ran his hand over his thick dark red hair and pressed his palm against the cowlick at the crown of his head. She could see the muscles of his jawline moving; he was grinding his teeth. He plunged his hands into his trouser pockets and sat down beside her, pushing her feet over with his knee.

"Barbara, I don't have the time this morning to go into all of this with you. I know that your feelings are sincere. I know that your beliefs are sincere. But I think you should know that my feelings and my beliefs are equally sincere. Also, I think you're mature enough to give some thought to the facts. I've got twenty-five years on you. I may not have learned much but I've learned a few things you don't know anything about. Hasn't it ever occurred to you that your old man might—just *might*—know a little more than you?"

She tried to use the weapons of silence and a cold stare, but he smiled, reached his hand to her knee and shook it lightly. "Babs—oh, Babs. Christ. I wish you were ten years old again. I'd whack the hell out of you and that would be it. But you're eighteen and you're all grown up and you know all there is to know and you have all the solutions." He glanced at his watch. "I've got one hell of a day ahead of me. I've got enough things to worry about without your adding to it. We'll talk it over tonight, okay?"

She clenched her hands tightly around her knees, raised her face to him. "I'm going, Dad. *I am going!*"

His face tightened and his voice, while still low, was unyielding. "Barbara, get one thing straight. You are still my daughter. You are still living under my roof. You will do what I say, whether you approve or disapprove of my decisions."

"I have responsibilities! You're the one who taught me that! You said every individual has to learn to be responsible—"

"Don't misquote me, for Christ's sake, not to my face." He rubbed the back of his neck angrily. "Learn to be responsible for *yourself*—for *yourself*—before you undertake the respon-

23

sibility of the whole human race." Again, the watch: the time racing him. He started to cross the room.

"I am going, Dad."

Now his anger burst forth, and he planted his feet wide apart, facing her, his finger jabbing the air. "Okay, now *I'll tell you*. You listen, and get this straight. Get yourself out of those clothes and put on a dress and stockings and some lipstick and get your goddam school books together and get yourself to classes today; and when your classes are over, you get yourself home and up here to your room and you stay here until I come home." The dark eyes, glistening, challenged him; he took a slow, deep breath. "Because if you make the slightest attempt to attend that goddam demonstration, I'll tell you what's going to happen. Two of my men are going to be there. There will be one detective at each side of you the minute you show up. And they will very quietly escort you to a car—very quietly so no one will even notice you. And there will be no reporters to ask you your educated sophomoric opinions and your learned intellectual judgments on society as you see it. Just two guys from my squad who will quietly and gently and firmly escort you home and will see to it that you remain in your room until I come home. Then I will write a letter to the Dean of Students at Sarah Lawrence and notify her that Miss Reardon, who was allowed to make an independent decision and take summer courses at Columbia, has now made another independent decision. She has decided to abandon all her great plans for a B.A. and an M.A. and a goddam Ph.D. that was going to qualify her to save the world from the mess her father and his generation have created. And that Miss Reardon, although she has never earned the price of a sneaker in her life, has decided to become self-supporting and independent. And that Mr. Reardon, as a thoroughly modern father, who has been footing all the bills up to this point, feels that his daughter is mature enough to know what the hell she is doing."

"You really would do that, wouldn't you?"

24

"You know it!"

She dropped her face to her knees, and when she looked up, her face was red and wet.

Reardon stood waiting impatiently. "I want your word, Barbara."

"Do I have any choice?"

"I just gave you your choice."

"Did you? No. You said, *'My way or my way.'* That's always my choice, isn't it, Dad?"

"I want your word," he repeated.

"Is my word any good? I mean, will you take my word?"

"I always have, Barbara, and I better be able to."

She stood up, planting herself in front of her father, her chin raised. "All right. All right, you have my word. *Your way:* like a good, obedient little girl. Daddy does all the thinking in the family. Daddy tells us what to think, what to feel, what to believe, what to say and what to do. Brainless little Barbara, and brainless little Ellen and brainless—"

"Watch it, Barbara," he warned.

"And brainless little Mother," she continued, defying him, "all do exactly what Daddy says!"

His reaction quicker than his control, Casey slapped his daughter sharply across the mouth, then whirled away from her and crossed the room. He pulled the door open, then turned, coldly regarding her stunned face. "Okay. Is that what you wanted? 'Daddy is nothing but a brute.' Okay, that's the way you want it—that's the way you got it!" He slammed the door behind him and, cursing, took the stairs two at a time.

Reardon yanked his dark brown suit jacket from the back of the dining room chair. His anger was directed at himself now. That was a hell of a demonstration of intellect over emotion he had just given Barbara. He bunched his fingers into a fist and jammed his arm through a sleeve. He turned so quickly that he collided with Ellen, who had just come to the hallway. For a fleeting moment, seeing her, he thought she was Barbara. It was a mistake he hadn't made for many

25

years. "Ellen? Give me a hand with this damn jacket, will you?"

She held it for him, eased it over his shoulders. He leaned toward her briefly, gave her a kiss on the forehead. "Thanks, Ellie. See you."

She held his arm. "Dad, could I talk to you for a minute?"

"Look, it's all right. Take that worried look off your face. Come on, Ellie, no problems with you, okay? I'm late as it is."

She nodded, not speaking. Christ, Reardon thought, how could the one face look so different on the two girls? The same small pale oval, the same dark hair and brows, the same intensely blue eyes, yet this was unmistakably Ellen, and because it was he had that old, vague feeling that he was giving her the short end of something. He reached impulsively to her long silky hair. "Okay, Ellen, make it quick. What's the problem?"

Her eyes didn't quite meet his. Her voice, low and barely audible, was apologetic. "Dad, that fashion show I told you about? You know, at Lord and Taylor's?"

"Yeah?"

"Well, I guess this isn't the right time, but . . ." She hesitated, then spoke rapidly. "It's being held in conjunction with the Peace Corps—it's an international show to interest college students in . . ."

Reardon nodded brusquely and pressed a bill into her hand. Ellen looked at the money, puzzled. "Will this solve *your* problem, Ellie? A twenty, okay? If you see something that this won't cover, use Mother's charge plate. Tell her I said so, okay?" Reardon stopped speaking, trying to figure what the hell was wrong. She smiled, but even in his acceptance of her brief cheek kiss, he caught that something: something. Well, he'd worry about that later. "Tell Mother I might be late tonight. See you, Ellie."

Detective Tom Dell turned the key and started the motor so that the black Pontiac was ready to move as soon as Casey

Reardon settled into the front seat beside him. Dell, who had been waiting patiently in front of the house for nearly forty minutes, noted that his boss had not returned his greeting.

Reardon's first words were a terse order. "Make a U-turn and take the hill slow."

"Opara's down there at the bus stop, Mr. Reardon," Dell assured him.

Reardon stiffened, turned so that he was confronting Dell. He spoke between clenched teeth. "If it wouldn't be too much trouble for you, Detective Dell, I mean if it wouldn't put you out too much, would you mind turning this goddam vehicle in the other direction and taking the goddam hill real slow?"

Dell kept his eyes averted from Reardon's face. "Yes, sir." It was going to be one of those days.

Reardon slumped in the seat and pressed his knees against the dashboard. He saw Christie Opara before she spotted the car coming toward her. She was leaning against the iron post that supported the bus-stop sign, the second stop from his house. Her hair, cropped short, was brightened to light blond in the glare of the sun. She dangled a folded copy of *The New York Times* between two fingers and turned her face up toward the hill. She didn't move or give any indication that she had seen him, and yet Reardon caught it all as they slowly rolled past her. The slim, long-legged girl pulled away from the post, her chin raised slightly in his direction. Though she was wearing large, round sunglasses, he could see the expression on her face. He glanced into the rearview mirror without adjusting it and saw that she had turned, staring after the car. Reardon could feel her anger and resentment and it intensified his own irritation. He swore softly and directionlessly and Tom Dell kept his eyes on the road.

This was starting out to be one hell of a day.

FOUR:

Casey Reardon flicked the switch on his air conditioner back and forth, impatiently waiting for the motor to turn over. He had a natural antipathy toward all mechanical appliances, and this malfunctioning air conditioner was no exception. He smashed the palm of his hand against the machine and drew forth a low moaning response, followed by a soft, tentative chugging and turning that did not promise much relief from the thick hotness of his large office. He surveyed the disordered condition of his desk. Various reports and case files lay scattered from one end to the other, exactly where he had left them the night before.

Reardon held his thumb firmly on the lever of his intercom. "Detective Ginsburg, come in here."

He released the lever before hearing any response and looked up expectantly as a shadowy figure filled the smoked-glass top of his door. "Come in, come in."

Marty Ginsburg was not smiling. He had been in Reardon's squad long enough to know that when Mr. Reardon walked through the squad office and directly to his own office without breaking stride, it was a morning to be very careful. And very official.

"Yes, sir?" he inquired politely.

"Where the hell is Stoney?" Reardon's hand swept above the disarray of his desk, then indicated the entire room. "You heard from him, or what? He taking a day off or what?"

"Stoner called in about twenty minutes ago, Mr. Reardon."

"That was damn nice of him. Where is he?"

"Well, he didn't exactly say . . ."

Reardon's hand moved roughly over his face in two quick motions, from his forehead to his chin, then up again, his fingers pushing through his thick, short red hair. His eyes, a clear amber, were very still and his voice was very cold. "Well, what *exactly* did he say or do you want me to play twenty questions and try to guess?"

Marty self-consciously tried to flatten his stomach so that the strain of material across his middle would not be too noticeable. "Stoney called about twenty minutes ago and said to tell you that something unexpected came up and that he had to look into it. And that he would be in touch with you as soon as he checked it out." Reardon stood still, not even blinking, and Marty impulsively offered a quick commentary. "He sounded kind of funny, Mr. Reardon."

Reardon's head moved slightly. "He sounded kind of *funny?* Amusing, you mean?"

Ginsburg wiped his forehead and tried to push the heavy dark hair back into place. "No, sir. He sounded—like something was really wrong. You know."

Reardon didn't know and there were too many possibilities for him to begin guessing. "You and Ferranti got that report ready for me? You're working on that parking-meter thing, right?"

Detectives Ginsburg and Ferranti had spent four days interviewing various coin collectors, field supervisors, minor executives and major executives relative to a missing sum of money due to the City of New York. They had been overwhelmed by the intricacies of a bookkeeping system that seemed to provide no checks or balances.

"We're working on it right now, Mr. Reardon. Boy, what a screwy setup those guys have. I'd say the shortage could range all the way up to a quarter of a million bucks during the last two years."

"How about saying it on paper," Reardon told him shortly.

"Yes, sir." He headed for the door, regretting that neither he nor Ferranti was a very good typist.

Reardon consulted his watch. "You heard from Opara yet?"

"No, sir, but she'll probably be buzzing in any minute." It was a routine attempt to cover for a squad member, but Reardon's eyes were like two glints of fire and Marty left the office quickly.

Reardon systematically went through the stacks of material on his desk, quickly scanning those things with which he was familiar, scrawling an illegible "R" in the upper right-hand corner of those reports which he considered to be complete, drawing large jagged question marks in the margins of papers that did not satisfy him. He felt a muggy draft of air aimed directly at the back of his neck; the air conditioner was making some progress after all.

He opened the second drawer of his desk and rested his feet on it, leaning well back in his chair. Rather than cleaning his smudged horn-rimmed reading glasses, he pushed them up onto his forehead and scowled at a sheaf of yellow lined papers. He had forgotten about the lecture he was scheduled to present to the National Conference of Law Enforcement Officials next week. He read the first few paragraphs out loud, then balled up the entire wad of papers and tossed them against the wall behind him, feeling some slight satisfaction when he heard them drop into the wastebasket. He wondered why the hell he ever let himself get drawn into these conferences—especially summer conferences. All those police chiefs and public prosecutors and public defenders from small cities and towns all over the country, arriving en masse surrounded by dowdy wives and damp sweaty kids, descending on New York in the middle of a heat wave. Like hell they were interested in "New Aspects of Law Enforcement: How Close an Interpretation of Recent Supreme Court Rulings?" What they wanted was to take Circle Line tours, see television shows, have specially reserved seats at Radio City Music Hall, gape from the top of the Empire

State Building, and eat roast beef instead of creamed chicken at the final banquet. His wife had stopped attending these things a long time ago. Reardon swallowed the last tepid mouthful of coffee from the ten-cent mug that was distinguished by the red marker legend: "*I Am the Boss.*" His wife had stopped a lot of things—a long time ago. He consulted his watch, then jammed the intercom lever. "Any fresh coffee out there?"

He waited for the coffee, rather than an answer. When a faint tap sounded at his door, he didn't look up. It would be Ginsburg with the coffee. He slid his cup across the desk, then raised his eyes.

Detective Stoner Martin was a tall, hard-muscled man whose appearance at any given moment could be described as "neat"; even if an assignment called for him to be dressed in torn or faded workman's denims, something about Stoner, his style, his way of holding himself, gave him a particular distinction. He was a dark-skinned Negro with an intelligent face and a low-pitched voice.

Reardon forgot his annoyance after his first glance at Stoner. He put his cup down and watched as the detective slumped into the chair before his desk. When he lit the cigarette that had been between his lips from the moment he entered the room, his hand trembled.

Reardon stood up, concerned. "Hey, Stoney—what's up?"

Stoner Martin raised his head. "They got my boy," he said quietly.

Reardon's mouth opened and he felt a numbness along his throat and down into his chest. "Johnnie?" he asked, thinking of Stoner's son.

Slowly Stoner shook his head. "No. Not Johnnie. My other boy: Rafe Wheeler." He raised a long index finger, held it in the center of his forehead. "Pow. Right between the eyes."

FIVE:

William Everett spooned the heavy oatmeal from his dish to his mouth with the precision of a man who did things according to an irreversible plan. One large dish of oatmeal, heavily laced with honey and stirred with cream, preceded by four ounces of fresh orange juice and followed by one slice of buttered toast and hot sweet cocoa, was the breakfast he had consumed every day of his life for the last forty years. It was, he maintained, the reason for his perfect health at age sixty-one and directly responsible for the successful delivery of the United States mail, day after day, regardless of the season, in that particular area of Brooklyn which was the responsibility of postman William C. Everett, Sr.

William C. Everett, Jr., had abandoned the gluey breakfast which, his father insisted, had contributed not only to his son's lean physical stamina but had somehow mysteriously seen him through high school and college and through two years of Columbia Law School.

The silence in the Everett kitchen, interrupted only by eating sounds, was not the customary, considerate silence among three people who were comfortable and contented in each other's company. It was a tense silence this morning, as it had been every morning this week, and it was to be interrupted at any moment by angry words. Lucinda Everett tried not to watch the two men, but this was impossible, and her glances, first at the stoic face of her husband as he concentrated on his breakfast, then at the controlled calmness of her son, made her want to cry out, to rush toward each of them. But Lucinda quietly sipped her tea and said nothing, waiting for the moment when her husband would scoop up the last spoonful, then place the spoon neatly in the emptied dish.

Billy, at twenty-two, was so like William in appearance, but Lucinda could not pinpoint the source of his intensity. The stubbornness, yes; but William's had been a slow, deliberate, mule-patient stubbornness, and she knew, though William would not—could not—admit it, that he, too, was frightened and puzzled by their son's determination.

As the spoon hit the dish and the dish was pushed toward the center of the table, William looked up and it began, as she had known it would.

"So, you're going to get yourself arrested today," he said.

Billy put his cup soundlessly on the saucer, his fingers clenching the handle tightly. He moved his chair back and his eyes met his father's. "Pop, please. Can't we let it go?"

"Going to get yourself arrested," the older man said wonderingly, as though this were the first time he had ever considered the situation. "Going to take four years of college and two years of law school and put it all right on down the drain." He shook his head over the strangeness of his son.

"Pop, every morning and every night for a week, you've said what you've had to say, I've said what I've had to say. Nothing's changed."

"Nothing's changed? Nothing's changed? Everything's changed. Every damn thing in this house has changed!"

It wasn't the unexpected loudness of her husband's voice that frightened Lucinda, terrified her. It was the fact that for the first time in thirty years of marriage she had heard her husband swear.

"Everything in the world is changing, Pop. Things don't change all by themselves. *People* have to make them change. *I* have to make them change. Can't you understand that?"

The older man stared at the empty oatmeal dish for a mo-

33

ment, lost in his own thoughts. When he looked up, Billy saw a face he had never seen before. It was an expression Lucinda had hoped never to see again. His voice trembled and he spoke with great effort. "You listen to me, boy. You just listen to me, you great world changer, you young damn fool! You see this hand? You see the color of this hand and the color of this arm and the color of this face?"

Billy felt his breath catch inside his throat and he could neither inhale nor exhale. He sat fascinated as his father clutched at himself, one hand tearing at an arm, plucking at hard leathery cheeks.

"Every day of my life, for more than sixty years, this is what I've seen in the mirror and this is what I will see until the day I die. You the only black man in this house? You the only black man raising up his people—fighting the hurts? What you know about it? Dear Jesus, what you know about it?"

He lapsed into old patterns of speech which his son had never heard before but which Lucinda remembered from some terrible time, long before their son had been born.

"You born and raised here in this nice house in Brooklyn and you grew up here in this nice house and your playmates—be they white or black—all welcome here and you welcome in most of their homes, so what you know about it?" The large dark fingers clenched into a fist which pounded the table so violently that the dish rattled and seemed about to fly into the air. "You think carrying your signs and singing your songs and lying yourselves down and getting arrested is the way? You think your father and your mother never did nothing in their lives?"

"Pop, no, really—"

William cut his son off sharply. "No, you shut your mouth and listen to me now and I'm going to tell you what you don't know. You fool boy. We waited to have you, all those years, till we could afford this house, and we bought this house before you were born, when your mama was carrying you and we were the *first*. It wasn't like it is now with agencies to call up and them sending all the fancy college men over with their writs and their civil rights saying nobody could deny us. No, sir. It was your mama and me and we stuck it out and her carrying you and half crazy with what they would do next." The old man's eyes were glazed, cast back upon things he had never forgotten but never before revealed. "With that telephone ringing and those filthy mouths whispering and screaming things at us, and paint smeared all over the steps and windows crashing in at night." He stopped speaking abruptly and a change came over him. His face relaxed, his body seemed to grow larger, straightening from the base of his spine to his neck and shoulders. His voice was normal now, quiet, controlled, and Billy, looking at his father's face, had never loved him more than at that moment. "We went through it, boy, every day of our lives. I went out that door and walked down that street with my head up and I pretended I didn't see the words painted on our front walk and pretended I didn't see that the little flower bed your mama had planted was all tore up and messed with garbage and excrement. I pretended I didn't see the signs in the windows of most houses on this block, big, hand-printed signs, all the same: THIS HOUSE FOR SALE—NIGGER NEIGHBORHOOD. We got through those days and some of them moved away and a few more black families moved in and we learned how to make it, just by being decent people and working hard. We just lived our lives, and by the time you got into school it had eased up and you never really knew anything about it. *Not really.*"

Billy did not look at his father or his mother. He could not, because his eyes were hot with tears and he couldn't trust his voice. Not that he would ever tell them what neither of them had ever known: the small things that he had lived with, pressing them back deep inside himself, the things his outraged love and sensitivity would never let him reveal. Why do I have to wear a white shirt and tie every day, not just on assembly day, like the other boys? Why isn't 95 on a math exam good enough, just because some other kid got 97? Why do I have to take violin lessons from a private teacher as well as the free lessons the school gives? Why do I have to be home, in the house, under your eyes, by eight o'clock, even in the summer? What's so *different* about me?

All the small things, eating on him through his childhood, unspoken and unmentioned, until he understood, and then it twisted inside of him until he came to terms with it: his own terms. He had finally formed his own image and could no longer spare them pain and anguish, because he had to be his own man. And do things in his own way now.

His hands slid along the table and reached for each of them and they sat for a moment in an exhausted silence, their hands joined. "Pop, I know." Quickly he amended his statement. "Okay, I don't *really* know and I owe that to you. To you and to Mama, what you took on for me. That was your way and your fight and you met it head on and I don't know if I would have had your kind of courage. But that was your part of it, and now this is *my* part of it."

His father pushed his hand away at the same moment that his mother tightened her grasp. There wasn't anger in his father's gesture or in his voice. There was something close to despair. "But if you kick it all away now, Billy—if you throw away everything we did—then what was it all about? Why did Mama and I go through it, to have you toss it all away?"

His mother spoke for the first time. "Billy, you get arrested and you'll never get admitted to the bar. Your papa and I— that's what it's all been for. You wanted the law ever since you was just a little feller in the junior high and you never once changed your mind. You kept in that direction and we been with you all the way. You get arrested and get a record against you and you can't never get admitted to the bar to practice law. You know that better than we do."

Billy released her hand, pushed his chair back and stood up; it was time to go. "There are times when a man has to think in larger terms. When you have to think outside of just 'me-mine.'" He saw his father's head snap up and kept his voice soft and even. "These are different times, Pop. People are joining together now, into organizations, into conferences, into committees. Not just one voice calling out, asking, pleading. Not just one man walking down a hostile street, pretending not to see, pretending not to know. But a larger force, moving together, getting laws passed, getting public opinion with us, touching the conscience, because we're not pointing and saying 'for me, just for me and mine.' We're saying 'for all of us.' Now, *for all of us!*"

William Everett was silent. There was nothing more to say. He drank his lukewarm cocoa and ate his hard, crisp toast, shaking off his wife's attempt to prepare some fresh breakfast. He would not look up at his son, whose hands pressed hard into his shoulders. He could not look up at him.

Lucinda held Billy's face between her hands, kissed him briefly on both cheeks then released him. "Take care of yourself, Billy," she said.

There was nothing more a woman could do. A man had to make his choices and a woman had to wait and pray. The silence in the kitchen was interrupted by the crunching, chewing noises as William mindlessly ate the stale toast. Lucinda lifted her face from the sink filled with dishes. She moved the starchy sheer organdy curtains to one side and watched the tall straight figure of her son moving down the front walk to the sidewalk. He bent suddenly, and in the glare of the sunlight she had difficulty seeing what it was that had stopped him. Then as her son stood up, she saw their big orange cat roll in the sunlight, his paws languidly stretching.

She watched Billy as he moved, easy and proud like his father, down the street of his home, and for some reason he stopped, turned back, and looked directly toward the window. Lucinda knew he couldn't possibly see her; the window was small and the sun was directly in his eyes. As her son stood and faced his home, then continued on his way, Lucinda's heart seemed to empty of all life and fill unexpectedly and painfully with a terrible and certain knowledge: She would never see Billy walk down this street again.

SIX:

Rafe Wheeler, whose lifeless body had been summarily collected and transported to the city morgue, had not been a police informer. He had been, for the thirteen months immediately prior to his death, a police officer.

The Police Commissioner, a bland, mild man in his middle fifties, held the silver patrolman's shield in the palm of his hand for a moment, regarding it without expression. Then he placed it on his desk beside a folder of material relating to Patrolman Rafe Wheeler. "A shame," he said for the third time, fingering a photograph that had slipped from the folder. "A good-looking boy."

First-grade Detective Stoner Martin did not raise his eyes from the edge of the Commissioner's desk. He didn't care to see the sincere effort the man was making to recall some faint vestige of the boy he had sworn into the Department in this very office. It had been a private ceremony, witnessed by the Chief of Detectives, Supervising Assistant District Attorney Casey Reardon and Detective Martin. Only Stoner Martin had ever seen the boy or heard his voice after that day.

Stoner sat wordless and motionless, shrouded by a sense of terrible failure, a failure for which Rafe had paid with his life. A good-looking boy, the Commissioner had said, because that was all the Commissioner could think of to say. He hadn't selected the kid from a list of prospective patrolmen waiting to be sworn in. He hadn't done the careful, meticulous screening of the kid from the day he was born on some sharecropper's farm in North Carolina, through his childhood in an orphanage and his adolescence with an elderly maiden aunt who owned a shack in Virginia. The Commissioner didn't *know* Rafe: busboy, shoeshine boy, clean-'em-up-boy, yes-sir-yes-ma'am scary-eyed little Southern black boy heading north to better things. The kid had arrived in New York two years ago: softspoken and twenty-one with no big dream, no big plan. Just a little old down-home kid with no living relative left, he had put on his one neat dark suit, a fresh shirt and narrow tie and got a job in the stockroom of a department store the second day he hit New York. A nice kid, the manager of the stockroom told Stony—gentleman, polite, intelligent. He spent his nights taking courses at City College, adding up a few credits—painfully, for he hadn't any special aptitude for academic learning, but he tried. A slow-moving, deliberate young man, taking life a step at a time.

The patrolman's exam represented no great dedication, no lifelong ambition, just an opportunity open to him with some good possibilities. Stoner Martin had made the selection; he had narrowed the choice to three boys and submitted his recommendations to Reardon, but it was Stoner who ultimately made the selection and had to make the approach.

It was a rotten deal, no matter what. If he had turned the offer down, they would have found some excuse to scratch him. (Rafe, you should have said no. Hands down—no.) They would have had to turn him down. By the time Stoner finished talking to him, Rafe knew too much. But Rafe Wheeler had listened, nodding occasionally, his smooth young face a mask revealing nothing, his bright eyes absorbing everything. Stoner hadn't conned him; he'd laid it right on the kid. It would be undercover all the way, from the private swearing-in ceremony to—whatever. When the boy spoke, his voice had the easy, expected lilt but something more, something unanticipated: a certainty, so that for all his careful background work, Stoner had somehow underestimated him.

"I'll have no identification with the Police Department whatever? You'll be my only contact?"

Stoner had nodded, catching the slight hesitation but not prepared for the next question, which was asked with an odd smile playing about the boy's lips.

"Did you pick me because I'm a little old dumb down-home boy with no connections, either back home or up here in the big bad North?"

"Strike the word 'dumb' and you got it."

Rafe had smiled and Stoner had smiled and accepted the hand offered to him and Rafe Wheeler had become *his* boy. And now Rafe Wheeler was lying, unidentified and unclaimed, in a refrigerated locker in the city morgue and Stoner Martin could not claim him and the New York City Police Department *would* not claim him. An anonymous donor would send a sum of money with instructions for Rafe Wheeler's burial in a plot in North Carolina, and the remainder of his $10,000 life insurance policy would be contributed to the Police Department's Orphans and Widows Fund.

"We've been going over Patrolman Wheeler's reports and your follow-up work of the last two months."

Casey Reardon's foot pressed on Stoner's shoe. Stoner looked up, startled. He hadn't realized that the Chief of Detectives was addressing him. "Sir?"

The Chief of Detectives was a tall, slender man with bright hair. There were still traces of blond but the silver that edged his sideburns sparked most of his thinning hair. He was a handsome man who would have been boyish except for webs of fine lines that extended from the corners of his eyes down into his cheeks. "From your work with Patrolman Wheeler, do you have any idea of what might be involved today?" His eyes were the color of granite flecked with bright glints of mica.

Stoner shook his head, shifting his thoughts away from Rafe because Rafe was dead and not what mattered at the moment. "No, sir, but it's tied in with the infiltration of the Freedom-for-All group. Patrolman Wheeler and a fellow named Eddie Champion"—Stoner's hand waved vaguely toward the sheaf of papers on the Commissioner's desk— "were instructed by the Royal Leader of the Secret Nation to infiltrate the FFA. There are five or six other members of the SN in the various chapters of the FFA—scattered around. That would be enough to stir things up from nonviolent to anything goes. All Rafe told me"—he dropped his head and spoke with his eyes closed tightly for a moment, remembering the soft voice, then the silence, then the dead telephone line—"all he had a chance to tell me was that there was going to be a shooting at the construction site."

"God damn it," the Chief of Detectives said, turning his back on Detective Martin.

Stoner stiffened in his chair, holding himself in; it was logical for the Chief of Detectives to be annoyed by the lack of specifics. "Rafe didn't know exactly what was planned," he said quietly. "He had only been a member of the Royal Guards for a few months. His partner, Champion, didn't trust him. Rafe told me two days ago that he and Champion had been given a top-secret assignment but all Champion would tell him was that it was something that would blow the top off this city." His brain was filled with the strange, almost comic-opera words, but the reality was present among the men in this room. The Secret Nation was headed by a Royal Leader, who was protected by a group of young men called the Royal Guards, who had powers of life and death over whatever victim they chose for whatever reason. The Chief of Detectives and the Commissioner had become used to the words and familiar with the reality of them through police reports describing violent death and senseless beatings and fulfilled threats, and they knew that the Secret Nation did, in fact, exist.

"Eddie Champion," the Chief of Detectives said thoughtfully. "You onto him?"

The detective's long fingers rolled into his palms and he raised his eyes. "I will be," he said. "They were staying at a dump on the West Side the last two days. I only had two contacts from Rafe. Champion stuck close to him and he couldn't get to me. We have people staked out at Champion's apartment uptown, at his girl friend's place—anywhere he might show."

"Will it be difficult to bag him on this shooting? Seems to me," the Commissioner said, "it will be tough."

"We'll bag him," Stoner said, "one way or another."

"There's only one way we want him," Reardon said, watching Stoner closely. "We want him *right*."

The Chief of Detectives was curious. "I thought none of the SN people were allowed to carry weapons. I thought that was rule number-one."

"It is. The whole idea has been that none of the people carry weapons. That's why they've been trained in karate." Stoney fought to hang onto the sense of his words, but Rafe intruded: *My Lord, Stoner, the things these folks are teaching us. My hands are like to break in half.* Stoner shifted in his chair and his voice was forced. "Rafe told me that Champion has been getting ready to make his move. There has been a lot of dissension in the group for a long time. The old man—the Royal Leader—has been having his troubles with some of his brightest boys. They have been getting edgy, hungry for action. For some of the blood and cracked skulls they've been promised. Word has been going around that some weapons have been collected. The old man has been getting more and more suspicious of everyone around him—and with reason. He runs a tight ship, strict chain of command. He trusts nobody. The penalty for any member of the SN who possesses a weapon is death. Originally, the rule was so that his people, if picked up by the police, were clean. None of his people have yellow sheets—that's rule number-two. Now it appears that the no-weapon rule is more for the protection of the old man. You get caught: boom, chop and you're out!" Stoner's hand slashed the air.

"Then why do you suppose that Eddie Champion not only had a gun but risked using it on Patrolman Wheeler?" the Police Commissioner asked.

"He was getting worried about Rafe: no special reason, just a general distrust—who's on what side of the split. He walked in on Rafe when he was contacting me. If he had chopped him instead, that would have been an admission that he was careless, nearly took a cop along on a big one. It would have shown poor judgment and that would just about eliminate Champion. The old man would have fingered him, and chop!"

"I suppose that's one way of eliminating incompetents," the Chief of Detectives observed sourly. It was a bitter, off-hand, casual comment and the Chief of Detectives didn't see Stoner Martin spring from his chair, his face contorted.

Casey Reardon had seen; his eyes never left Stoner and he moved swiftly, his hands lunging for Stoner's shoulders, pulling him back. The Chief of Detectives turned, startled at the sudden commotion behind him.

"He didn't mean *that,* for Christ's sake. Get hold of yourself, Stoney," Reardon ordered as he forced the detective back into the chair. Stoney, speechless, breathed in short, shallow gasps.

The Chief's face seemed etched by a million hair-fine wrinkles. "Did you think I meant *Patrolman Wheeler?* My God."

Stoner breathed his words in tight spurts. "That kid did one hell of a job. You got two other boys in that SN. What information have they given you? What have you learned about this Secret Nation from them? Rafe Wheeler told us all we really know. He died telling me. You think he was incompetent?"

"No, I don't. I think he was one hell of a cop and I wish we had a hundred more like him," the Chief said. "I wish we could put what he did in headlines and in all official Department reports and that we could put him up for promotion. But we can't do any of those things. All we can do is work with what we've learned through his efforts."

Stoner lit a cigarette, brushed Reardon's hand off his shoulder. "Okay. I'm just uptight about this whole thing. Sorry."

The Commissioner cleared his throat and indicated several large sheets on his desk. "The Chief Inspector has been notified to put a large contingent at the construction site and we have emergency service vehicles close at hand. But a shooting—it could be anyone. The target, I mean." His hand swept the room as though a bullet might be aimed from or to any corner, and no one contradicted him. "Well, then, we can only exert as much readiness as humanly possible. Chief, have you made arrangements to give Mr. Reardon all the assistance he needs in running Champion down?"

The Chief of Detectives held his hands palms up. "Whatever he wants."

"I got all the people I need, Commissioner. Our main hope is to find Champion. I've sent some of my people down to the demonstration and the Chief gave me an additional twenty men. If you don't need us here, Detective Martin and I will get down to the site now."

The Commissioner stood up and they all got to their feet. "If only this heat would break. This damn New York heat. Too many hot, uncomfortable, unhappy people on the streets as it is."

Stoner Martin felt cold: cold in the air-conditioned room, right to the base of his spine, as though he were lying in a refrigerated tomb. He nodded briskly at the Chief of Detectives and followed Reardon's quick jerking exit signal. They walked through the elegance of the mirrored waiting room and both felt assaulted by the hot thick air as they passed through the wide, breathless corridor.

As they entered the waiting black Pontiac, Tom Dell started the engine. Reardon dialed his office, his eyes on his watch. "Any word from Opara?" he asked whoever took the call. He swore softly into the receiver, his eyes remaining on it after he replaced it in its cradle.

"You coming with me, Casey—to the site?" Stoner asked.

"Yeah," Reardon said, and gave terse directions to Tom Dell. He was silent for a moment, then turned to Stoner and said softly, "In addition to everything else, we might run into Christie Opara and my daughter Barbara up there."

SEVEN:

Detective Christie Opara was part of the hot, jostling, disagreeable subway rush-hour crowd, her body prodded, shoved and resented, suffering the countless discomforts and annoyances. Yet her mind remained cool and clear and free of all physical distractions. It was a matter of concentration, and her attention was centered on the odd detour that Casey Reardon's daughter had taken. Christie had watched Barbara Reardon board the bus at the top of the hill, had gotten on the bus behind a woman with a large shopping bag, paid her fare, sat at the back of the bus, keeping the girl in view. They had both entered the subway, Christie using a token instead of showing her shield. They had detrained at the proper station for transfer to an uptown train to Columbia, and then the girl had hesitated, turned and walked to the downtown BMT platform.

Christie had long ago lost any scruples about throwing her slight but strong and wiry body into a crowd. When Barbara Reardon boarded the train, Christie wedged her way into the jammed mob and felt the doors, sticky and warm, close against her shoulders. She kept her eyes on the dark ponytail which was tied with a red ribbon. It was all she could see of the girl at this point; it flashed back and forth within the swaying train. The rest of her was hidden, the bright red cotton dress obscured on all sides by anonymous shoulders and torsos.

As the train rocked, the crowd moved, subtly changing position and stance. Barbara was forced to turn and Christie looked beyond the girl, keeping her expression impassive and blank: the kind of face that would not register on the awareness of her subject.

The crowd thinned out considerably by the time the train reached Delancey Street and Christie sat gazing at *The New York Times,* but she was not reading. She kept the bright flash of red dress under observation, then moved for the door when Barbara exited. This delayed action caused some slight consternation on the part of a small, elderly man who was attempting to enter the train, his arms filled with bulky, string-tied packages. Christie ignored the muttered complaints about her stupidity. The important thing was that at no point throughout the trip had Barbara Reardon noticed her.

As her face was hit by the bright glare of sunshine, Christie made two slight adjustments in her appearance. She tied the small navy kerchief around her head and put on her large, round sunglasses. She dropped *The New York Times* in the Department of Sanitation basket on the corner of Delancey and Sheriff Streets, adjusted the straps of her handbag so that it became a shoulder bag and walked briskly, staring straight ahead of her. Barbara Reardon knew exactly where she was going and she walked rapidly through the languid, heavy, East Side summer streets.

Christie moved easily through the littered sidewalks on the opposite side of the street so that Barbara was diagonal to her. The girl stopped once and turned, looking over her shoulder, but for what reason Christie could not know. As the girl turned, Christie's attention was engaged by the merchandise in the window of a yard-goods shop.

Barbara continued east and her destination became apparent, not through any sense of calculation on Christie's part but by the change in the inhabitants of the street. There were groups of young people, all moving purposefully in the same direction: toward the East River Drive or, more specifically, toward the construction site for the Abraham Lincoln Low Rent Housing Development. There were flashes of brightly lettered placards: FREEDOM-FOR-ALL. The words recalled the radio commentator's voice; she had, after all, absorbed what he had said. This group had picketed all week and was planning a massive sit-down demonstration at the site today. Christie walked faster; the young people were filling the sidewalks, spilling over into the gutters, and Reardon's daughter was getting too far ahead.

The narrow street ended abruptly, unexpectedly, on a vast open area, newly cleared of tightly packed tenements. It had a startling, barren look, gleaming and bright and unshadowed with the drive and the river as its far boundaries. Formless areas were still identified by street signs proclaiming intersections which no longer existed, but the more important designations seemed to be displayed in large, carefully hand-painted signs which proclaimed FFA: QUEENS LOCAL, FFA: BRONX AFFILIATE, FFA: BROOKLYN COLLEGE-BROOKLYN HEIGHTS, countless signs indicating localities and colleges and universities throughout the city.

Christie kept her eyes relentlessly on the red of the girl's dress but she realized she would have to move in very close now. The color was beginning to flicker in and out among the press of bodies and, worse, other flashes of red—open-necked sports shirts and casual cotton knits—were interfering with her observation. It was a good-natured crowd and the jostling was friendly, and the press of bodies yielded to her steady insistence as she cleared a narrow path for herself with sudden lurching detours, her body seeking openings in the tightening wedge of demonstrators.

Barbara Reardon was greeted by smiling faces, excited young men and women speaking in unnaturally bright voices. Christie responded to anonymous remarks directed at her, shrugged helplessly, smiled easily, pointed over the top of the crowd, explaining, "I can't reach my group—Upper Manhattan—" The conversation around her was friendly and accepting. Christie kept within touching distance of Barbara

Reardon and tried to calculate what the group was about to do.

More importantly, she tried to visualize the larger picture, for she had seen police barricades directly across from the building site, and behind those police barricades she had seen something that these kids apparently had failed to note: the beginnings of a mob.

EIGHT:

Sergeant Stanley Frankel did not like the situation. He did not know any of the twelve men assigned to him, and as they sat inside the police van, facing him, he had no way of knowing what they were thinking or what they were feeling. They were an unknown quantity and Sergeant Frankel did not like unknown quantities.

"Now, I'm going to tell you in all candor," Sergeant Frankel said, "that I have no idea why you men were sent here or why it was decided at the last minute to beef up the force. For the last four days there have been what we can term 'peaceful demonstrations,' and no arrests have been effected because no arrests have been warranted." Sergeant Frankel noted the quick exchange of glances between two patrolmen at the rear of the van. He aimed his remarks directly at the center of the van. "These kids out here are within their rights when they march around and carry their signs and chant their slogans. As long as they don't interfere with the conduct of business, as long as they don't block entry into or out of the construction site, they are okay. Our job is to just keep them moving." Sergeant Frankel felt the beads of sweat across his forehead join into a thin trickle of moisture which worked down the side of his left temple. He raised himself from a squatting position, and as he did so, twelve sets of eyes followed him. He had pretended not to hear their initial remarks when he introduced himself. After all, he knew he was a twenty-four-year-old kid who looked no more than seventeen. But he also knew, as they did from the TPF insignia at his collar, that he had been on this assignment because of his special training. All members of the Tactical Patrol Force had to meet certain specifications, the first relating to height. Sergeant Frankel was over six feet tall, with stiltlike legs and a wiry body. He also had two and a half years of college, two years as an Army MP, and special training at the Police Academy which gave him a certain understanding of the present situation. Why these extra men had suddenly been tossed into the line was a puzzle, but Sergeant Frankel had to work with what they sent him.

"Now, it is going to be real hot again today. We can expect it to break a hundred, so the weather is against us all the way. It's hot, it's humid and the kids are planning to lie down."

"We know what they're planning?" a hard voice asked.

Sergeant Frankel nodded. "Yes, our CO had a conference with four of the student leaders last night."

"A *conference*, for Chrissake."

Sergeant Frankel sucked in his breath; his stomach was so flat it was nearly concave. "Now listen. These kids are not criminals. They've told us their plans and they've been advised of the position they'd be putting themselves in. Whether they go through with it or not remains to be seen. But if they do, then our job will be to lift them bodily and place them in the vans."

There was a groaning, a flexing of shoulders and arms and a soft, long string of swear words. The young sergeant moved to the center of the van. He placed his feet wide apart and took a long, slow look around, meeting each pair of eyes, trying to memorize each face and to calculate where he might lean and where he would have to be careful. The top of Sergeant Frankel's hat nearly touched the ceiling. His face tightened and he jabbed an index finger as he spoke. "If and when we get the order to place the demonstrators under arrest, you, you, you"—he turned, then pointed again—"and you, you and you, will be assigned to lifting bodies. The rest of you men are assigned to crowd control." He reached under one of the seats for his clipboard. "All of you men sign the roster: name, shield number, command, and indicate your specific assignment with either 'l.b.' or 'c.c.' I'll be back in a minute—stay put."

Lieutenant Ralph McDermott was thirty-six years old. He wore his shiny peaked uniform hat tipped forward over his forehead, his chin raised in such a position that he seemed to be glaring at Sergeant Frankel. "Hey, Stan, what kind of group you got in there?"

"Lieutenant, what the hell is cooking? Why they sending in precinct men? Even if these kids flop, we could handle it."

McDermott, his shaded eyes on a level with Frankel's, raised his shoulders. "I don't know what gives, but they're beefing up the whole area."

"We got anything really serious here? Seems to me we're getting ready for something heavy."

"Son, the New York City Police Department is *always* ready for something heavy. Let me give your guys a look and a little pep talk."

The sergeant preceded the lieutenant into the van and motioned for the men to remain seated. "This is Lieutenant McDermott of the TPF, in charge of our sector of the operation."

The upper half of Lieutenant McDermott's face was shadowed by his hat, but the men noted the firm, square jaw and tight lips and their silence was respectful. He might be one of the new-breed boys but he looked like he knew what it was all about. They were surprised by his quiet voice.

"Sergeant Frankel has briefed you men, and I just want to add my few words to his. This is a tight setup here. We will all be under heavy pressure. There are more goddam cameras and news photographers and reporters than you've ever seen assembled in any one place, so we are going to be under constant scrutiny. If the order comes to lift bodies, that is exactly what you are going to do: *lift* them." He tilted his head back slightly and two pale eyes surveyed each face in the van. "You will not shove, kick, gut-punch, pinch, jab or use unnecessary force. Further, you will not make any remarks, comments, statements, et cetera. Clear?"

One patrolman, directly in McDermott's line of vision, started a comment to the man next to him, but he swallowed the wisecrack and McDermott's eyes stayed on the man's throat for ten full seconds before his face relaxed. "Okay. Now one other thing. There are some hecklers in the crowd. Some of the heckling will be directed at us—at all of us, at our blue uniforms. The demonstrators will probably call us anything from pigs to fascists; that's standard. The construction workers and their sympathizers will call us anything from finks to cowards." He leaned his head back again, folded his arms across his chest. "Now, I trust that you gentlemen are thick-skinned enough to accept a little name-calling with good grace?"

There was a small rumble of polite laughter and McDermott nodded and signaled Sergeant Frankel to leave the van with him. He waited until the door closed behind them. "It might be a rough one, Stan. I wish to God they'd left the job to us."

Christie had seen the young student leader many times on television, so that she was familiar with his face and with his voice, which, while soft, could be heard quite clearly because of the hush that encircled him. What impressed her was the aura that radiated from him: an aura of calm serenity yet certain determination. He stood among them, the center of it all, the leader of it all, and there was no slightest trace, no hint, of the excitement that surrounded him. He scanned the faces around him but his own face reflected nothing of the mood of the students; he was sober and calm

53

and controlled and intent. His words had a quieting effect, which did not destroy the purpose of his followers but rather clarified their aims.

"Now, there will be the most total media coverage given to us today," Billy Everett said, "and this is our immediate aim: to catch the public eye and the public mind, and thereby to catch the public conscience. We have *elected* this course of action." He paused, his eyes finding the nod of understanding. "We have *elected* this course of action freely. We must remember and hold onto that. The police officers assigned here will be doing their sworn duty and *they* have no choice. The choice was ours and we have made it. This must be a *moral* demonstration and I rely on you—as we must rely on each other—to keep this fact in mind: *We have made our choice!*"

Those words, spoken slowly and distinctly, worked through the crowd, from the circle immediately around him, back steadily to the vast group of anonymous faces. The words spread into a rallying cry until the entire area reverberated: *"We have made our choice!"*

Billy Everett nodded in response to some question put to him. He smiled, scanned the faces around him, consulted his watch and turned against the bodies that seemed to hold him fast. "Let's move out now," he said. Hands reached out, pressed his shoulder, his arm, patted his head with rough affection, and Christie noted that he seemed genuinely surprised and touched, for he, in turn, reached out for the others.

Reardon's daughter stayed close to the standard-bearer for the FFA: BROOKLYN LOCAL—Billy's local—and she caught his arm and exchanged some words with him and he smiled and nodded. Christie stayed, unnoticed, within physical contact of the girl because should one person come between them the girl would be swallowed in the press of moving bodies.

The demonstrators moved across the wide-open area of rubble in a loosely formed line. As they approached the row of wooden police barricades that fenced the construction site on one side and the improvised roadway on the other, the ranks of demonstrators began to tighten. There was another row of barricades on the far side of the road, to hold back a large group of spectators. Tall, immaculately groomed TPF men stood with their backs to the crowds, a long, even line at arm's distance from each other. They faced the demonstrators and seemed alert, but not too tense. A police captain and lieutenant, the gold on their caps and at their shoulders sparked by the sun into gashes of flickering light, stood directly across the road, but their eyes were not on the slowly moving line of construction trucks coming toward them, nor on the police emergency vehicles that were parked to one side of the road. Christie noted that the lieutenant's lips were pressed into a tight, thin line. The visor of his cap hid his eyes but she knew they were fastened on Billy Everett. The captain's face was flushed to a dull, dry pink and he licked his lips, then moved to face the demonstrators.

He held up a white-gloved hand. He looked uncomfortable in his heavy, navy blue uniform, not as fortunate as the patrolmen, who wore short-sleeved summer uniforms. "Okay, now, you people, that's about far enough. You know what the limits are. You are not to move beyond the barricades."

Billy Everett stood absolutely still, the edge of the barricade against his hip. Christie heard the long slow intake of breath as he raised his face for a moment toward the sky. His skin was light tan in the sharp glow of the sun. He released his breath in a sad, regretful sound and a muscle was working at his jawline. He glanced down the road at the four trucks that were creeping along the dusty, littered road. His voice was almost apologetic, yet firm.

"Captain, I regret the actions we must take even more than you do. I regret the inconvenience we must cause you and your men."

In a quick, graceful, unexpected motion, Billy Everett ducked his body down and emerged on the other side of the barricade, and before anyone could stop him he moved the barricade aside. As the young people surged through the opening, the captain's hand gestured, a quick half-wave, and his signal produced immediate action. Four of the TPF men came forward toward the opening.

A young TPF man, his face smooth and earnest, his voice friendly, said, "Hell, Billy, come on. You don't want to get locked up."

Billy smiled at the officer, touched his elbow lightly. "That's the way things are."

Several of the barricades were pushed aside and the captain signaled for the police emergency trucks. The demonstrators swept onto the improvised road and ranged themselves around their leader, who lay stretched flat on his back at the feet of the police captain.

Christie's hand grasped the shoulder of Reardon's daughter; she tried to hold the girl back, but Barbara Reardon, if she felt the pressure at all, must have thought it was just part of the general jostling for there was physical contact all around them in the rush to be part of it. Mechanically, Christie lay down beside the girl but kept her head up high enough to watch the action. Men with earphones clamped across their heads were stepping over prone bodies, stretching cigar-shaped microphones at arm's length, trying to duck so that the zoom lenses behind them could close in on the captain's face and catch his words and expression and gestures. There was a series of blinding flashes as the newspaper photographers aimed straight down at the demonstrators and Christie leaned forward, hiding Barbara Reardon's face with the back of her head. She heard the low heavy rumbling as the trucks approached. The drivers, slowing their vehicles, leaned their heads out of the cabs and began shouting, adding their words to the insults from the crowd of spectators.

The captain's voice was harsh and thin as he addressed them and did not quite carry over the noise from the hecklers. "You are committing an act of disorderly conduct. If you will all rise to your feet now and clear this roadway, these men can get on with their jobs. If you refuse to rise and clear this roadway, I have no other choice but to place you all under arrest."

Billy Everett raised himself on one elbow. "Captain, will the union officials accept members of minority groups into their training programs? Will they accept qualified men, regardless of their race, into their unions? Until such time, we have no alternatives."

The captain's face was expressionless. "Very well, you are all under arrest."

Christie turned her head and watched the progress of the police vans. Her mouth felt dry and sandy from the heat of the sun and the dirt of the road. Barbara Reardon lay beside her, her face pale, her eyes half closed. She was breathing in shallow, quick gasps of air. The sounds from across the road, which had been a humming noise, took shape. The words were ugly and hard. A loud masculine voice could be heard over the other voices: "String the bastard Commies up!"

The crowd cheered and picked up the cadence until the words became a chant: "String the bas-tard Com-mies up!" Intermittently there were loud hoots and catcalls and threats and insults, but all around her Christie saw that the demonstrators appeared to be calm and under control. A chant spread among them now, rising over their heads, and Barbara Reardon, her lips dry and trembling slightly, her eyes closed tightly now, repeated the slogan: *"We have made our choice!"*

Christie calculated quickly. When they were on their feet, as they approached the vans, she would identify herself and claim to take Barbara into custody herself. There wouldn't be any questions asked; the uniformed men would be grateful to have her assistance. Arresting a female was a rough deal for a man. She'd get the girl out of here and—

Through all the noise there was a sudden crashing sound, the sound of glass smashing with a terrible finality. All heads turned instinctively toward the first construction truck, which had been pulled to a stop on police orders. Slowly, as if in a trance, the driver emerged, holding his right hand up to his forehead, bewildered at the red blood that gushed between his fingers and streamed down his face. The TPF men moved closer together, and without instruction they extended their arms to form a human chain, holding the mass of spectators. They were forced a few inches from their original position, but they held firm a distance of fifteen feet from where the demonstrators lay. The sight of blood seemed to infuriate the crowd and they strained against the police line. A voice called out, "They want blood, we'll give them blood —some of their own!"

At the explosive shattering within the group, Christie turned her body instinctively so that her shoulder pressed against Barbara Reardon's face. "Keep your head down!" she instructed the girl. "For God's sake, turn over onto your stomach and keep down!"

There were sharp startled cries of shock and pain as a series of missiles—bottles, beer cans, stones, pieces of chain —was sent raining down among them. Christie heard the furious voice of a technician who had just realized that his television equipment had been damaged. The captain was shouting his orders now and his vocabulary, which had been so careful and so official, was breaking into urgency and would have to be censored before any footage of him could be shown on the late news.

A hand grasped Christie's shoulder, half pulled her to her feet, and without looking up she grabbed at Barbara Reardon. "Come on, let's get up now. Barbara, get up!" The girl stayed where she was, as unrelenting as the other demonstrators. In a kneeling position, Christie traced the path of a broken bottle: It was going in the wrong direction. Someone within the group was responding to the attack. A cry of fury and pain came from the crowd of hecklers; they hadn't expected to be assaulted.

Billy Everett rose to his knees, his face pained and worried for the first time. His lips formed the word "No," but his voice could not be heard over the growing reaction from within his own group.

"How long we going to take it? How long we going to lie back and take it?"

This was something new. Christie's attention spun about, trying to pinpoint where it was coming from. An odd fact registered in her brain. First one voice would call out in anger; then, as though in answer, from another section of the half-kneeling, half-lying bodies, another voice picked it up. As though it had been planned. Another missile, a piece of chain, soared through the air, back into the crowd that had sent it. There was a shriek as the chain hit a target. There was a move as irresistible as an ocean current and the TPF men, reinforced by regular patrolmen, leaned backwards, then toppled forward. Their hands lost contact with each other and the mob, faceless, waded into the prone demonstrators and heavy shoes kicked out and directionless fists struck. A solid body of blue uniforms surged into the mob, forcing them back and away. Some demonstrators were shoved into the mob, and some of the mob were herded back into the crowd of demonstrators. A hand pulled Christie to her feet; an arm shoved her back to the ground again. She had a deathlike grip on Barbara Reardon's arm, and as they lunged, directionless in the mass of bodies, Christie's cheek hit against Billy Everett's shoulder, then a blue uniform shirt pressed against her face. She could no longer see Reardon's daughter, but her hands never left the girl.

The police officers grappled with arms and legs and bodies. Billy Everett, tall and lanky, seemed to be struggling against them, his arms slipping free of their grasp. He turned into the group of his demonstrators. They were alien to him. They had the face of the mob. Voices all around him were screaming words he could not understand, shouting back the anger and the threats and the demands that were hurled at them.

"Kill the bastards!"

"Give them what they gave us!"

59

"No more lying down. Let's do it their way!"

"No," Billy Everett called out, "no. We have made our choice!"

"Get the goddam vans pulled up and load them in. Fast!" the police captain ordered; then, his white-gloved fingers trying to hold Billy's arm, he told the police officer nearest to him, "Put the friggin' cuffs on this bastard!"

Billy Everett felt his arms being pulled behind him and he turned, puzzled, and tried to raise his hands to his friends. A cry went up, directly in front of him: "The bastard cops put the cuffs on Billy!"

Billy shook his head wildly. "No, no. It's okay," he said, but his voice was lost.

Barbara Reardon pulled herself free without looking at Christie and she caught Billy's arm and held fast, ignoring Billy's words which tried to tell her, to tell them all, No, this isn't what we want; this isn't our way.

Christie threw herself at the girl and spun her about. The girl's face was a white, frozen, unseeing mask. Christie's eyes went to Billy Everett's face at the exact moment that the air was ripped by the explosion of a revolver. Billy Everett's face suddenly tightened into a bewildered, stunned expression. His mouth fell open and he went down without a word, but Christie did not watch his descent to the dirt. Her eyes saw something that her brain could not interpret: A long brown hand smashed a .38 service revolver into the empty right hand of a patrolman, and Christie, without blinking, moved her eyes from that brown hand upwards, and for a fraction of a second, over the shoulders and bodies around her, Christie was confronted by the oddest eyes she had ever seen. They were glazed and nearly yellow, and strangest of all, they were somehow familiar.

Even before Billy's dead body had fallen, a voice cried out, "They killed Billy. The cop shot Billy!"

Barbara Reardon turned, and her voice was a low wailing sound as she picked up the chant: "They killed Billy! Oh my God in Heaven, the cop shot Billy!"

NINE:

Christie Opara moved about the living room, touching familiar objects without seeing them. Her body ached from stretched and twisted muscles, and her right elbow and both knees stung and burned where the skin had been rubbed off. She sat on the couch and stretched her bare legs before her and examined the messy wounds. Christie felt a longing to be with her young son. Poor Mickey, how many skinned knees had she shrugged off with a quick dab of antiseptic and a Band-Aid. She hadn't remembered how these things could sting.

She heard a car pull up in front of her house, heard the motor cut off and the sharp slam of a door. Rising quickly, Christie pulled the edge of her sleeveless shirt down over her shorts and opened the door before Reardon rang the bell. Not that the soft chimes would disturb Barbara. The girl was still in a deep sleep. Reardon looked directly toward the stairway, his chin lifted inquiringly.

"She's still sleeping," Christie said. "Mr. Reardon . . ."

He walked past her and into the living room. "This has been one hell of a day," he said, more to himself than to Christie.

"Mr. Reardon . . ."

"What have you got that's cold and comforting?"

Christie could see his face clearly now. Beneath the remnants of freckles and under the sparkle of short stiff bright red bristles that crossed his square chin, there was a faded look, the paleness of exhaustion. The lines across his forehead were like deep bloodless cuts, and his eyes, shaded by the thick orange lashes, were almost colorless. She tried again to get his attention, but he leaned back in a chair, loosened his tie and rubbed the palm of his hand over his forehead. "Let me come to, Christie. Be a good girl and get me a drink."

In the kitchen, Christie measured out a shot of Scotch. She yanked at the ice tray, then jumped on one foot as the tray slid from her grasp and crashed on her bare toe, heavy as a rock. She retrieved two ice cubes, rinsed them, dropped them into the glass and sloshed the liquid around, then added water, then wondered if he would have preferred it straight. She hoped the drink would revive him. It had taken all day to reach him by telephone, and when she started to speak he had asked if Barbara was all right, then, reassured, told her anything else would have to keep.

When Christie entered the living room, it hit her immediately. He had made the room his own. He flicked the television on, then turned it off. He glanced without interest at a collection of art books piled at one end of the bookshelves which lined the long wall of the room, then turned and reached for the drink.

"What about you?"

Christie shook her head. Reardon held the liquid in his mouth for a moment before he swallowed. He sat down in an easy chair and watched as she sat stiffly on the couch directly opposite him.

"This is one hell of a situation," Reardon said, his voice accusing her.

Christie cradled her throbbing elbow in the palm of her hand and agreed with him without accepting responsibility. "Yes, this *is* one hell of a situation." She hadn't anticipated Reardon's anger, but it was present. Through his exhaustion she could sense it and she felt on guard, and because of that she was angry, too. The urgency of the information she had to relay to him receded.

"Jesus, Opara, couldn't you have gotten her out before this thing happened?"

What reached her was not only his irritation; it was the underlying, subtle tone of disappointment. "Mr. Reardon, you didn't give me any idea what to expect. If you had—"

"I didn't think I'd have to spell it out."

"I'm not clairvoyant, Mr. Reardon and—" She stopped abruptly because anything she said would sound defensive.

Reardon's eyes narrowed and darkened. The drink seemed to have stimulated him. He pulled himself upright and put the glass on the table beside him. "Okay, let's start again. I didn't tell you because I didn't really think my daughter would go to the construction site. If she had gone to school, there wouldn't have been any reason for you to know the possible alternatives, right?"

He always made things sound so logical, after the fact. "Yes, that would be right, except that she *didn't* go to school."

Reardon reached for the drink again, but his eyes never left her face. "Well, we're agreed on that. Now, I know you are practically bursting to tell me what happened, and from our telephone conversation I assume Barbara is okay, so . . ."

"Yes, she's okay." Christie was filled again with the information she had to convey to him. "I tried to get you all day to tell you—"

Reardon held his hand up. "Relax. You're here. I'm here. Let's take it a step at a time, right? Nice and easy."

Her eyes were glaring at him and she bit her lower lip, but she nodded.

"Right. Now, tell me about it. First, about Barbara. What did she see?"

"I'll tell you what she *thought* she saw. She thought she saw the patrolman—what's his name? Linelli—shoot Billy Everett."

63

His question was sharp and precise. "What does that mean: 'She *thought* she saw'?"

"It means that your daughter got caught up in the hysteria. There was a shot. Someone began to scream, 'The cop shot Billy.' Then everyone, including Barbara, was screaming it, over and over again: 'The cop shot Billy.' She's absolutely convinced she saw it."

"You sound absolutely convinced that she didn't see it. *Why?*"

She had waited all day to tell him and now she hesitated and savored the fact that she was about to shake Casey Reardon, who always knew everything. "She didn't see the cop shoot Billy Everett because the cop *didn't* shoot Billy Everett."

She had known Reardon long enough to expect no overt reaction, yet she was annoyed by the casual way he lifted the glass to his lips, swallowed, rotated the glass between his palms. But his voice changed. It had the familiar cold alertness, the special, sharp District Attorney's demand for information. "Did *you* see who shot Billy Everett?"

"Yes."

Reardon closed his eyes for a moment and frowned. Christie wanted to speak, but she waited for him. Let him ask. He put the glass down and stood up, not facing her. "How close were you to Everett?"

"I was facing him, within touching distance. Your daughter was wedged between us, facing me."

His eyes studied the carpet thoughtfully. "Go on."

"I was looking directly into Everett's face. There was a lot of commotion; missiles were flying back and forth."

"Get to the shooting," he said impatiently.

"Right. I was looking directly into Everett's face. There was a shot and—"

"No good," he said, interrupting her tersely. His eyes were on hers again. "Did you see *who* fired the shot?"

"Yes and no." Christie spoke quickly, anticipating his objections, but he let her continue. Her voice had the flat, unemotional quality of a testifying witness. "At the instant of the shot my eyes were on Everett's face, but I looked immediately at something that caught my attention. I saw a hand holding a police service revolver and—"

"You saw a *hand?* For Chrissake, you going to identify a *hand?*"

Christie inhaled in sharp annoyance and broke the quiet cadence of her recitation. "Mr. Reardon, will you let me finish? You keep interrupting and—"

Reardon sat down again. He waved his hand. "All right, all right. Go on."

"I saw a hand holding a service revolver and then I saw that hand jam the revolver into the officer's right hand."

For the first time her words had some visible effect on him. He sharpened and tensed and leaned forward. "Did you see the face that went with the hand?"

"Yes, sir."

"Well?"

"Oh. I thought you wanted to keep asking me specific questions. You want me to continue?" Her voice was innocent but Reardon caught the needle and he wasn't amused. "Well, he was a Negro male, light tan skin, thin nose and lips, twenty to twenty-five years old. And, he had, well, his eyes . . ."

"What about his eyes?"

"Well, they were . . . peculiar."

Reardon whistled between his teeth, rubbed his thumb over his mouth. "Peculiar? In what way? Were there three of them? Were they crossed? *What about his eyes?*"

"Well, they were . . . yellow."

"*Yellow* eyes? He had yellow eyes? What the hell was this guy, a cat?"

Christie ran a fingertip lightly over her skinned knee and spoke quickly, not looking at him. "They were sort of . . . they were the color your eyes are sometimes, Mr. Reardon."

"The color of *my* eyes? *Yellow?*"

She looked up and nodded. "Well, sometimes, your eyes

65

look, well, yellow. Yellowish. And that was what struck me about this man. That his eyes were . . ." Christie shrugged and her voice faltered. "You know . . ."

Reardon dug at his eyes for a moment, muttered something to himself, then spoke to Christie. "All right, let's leave it at that—the guy has yellow eyes. How was he dressed?"

"He wore a white cotton knit shirt. I couldn't see his trousers."

"How tall?"

Christie considered for a moment, then stood up. She held her hand over her head. "I'm five-five; I'd say he was just under six feet."

"That is one hell of a story," he said quietly. The mocking sarcasm of his remark startled Christie.

"That is *exactly* what happened, Mr. Reardon. *I saw it!*"

Reardon was unimpressed by her vehemence. "I have twenty-five college students who are ready to sign sworn affidavits to the effect that *they* saw Patrolman Linelli shoot this kid."

Christie crossed the room to the desk that jutted out from the wall of books. She picked up several typewritten pages and handed them to Reardon. "I've put it all on paper and I'm ready to swear to what I've just told you."

Reardon glanced at the papers and wordlessly rolled them into a cylinder which he tapped lightly against the arm of the chair. The gesture infuriated Christie. She had waited all day, tried desperately all day to reach him, to tell him that the reports that blasted on radio and the TV news were wrong. Patrolman Linelli had been framed. She had seen what really happened. And now he was dismissing her statement with a careless lack of enthusiasm. Her mind raced, searching; then she stood in front of him. "What did Patrolman Linelli say?"

Reardon gave a quick nod of approval; she had found the logical question. But his voice was flat and noncommittal. "Patrolman Linelli said that there was a scuffle and that there was a shot and that suddenly his gun was shoved into his hand. His right hand."

Christie spread her hands out. "Well, then, there you are."

Reardon shook his head slowly. "No, not really. Yes and no, as you said before. We know Linelli didn't fire the gun. There was no chemical evidence to indicate that he had fired any weapon within the last twelve hours prior to the shooting, but—"

"So what's the problem? *I* saw what happened!"

Reardon made a short clicking sound of annoyance between his teeth. "You know, Opara, sometimes I wonder about you."

"What's that supposed to mean?"

"You're acting like a little kid. Here's the fact of the matter, so boom-boom-boom. There's the solution. For Christ's sake, grow up. I've got twenty-five emotional demonstrators coming in tomorrow to swear they saw the cop shoot the kid. We've had civil rights leaders from all over the city and state demanding that we arrest the cop forthwith and release the forty people who were arrested today. In about fifteen minutes that TV set will be blasting all over the city, calling for action. And speaking of action, the entire PD and the Fire Department are on riot alert. City Hall is being picketed. Police Headquarters is being picketed. There are mobs of hot, angry, emotional people on the streets of Harlem, Bedford-Stuyvesant, Jamaica and God knows where else. And what have I got? I have Patrolman Linelli's story, and now I have your story about some mysterious hand and some mysterious face."

He watched her green eyes narrow, saw the deliberate intake of breath. Reardon laughed suddenly: a harsh, humorless sound. "Relax, Christie. *I* believe you. But at this point I need more. It would come out as one police officer covering for another. We've been moving all over the goddam city today looking for something tight, something concrete. I'm not going to throw you into the lion's den without something strong to back you up, and back me up and back the whole damn case up. We got other lines out." His eyes flickered over her and he reached out toward her leg. "What the hell did you do to yourself?"

Christie sat back on the couch and bent over her skinned knees, touching them lightly with the tip of a finger. "It was rough out there, Mr. Reardon."

He gently lifted her toe with the tip of one shoe. "Didn't you wear shoes this morning, either?"

Christie looked down at the red bruise on her large toe. "I dropped the ice tray on it."

His voice was serious again and he sounded tired. "How'd you get Barbara here?"

"She seemed to be in a state of shock. After the shot there was a terrific commotion. We all seemed to fall together. I just latched onto her and pulled. She didn't realize what was happening. I just shoved and pushed until all of a sudden we were clear. We were a full block away before she stopped, and I showed her my shield and told her you had sent me. We caught a cab at Delancey Street."

Reardon nodded in admiration. "I don't know how you managed, Christie. It was desperate."

"Were *you* there?"

"Stoney and I got there about fifteen minutes after the shooting. It was hell."

"Well, we managed somehow. She never said a word until we reached the house and then she began to react. She couldn't stop talking about it. She kept saying, 'The cop shot Billy.' Then she went into a cold sweat and starting shaking. I couldn't reach you, so I called my doctor. Told him Barbara was a friend of mine who'd just got word that her fiancé was killed in an accident. That her family was out of town. He gave her a shot to knock her out—until I could reach someone."

Reardon took the last of the drink, put the glass down. "Thanks, Christie."

She nodded. It was the first time he had ever thanked her

for anything. Reardon glanced at his watch, then crossed the room and switched on the television. It was a small portable, set into one of the bookshelves.

A sudden burst of frenzied voices filled the room, but it was an artificial sound: chanting from a half-remembered dream. Christie rose and watched beside him. Placards waved wildly across the screen. There was a rush of bodies, a quick, fleeting glimpse of Billy Everett's face; his voice was heard briefly, calling out to his followers. The camera seemed to spin; there was a smeary streak across the screen, then first one face, then another, came into half focus as an expression of horror spread through the scene and the shouting became a terrified cry and the voices picked the words up with a dreadful clarity: "The cop shot Billy!" The sound dropped down and the strong voice of the commentator, dramatic and incisive, narrated. "That was the scene this morning at the site of the Abraham Lincoln Low-Cost Housing Development on the lower East Side at the moment that civil rights leader Billy Everett was shot. Now, with an on-the-scene report from Harlem, here is Tim Daniels."

A good-looking, intense young man appeared on the screen, clutching a small microphone. He hunched over and spoke directly into the mike as the camera panned around the area. "I am speaking to you from 125th Street and Lenox Avenue. There are angry people on these streets tonight and their mood is ugly. There is violence in the air and there have been several eruptions of violence in the streets. Several store windows have been smashed; several bottles and other missiles have been hurled from roofs. Miraculously, none of the police officers—who are the obvious targets—have been hurt. So far." His voice became ominous. "Police reinforcements have been sent in in large numbers; the people have been kept moving, but the crowd has been getting larger by the minute."

The camera swept past the commentator and there were masses of dark, angry faces. A zoom lens zeroed in on a placard: a crudely drawn cartoon of a policeman, his face ugly and cruel, his hand holding a smoking gun against the head of a grotesque figure. Beneath it were the words:

INDITE MURDERER LINELLI

After a commercial, a series of interviews followed. On tape a Negro minister, long active in the civil rights movement, his voice sorrowful, his words sad, warned the city that the Negro community would no longer tolerate the murder of its sons. A Negro youth leader, his face twitching with rage, demanded that the Mayor and the Police Commissioner arrest Linelli for murder, or turn him over to the people on the streets. "We know how to take care of his kind," he said.

A familiar state senator, up for reelection, spoke with much feeling; he pleaded for calm and law and order. He assured his fellow citizens that justice would be done.

The Police Commissioner appeared on the screen for a brief moment as he pushed his way past newsmen who lined his path from his limousine to Police Headquarters. He was surrounded by several tense, alert plainclothesmen who kept their backs to him and their faces to the crowd. As the microphones were pushed up to his face, the Commissioner shook his head. "We are currently investigating this matter. I have no further statement at this time."

"When will you have a statement, Commissioner?"

"Where is Patrolman Linelli now, Commissioner?"

"Is he going to be charged?"

The Commissioner left a trail of unanswered questions as his men shouldered him into Headquarters.

Reardon snapped off the television and said, more to himself than to Christie, "That poor bastard."

"Who? The Commissioner?"

"Not the Commissioner," Reardon snapped. "Linelli. He was set up. It was all planned and he doesn't know what hit him."

Christie watched Reardon pick up the empty glass, then

put it down again. "Mr. Reardon, did you have prior information?"

"What do you mean?"

"Did you—did you know that something like this was going to happen?"

"Anything might have happened, right? Look, Christie, you're involved in this and God knows I didn't expect you to be, but you are. Let's kind of ride it out for a while and see where it goes, okay?"

She considered for a moment, then took the glass from his hand. "Do you want another drink, Mr. Reardon?"

"Yeah, that's what I want. Another drink. And for God's sake, Opara, pour the Scotch *over* the ice, will you?"

TEN:

At first Barbara Reardon thought the voices were part of her dream. She felt an unnameable panic, which dried her throat, tightened her chest and churned deep inside her stomach. The chanting sounds stopped and she pulled herself up in the bed, trying to fight off the heavy sleep. She recognized the familiar voice of the television commentator, and while she realized she was awake, she could not quite grasp where she was.

It was her father's voice that cut through the heavy confusion. Though the dimensions of the room, outlined by the glow from the small lamp beside the bed, were unfamiliar to her, she remembered that she had been brought to the home of Christie Opara. There was a dull ache in her upper right arm. Her fingers lightly felt a small swelling. A doctor had come, injected her with something, and she had fallen into a sick, whirling sleep composed of sounds and pain and confused streaks of color and then total darkness.

Billy Everett is dead.

The words moved on her lips with startling clarity and shocked her into a cold and total consciousness. Billy Everett was dead and she had to tell her father about it. She moved across the room and into the hallway, puzzled by the difficulty of her movements. Her body did not seem to respond, as though it had been drugged separately from her brain,

72

which was starkly alert and aware of the devastating fact: *Billy Everett is dead.*

She was not aware of the thumping sound of her footsteps on the stairs, only that her father stood waiting below.

Christie moved instinctively to assist the girl, but Reardon raised his arm, barring her way. He stood motionless watching his daughter. He seemed as frozen and as immovable as a statue, and Christie felt a terrible urge to shove him, to make him move, to make him reach out for the girl.

As she reached the last step, Barbara's face was nearly gray. There was a wide circle of white completely surrounding her mouth where the blood seemed to have deserted the skin. She stood unsteadily, one hand touching the post; then she blinked quickly, as though trying to focus her large, abnormally shiny eyes. She let her hands fall heavily to her sides and stood uncertainly.

Reardon made no gesture, no move. He didn't even seem to be breathing; yet, somehow, something communicated itself between the father and daughter, for at the exact moment that Barbara silently mouthed the word "Dad," Reardon's arms raised and the girl hurled herself against him.

Christie turned away. She had never imagined that Reardon's hard face could reveal his feelings so nakedly. He held his daughter tight against him for a minute; then, when her sobs grew stronger and less controlled, he thrust her back abruptly. "Okay," he said, "take a couple of good deep breaths." His daughter stared at him blankly and he grasped her shoulders and shook her roughly. "Barbara, snap out of it."

Barbara inhaled through her mouth and let the breath out in a series of gasping sounds, then let her father lead her to the couch, where she sat stiffly.

"Well, you sure screwed things up today, didn't you?"

The girl's mouth moved, but no words came.

"You had to be part of it, didn't you? Well, you were part of it, all right. Was it fun?"

Christie, shocked by his tone, said, "Mr. Reardon, she's still a little sedated and I think she's still in shock. Don't you think you should—"

"I think you should cut out of this, Opara, right now!"

Barbara turned toward Christie in confusion, but her father's voice forced her to face him again.

"Well, come on, tell me about it. Lots of excitement, right? You were right in the middle of a bit of history today, weren't you?"

Barbara's voice was thin and hollow. "It was terrible. It was awful." She tried to say more, but seemed unable to get any words out. Reardon kept jabbing words at her, not stopping for her to speak. Finally she stood up—found herself standing up, her face close to his, her voice finally her own. "*Will you listen to me!*" she demanded, stunned by the sudden silence, for her father had stopped speaking.

"Okay," he said calmly, "I'm listening, Barbara."

Her words came as her memories came, clear and terrible. "I saw a police officer shoot Billy Everett." She turned her face to Christie. "I *saw* that, no matter what my father told you to tell me. I *saw* it."

Reardon's face relaxed and his voice was almost gentle. "Barbara, why would the police officer shoot Billy?"

The girl shook her head. "No, Dad, no. Don't try that. I *saw* the policeman shoot Billy. Don't try question-and-answer games with me. It won't work."

Christie was surprised that he let it go. "Okay, we won't talk about that part of it now. What else did you see today? What else did you *learn* today?" He reached out and turned his daughter's face to his. "Come on, I want to hear you. I want to know if it was a worthwhile experience after all."

Though his voice was soft it was insistent, and Barbara knew that he was demanding that she tear into herself and that she would have to make certain admissions to him. More importantly, she knew he would force her to make certain admissions to herself. "It was terrible. The whole thing."

"Go on," he insisted.

74

She pulled his hand from her face, and Reardon saw a flash of anger. "All right. The people were like *animals*. Everyone seemed to go crazy. *Everyone.* There was a terrible violence all around us. *We* were part of it, too. Is that what you want to hear? All right, then, *we* were part of it too."

Reardon ran his hand over his eyes, dug at them roughly but said nothing.

"We hurled bottles back at them and chains and stones back at them. It all seemed to fall apart, the whole thing. *We* became a mob, too."

"What the hell did you think would happen?" Reardon snapped. "A large group of people, unlawfully demonstrating with the sole purpose of interfering with a lawful enterprise, refusing to obey direct police orders, with *weak* leadership—"

"Don't you say anything about Billy Everett," she warned him.

"Was he in control of his people?"

"Don't say anything about Billy," she repeated.

"He didn't know a goddam thing about the group of people he was supposed to be leading. He didn't know that his own group had been infiltrated by a handful of dangerous people who were intent on turning this into the situation it has become. He didn't know that his people *could* be turned so easily to violence, and that was his responsibility—to *know*." He turned to Christie and realized she had followed what he had said fully. "Yes, we had information. But not good enough to have prevented what happened. Just enough to have anticipated some kind of trouble." He turned back to Barbara. "Don't shake your head at me. You don't know anything about it. God damn it, you gave me your word you'd stay away from there today!"

The girl's voice was cold and slightly taunting. Her eyes flicked toward Christie, then back to her father. "Why did you bother to ask for it? You didn't trust me anyway."

"Apparently I was justified, wasn't I?"

They glared at each other, father and daughter, and it occurred to Christie that they were evenly matched. The girl, fragile and pale, her black hair dark against the whiteness of her skin, her blue eyes luminous and angry. And Casey Reardon, radiating a kind of street toughness, his eyes deepening to a honey color, his head held to one side: neither of them giving an inch, both of them certain and sure.

Christie reached out and touched his arm. "Mr. Reardon, I think we could all use some coffee."

"I think my daughter could use some more brain cells, not coffee," he said shortly.

Barbara sank back on the couch, weariness buckling her knees. Her small hands clenched into fists, trying to hold onto a rapidly fading sense of control. "I don't know why things went wrong," she said. "I don't know why some of us responded to the violence. But I know that most of us didn't. Billy didn't. I know that the policeman shot Billy without any provocation and—" Barbara suddenly clamped her knuckles over her mouth, and for a moment her body was rigid and her breath came in an anguished cry. Casey pried her hand from her mouth, sat beside her, his hand on her face, but she pulled back from him. "My God," she said, "Billy is dead. It's not possible. Billy is dead."

"Get the coffee, will you, Christie?"

She hesitated for a moment, but something about Reardon —not his voice, which was still harsh, nor his face, which was set and expressionless, but possibly his hands, which reached out and kneaded his daughter's clenched fists—reassured her.

He brushed Barbara's dark, disheveled hair from her face and touched her cheek. "Daddy," she said, her voice young and frightened, "Billy Everett is dead and I loved him. We all loved Billy. Billy was my brother and he's dead."

Reardon cupped his daughter's face in his hands and said softly, "Sure, baby. We're all brothers and we all love each other and we all die sometime, right?"

ELEVEN:

At first, Christie thought she had gotten off at the wrong floor. The narrow corridor was filled with desks, some regulation, some improvised with boards set up on wooden horses. The men behind the desks were obviously detectives, their eyes narrowed and intent and wary upon the young people sitting across from them, their voices so soft and intimate that they did not interfere with interrogations taking place not more than twenty-four inches from them.

Detective Sam Farrell, a large man with narrow hips and wide shoulders, plunged into the corridor from the door marked DISTRICT ATTORNEY—SPECIAL INVESTIGATIONS. He collided with a desk placed immediately outside the office, rubbed his side absently without noticing that he had knocked a stack of papers to the floor.

"Hey, Christie, how about all this, huh?" Farrell's whisper carried the length of the corridor and his round, clear blue eyes circled the area. "Boy, are we jumping here today."

"Where'd we get all the extra people?" Christie asked, for she did not recognize the detectives.

"Oh. Yeah, them. They're Headquarters people. Mr. Reardon wanted some detailed statements from anybody we could lay our hands on. There's more of them inside. We got everybody in the squad on this. Boy, the guys who were on vacation are fit to bust. Mr. Reardon recalled everybody." Farrell was cheerful. His vacation had been in July, and instead of the usual deadening lull of August he had returned to a burst of activity that suited his need for constant motion.

"Oh, yeah. Mr. Reardon's been asking for you. Twice so far." Christie glanced at her wristwatch; apparently Mr. Reardon had the squad in early, but he hadn't told her anything about it. Farrell thumped her on the shoulder. "That was about an hour ago. He's got some people in his office now, so it's okay."

There was a soft humming sound of voices from every section of the squad office and Christie wandered from desk to desk, exchanging nods with the squad men, listening for a moment to the questions, gauging the climate of the interrogations so precisely that she could hear Reardon's instructions as clearly as if she had sat in on the briefing: Keep it calm, keep it low-pitched, work around the main question, lead up to it.

Marty Ginsburg sat hunched over his battered relic of a desk in the far corner of the office, his heavy face damp with perspiration. He seemed to be strangling beneath his tightly knotted tie, and his eyes kept flickering between his notebook and the large bosom of the young girl sitting beside him. The girl was dressed in a jersey shift that barely covered her thighs, but Marty wasn't looking at the lower portion of the girl. His eyes were drawn irresistibly from the wide pale mouth down to her breasts which were outlined by the clinging jersey. They were pushing up out of the low wide neckline and Marty was finding it difficult to concentrate on his questions. He looked up at Christie, raised his eyebrows and shrugged. Christie glanced at the girl, then smiled to herself.

"Boss was looking for you," Marty told her, "but he's tied up with some VIPs right now."

"So I've been told," Christie answered.

Marty wiped his forehead with the back of a heavy hand, and his eyes, as though they had a life separate and apart from his will, moved again, examining that incredible fullness before him.

Detective Arthur Treadwell sat stiff and erect at Stoner

Martin's desk. It wasn't often that he had occasion to be in possession of his partner's desk, but Stoner wasn't around and Detective Treadwell treated his opportunity with respect. His hands never touched the Royal, which was tuned and timed to Stoner Martin's special rhythm and would rebel against the pecking and halting of any two-fingered typist. He jotted notes on a legal-size pad, neatly in small cramped legible swirls of green ball-point. His large round face, speckled with soft brown freckles, betrayed nothing, did not react in any way to the pretty young Negro girl who had just slapped the flat of her hand to the surface of the desk.

"I was *there*, Detective Treadwell. You weren't!"

"Which is why I'm asking you questions, miss," Treadwell said in his reasonable, noncommittal manner. "Hey, Christie, how you doing?"

Christie noted that Art looked weary: the weariness of a forty-five-year-old man, with two teenage children, who had half warily and half delightedly become the father of an infant daughter two months ago.

"How's it going, Art? The baby, I mean."

Arthur exhaled between clenched teeth and shook his head. "Out of practice with all that, I guess. All night again."

"When the heat lets up, it'll be better."

The witness tapped her fingers impatiently against the surface of the desk and Art turned back to her. Her angry dark eyes saw him only as a policeman, an enemy, incapable of spending a sleepless night because of an unhappy baby. "Sorry, miss, let's get back to it. Oh, Christie, Mr. Reardon was asking for you."

"Yes. I know. You got something you want typed up? I understand he's busy right now."

Gratefully, Detective Treadwell vacated the desk, leaving the Royal to Christie's quick and experienced touch. She worked steadily for nearly an hour, watching the parade of students and witnesses who came to sit beside each detective, answering the questions in varying degrees of anger or eagerness. As she typed up a succession of statements, pre-

79

paring them for signatures, Christie felt the heaviness of words pressing down on her. One after the other, they all claimed to have been witnesses to the shooting of Billy Everett and they all claimed to have seen the policeman shoot the boy.

There was a sudden flurry of applause and then a low, affectionate cheer as three men walked from Mr. Reardon's office and stopped momentarily in the squad room. The men, all familiar civil rights leaders, raised their hands, motioning the students back. The largest of the three men, an immense man, heavy but not fat, with pale tan skin and coal-colored eyes and a deep, eloquently resonant voice, faced into the room, waited for a timed moment, then held his hand out for silence.

"My young friends," he said in his familiar platform voice, "just answer all the questions put to you. It is up to you and to all of us to see justice done, and *it will be done!*"

There was a growing cheer rumbling from the corridor, for his voice had carried, and his many admirers pushed into the office. Reardon's door opened and he strode quickly to the side of the three civil rights leaders. Reardon looked tense and pale. He placed his hand lightly on the shoulder of the speaker, the Reverend Dr. Alfred Morse, and when the man turned expectantly, Reardon shook his right hand firmly and his lips smiled, but Christie saw that Reardon's eyes were like frozen amber. Casually, still holding the minister's right hand, Reardon turned him about toward the door and moved with him and the other two men. Photographers were waiting in the corridor and Reardon released the hand and turned his back as the flashing of photographers' bulbs began and students rushed to be included. Reardon reentered the squad room and with a jutting of his chin signaled Christie into his office.

Reardon snatched the phone from the corner of his large oiled-walnut desk and dialed a number impatiently. Christie could hear a cheerfully feminine voice identifying the office of the Director of Public Relations.

"Put your boss on the phone. This is Reardon."

As he turned, sitting on the corner of his desk, he told Christie brusquely, "Sit down." His voice was low and hard into the phone. "George, you get those goddam photographers and newspaper people off my floor within the next three minutes or I'm going to have your ass in a sling!" Without waiting for a reply, Reardon smashed the receiver into place. He walked to the window and stood for a moment staring into the glare of the street. Christie could not hear what he was saying, for the torrent of words, directed nowhere, was an inaudible whisper. To Christie, the ring of the telephone was so unexpected and loud that she felt her breath catch in her throat, but Reardon turned from the window with a tight, expectant smile.

"The little bastard," he said, looking at the phone. He picked up the receiver. "Reardon. Yeah, George. I don't give a damn who told you what. This is *my* floor. You want pictures, take them upstairs in your own department. I'm conducting an investigation down here and these news people are interfering." Reardon sat in his swivel chair, leaned back and held the receiver high over his head. A high-pitched voice squeaked into the room, and Reardon—his eyes closed, then staring at the ceiling—waited for the talking to stop. He lowered the receiver to his ear and his voice was reasonable and his words, while spoken rapidly, were clear. "George, let me put it this way. If those bastards aren't gone by the time I walk out into my hallway, I'm going to have my people throw them out bodily. And, George, that wouldn't be good public relations at all, would it?" Reardon listened for a moment, then winked at Christie. "That's the way, George. You cooperate with us and we cooperate with you. Just one big happy family. Right, George?"

Reardon replaced the receiver, glanced at his watch, then at Christie. "What time did you get here?"

"I've been here since nine, Mr. Reardon. I was told you were looking for me, but that you had people in here. I didn't want to interrupt."

He considered this for a moment. Christie decided that his irritation today would be all-inclusive and not personally directed at her. "Very thoughtful of you," he said sarcastically. "You know where the morgue is?"

"The morgue?"

"The morgue. You know, where they keep all the dead bodies—the morgue."

"Yes, sir."

"That's fine. You get down to the morgue right away. Stoney is waiting for you. There's a body we want you to look at."

"A body?"

"A body. A stiff. A dead person. Right?"

"Yes, sir."

"You look at it and then you tell us what you think."

"What I *think*?"

"For Chrissake, Opara." The phone rang. "Reardon. Yeah, right, Tom. Be with you in five minutes, as soon as I finish playing Little Sir Echo with Detective Opara."

Christie's right leg was crossed over the painful soreness of her left knee. She wanted to shift position, but didn't want to distract him in any way. She had no idea what he had been talking about: a body at the morgue. She wanted to ask, but Reardon seemed to have forgotten she was present. He moved about his desk, collecting papers, mumbling to himself as he stuffed reports into his briefcase. Finally he stretched, adjusted his tie, put on his jacket. Christie stood up and her right leg, numbed, buckled unexpectedly. She grasped the edge of the desk to keep from going down. Reardon glanced up, his face annoyed. "What are you doing?"

"My leg. It went to sleep. I have a trick knee." She hadn't intended to say that; the words had come from her lips in response to his expression, which seemed to demand some explanation.

Reardon stared as though she had spoken in an unknown language. "A trick knee?"

"I had a shattered cartilage when I was a kid and had my knee operated on. Every now and then, it buckles on me. Like when it gets numb."

Reardon ran his hand roughly over his face and shook his head; then the quick glance at his watch brought him back into focus. He spoke as though he hadn't heard a word that had just passed between them. "All vacations have been canceled indefinitely. If you hadn't been notified, you're notified now, right?"

"Right." She mimicked him without intending to, but he didn't notice.

"Next: Your statement was delivered to the PC this morning and the Mayor should have it by now. The way it stands, with all those kids and their statements, the grand jury would indict this cop and throw the whole thing into open court. Your story is being kept completely under wraps for now. The squad is conducting a complete investigation—we need something substantial." This reminded him of something else. "After you meet Stoney at the morgue, both of you come back to the office. I'm having a meeting with all squad members at one P.M. sharp."

"Yes, sir."

He moved from behind his desk, his briefcase jammed under his arm, but Christie didn't move. The words gathered inside her brain until Reardon stopped. "Yeah? Now what?"

"Well, I just wanted to ask you." She hesitated for a moment, searched for the careful words. "What about Barbara?"

Reardon, for the first time that morning, was not only looking at her; he was seeing her. "*What about her?*"

Christie's hand traced a pattern in the air; then her fingers tightened around the edge of the chair before her. "Are you taking a statement from her?"

"Didn't you tell me she had her back to Everett?"

"Yes, but—"

"Detective Opara, I would advise you to let me handle this

83

particular matter. And just in case I haven't impressed it on you, the matter of my daughter's involvement is strictly confidential as far as you are concerned."

Christie's voice was even colder than his. "Mr. Reardon, I consider everything I do in connection with my work in this squad as confidential. Not more confidential or less confidential or top confidential or—or—just confidential. *Everything!*"

Her eyes were bright green sparks of anger, and Reardon regarded her silently; then, unexpectedly, he laughed a short, hard, brittle laugh. He reached out for her shoulder, turned her toward the door. "Relax, Opara. Come on, move. Stoney's waiting for you."

She moved stiffly ahead of him and stopped at the door, waiting for him to open it. His voice was directly in her ear, warm and breathy and unexpected. "How the hell did you shatter your cartilage?"

Christie moved slightly so that he could open the door. "Playing basketball. In high school. I—I fell."

Reardon's arm reached beside her and his hand rested on the knob for a moment. His eyes glinted and he smiled. "Basketball, for Chrissake." He pushed her lightly with his shoulder. "Come on, come on. Let's go."

TWELVE:

The morgue had a coolness unaffected by any season. It was an isolated, timeless place, and the people who worked there looked as if they had never emerged into the real world. The attendant, studying Stoner Martin's request slip, affected a cheerfulness and a casualness that seemed unnecessary. He whistled brightly as he carefully copied their names and shield numbers in his gray cloth-covered ledger. He slid a round metal ashtray across the black rubber counter toward Stoner.

"The butt," the attendant said. "Dinch the butt. Don't want to fill the air with smoke and have our guests getting lung cancer."

Stoner Martin pressed the lit end of his cigarette into the ashtray. Christie had never seen him like this before. She had sought him out through the long, complicated corridors, following the signs that directed her to this lowest level of the building, and felt a wave of relief at seeing the tall, easy, familiar figure. Then Stoner had turned and the face confronting hers was that of a stranger: expressionless, withdrawn, nodding at her without recognition. His brief words of greeting seemed to crackle as though his tongue had dried and moved within his mouth with great effort. His eyes were dull and bloodshot. All the sparkle was gone.

"Just got to get the okay on this slip, and we go," the attendant said, disappearing into a small inner office.

"Stoney, what's it all about?"

Stoney's fingers played with the dead cigarette butt. "We'll just take a look first, then we'll see."

"Well, here we go," the attendant said. "Just down and around. Hey, still hot out?"

Stoner, stiffly: "Yeah."

"Ought to get some of those people off the streets and down here. That'd cool the situation off, huh?" Then, fearing they hadn't understood his full meaning, he added, "We'll get some of them down here before it's all over, huh?"

Neither detective answered and the attendant began to hum. He led them into a room that was wide and high and seemed to be lined on both sides with large filing cabinets. He consulted the slip of paper, then thumped the flat of his hand against a locker. "Yup. Here we go."

Christie's vision was blurred. Everything down here seemed green. The walls were green; the dark tile floor, which actually was black, seemed dark green; and the face of the dead man, at eye level as the attendant tugged and slid the body out of its chamber and uncovered it, seemed green. Christie closed her eyes for a moment, then opened them, looking not at the dead man but at Stoner Martin. His mouth was slightly open and he looked drained and empty.

Christie forced herself to look at the dead face: to *see* it. The face, neither young nor old in death, was smooth and pale brown. The only blemish was a dark, caked, small hole in the center of the forehead. The mouth was slightly opened, as though about to speak. The eyes, deep-set in concave sockets, were open in death; they had a dullness, an unseeing, lusterless haze.

The attendant, standing on the opposite side of the body alongside Stoner Martin, asked her, "Well, you know him?"

With a gesture, Stoney motioned her to remain silent. With a slight movement of his eyes, not quite meeting hers, not quite abandoning the face of the dead boy, he told her. Christie shook her head. "No, I don't know him."

"Well, neither does anybody else. Except somebody sent in

money for his burial. Maybe the guy who shot him. You should have seen him when we got him. His head was that big." He held his hands extended six inches from either side of his own head. "Man, when they get it in the head, you should see the swelling. His own mother wouldn't have known him. We did a nice job—considering."

Stoner Martin's face was as tight as a mask, and a gray haze worked down along his dark cheeks. His eyes remained on the boy's face.

"Tell you something about this one," the attendant said, his eyes without pity or curiosity. "Must have had it pretty rough as a kid. Got lash marks across his back and shoulders. Old scars. Must have had it rough."

Stoner Martin closed his eyes; his hand touched the cold metal beneath the body of the boy who had been an orphan.

"Well, he's being shipped south tomorrow morning. Guess that's where he comes from. He should have stood there." The man pulled the sheet over Rafe Wheeler's face.

Poor little back-home boy going back home. Stoner Martin reached his hand out. The attendant didn't see the gesture but Christie Opara did. The long, dark fingers smoothed the sheet over the top of the dead boy's skull and lingered for the barest instant, bent to the contours of the head, gently, and then withdrew as the attendant slid the body back into the refrigerated wall with a loud metallic finality.

They went back to the high reception desk, signed the book, lit cigarettes, followed the signs that led to the street exit. Christie dug into her pocketbook for her sunglasses. The sun hit into her eyes like sparks but Stoney didn't seem to notice. His eyes were wide and vacant and unblinking.

"Stoney, who was he?"

He stood motionless and his breath was heavy. "Who was he?" he repeated, as though asking himself. Then, with great effort, he asked Christie, "Who did *you* think he was?"

"I'm not sure—not positive, but—"

"That's okay. Say it anyway."

"Well, he *looked* like the boy who shot Billy Everett."

Stoner raised his hand across his eyes as though he were just aware of the harsh light and he shook his head. "He isn't. How about we get some coffee?"

The luncheonette was filled with cold rancid frying odors and civil service employees from the various municipal buildings in the area on coffee breaks. There was evidence of old hamburgers and french-fried-potato drippings on the dull red tabletop and on the stained green apron of the waitress who stood, one heavy hip jutted out, one large hand poised over her pad.

"Just coffee," Stoney said without looking at her.

"You have just coffee and you sit in a booth, cost you twenty-five cents a cup. That's the rule." Stoney waved a hand at her and she said, "Okay. It's your money."

Slowly, he began speaking, the words coming in a soft, thick rush, an almost whispering sound, aimed at the surface of the table, slightly disjointed, slightly incoherent, compounded of grief and exhaustion and self-accusation. Christie pieced the story together from the fragments and the sudden complete sentences which were followed by sudden silences. He lifted the cup of lukewarm black coffee to his lips, put it back on the saucer untasted, unaware of the puddle of liquid that splashed on his jacket sleeve. Christie did not know how to comfort him. She sat quietly and let him talk.

"It was a dirty trick on the boy. My God. He was too soft. Hell. All my fault. You know what? Hey, you know what? Rafe Wheeler didn't even exist until I got him." He raised his face for the first time, the words forming the thought that had just occurred to him. "I created him, from the first day. Showed him a whole new rotten world, and there he is now, like you saw him. That's what I did. Created and destroyed Rafe Wheeler, who was just a nice, gentle kid who never . . . he didn't know *nothing*. My God, but that boy was ignorant when I got him. But I sure taught him. Yes, indeed, I taught him all right. I did. Jesus."

Christie looked up. The waitress was behind the counter

whispering to the counterman, her eyes on them. Christie signaled and asked for two more cups of coffee. The waitress brought the coffee, slammed the cups down, lifted Stoner's still-full cup. Her eyes were two small beads of accusation, her mouth an uneven, greasy orange slash of resentment. "What's the matter with this cup?"

Stoner Martin looked up, puzzled.

Christie stared at the woman who stood there glaring at Stoner, her eyes sliding and dirty on Christie. Impulsively Christie reached her hand across the table; her fingers tightened on Stoner's hand. "My husband doesn't like cold coffee in dirty cups," she said, her eyes steady on the woman.

The waitress hurried away, eager to relate this information to the counterman. Christie turned back to Stoner and released his hand. There was a familiar smile confronting her, a brightening and deepening of his black eyes and a bell-like clarity in his voice. "Well, my God, little one, but you certainly are a nut."

"That miserable slob," Christie said. "That awful woman, she—"

"Hey, watch it, now, Christie. Don't say anything you wouldn't want quoted."

"She just—well . . ."

Stoner took a swallow of coffee, put the cup down. "This is miserable stuff. Our girl over there probably poisoned it in the interest of future generations," he said lightly.

Christie smiled. It was all she had had to offer him: a momentary protection. It was all he had needed. He was Stoney again. "Listen, Stoney," she said earnestly, "don't leave her a tip."

For the first time in many hours Stoner Martin laughed: a warm, big, full sound. He bounced a coin on the table and pulled Christie's hand away as she tried to retrieve it. "Christie, leave it." His eyes were serious again, but clear, and his voice was low and controlled. "Listen, kid, I did a lot of running off at the mouth. More than I meant to—more than I should have. But—well, the man is going to brief everyone at this meeting and give a complete rundown and a lot of stuff, so—"

Christie interrupted. "Stoney, all I know is that Rafe Wheeler was someone you cared about very much. You needed a shoulder—I've got two of them. I'm glad I was handy, and I hope I helped a little."

"Helped a lot, little one—helped a lot. Well, like the man says, let's move. Come on, come on, let's go. But first"—he reached down, forced her clenched fist open, removed the quarter and carefully held it up to the woman behind the counter, smiled and placed it on the table. "Okay—now!"

THIRTEEN:

Eddie Champion stretched his hard body against the clean white sheets and felt a chill of pleasure. The air conditioner sure cooled things off. His fingers absently traced a series of thick, ropy scars along his left shoulder and down his arm, but the pain was dull and didn't particularly bother him. The stitch marks from his lower throat to his diaphragm never bothered him. Only his knees ached, and Eddie stiffened his legs, pulled the kneecaps up tight, then released them. He sat up in bed and rubbed his knees, his fingers automatically working over his old wounds.

When Eddie Champion was three years old, his twenty-year-old mother pushed the button for the top floor of the housing project from which she and Eddie and her two-month-old daughter were about to be evicted. It was a cold, ice-gray day, but neither mother nor children were adequately dressed for the blast of frigid air that assaulted them as they pursued their way to the edge of the roof. They did not remain on the roof for any length of time, as far as witnesses could determine. Actually, the young girl, staring straight ahead, seemed unaware of the climate, so intent was she on her purpose. Without breaking stride, she crossed to the edge of the roof and shifted the infant to her left arm while her right hand caught hold of Eddie's polo shirt. Without hesitation, she hurled her small son out into space and then, not watching his descent, the infant still in her arm, she followed. Eddie Champion's mother and baby sister were killed on impact. Eddie was not.

Eddie Champion had no real recollection of the incident on the roof nor of the long periods of hospitalization during which orthopedic surgeons performed a total of sixteen operations on various parts of his body that had been smashed or broken upon making contact with the concrete. His memory went back as far as his later childhood years, which were spent in an upstate Catholic orphanage, to which he was sent because when his small clenched fist was pried open upon his arrival at the emergency ward of Bellevue Hospital, a miraculous medal was found impressed in the palm of his hand. Whether the medal had been placed there by his mother or had been pulled from the neck of his rescuer was not determined, but it was decided that the boy should be reared by the nuns.

Aside from the fact that he was the only Negro boy at the upstate orphanage—in addition to three Negro girls—Eddie's great attraction for the other children was the interesting series of stitches that seemed to outline the various joints of his body. When he reached adolescence, he had become used to, though not hardened to, the appellation "Frankenstein"—for he did seem to be some strange put-together creature.

Eddie grew lean and hard and fairly straight and for the most part could move without any limp or other impediment. His recovery was considered something of a medical miracle. When he left St. Anne's at seventeen, he was considered polite, soft-spoken, fairly devout and reasonably intelligent. He had a general high-school diploma, the ability to take a piece of machinery apart and put it back in working condition. He had a letter of recommendation from Father Ryan, dean of senior boys, and a room reserved in his name at a Catholic youth shelter in midtown Manhattan. He also had a brain that periodically sent unspecified waves of panic and terror racing through every part of his being.

He had left St. Anne's with a series of resolutions: first,

that he would never again spend a night under the auspices of a church whose main communicants—to his knowledge—were pale, mean-faced, narrow-lipped Irish and Italian bastards whose main aim in life was to torment him. His next resolve was that he would never again permit anyone, black or white, to call him by the monster's name. His third resolve, less tangible, was that he would find some way to get even with a world that had inflicted cruelty, rejection, pain and humiliation upon him.

Eddie Champion's collection of terrors drove him through the black streets of the Harlem ghetto, searching. He avoided the easy, obvious escapes available to him: drugs, liquor, open violence, for these things would harm him. It was not his intention to add to his own injury. His intention was quite the reverse.

His first shock was that he was a stranger among his own: an alien in his own land. This added to his anger and hatred. His isolation was far more painful on the streets filled with black boys and girls, men and women. In the orphanage he had at least known who he was and what was expected of him. Street life terrified him, and his days were spent pushing iron clothing racks, jammed with cheap cotton dresses, from one warehouse to another, determined not to let the noise and the rush of humans and vehicles frighten him. At night he found something unanticipated and unbelievable: a youth center in the heart of the ghetto, run with hard self-confidence by tough, wise, bright, young black college students.

Eddie Champion knew he was different from the other boys who came night after night to clown around, shoot some pool, talk dirty, and bang drums or—on occasion—each other. What he didn't know was that his difference was carefully noted and duly reported to people he didn't even know existed. He was approached, after a few months, by one of the most popular of the youth counselors, a senior at Brooklyn College. He had been selected as an ideal candidate for membership in the Secret Nation.

Eddie felt safe within the stringent rules of the Secret Nation. His deep, long-suppressed anger found direction, and within two years he had become one of the best-trained, most skillful and most devoted members of the select group, the Royal Guards, whose purpose was simple and clear: the elimination and destruction of any and all enemies of the Royal Leader of the Secret Nation.

Eddie Champion glanced around the large spotless room. The Royal Leader's sister was a good housekeeper. He visualized those large strong hands rubbing a shine into the furniture, her hard face expressionless, every muscle of her heavy body straining at her task beneath the loose white garment that reached to the tops of her flat, shapeless shoes. Her robe was almost nunlike and her eyes were the coldest and most calculating Eddie had ever looked into. She had led him to this room after his brief meeting with the Royal Leader, provided him with a cold supper on a metal tray, appeared soundlessly to remove the tray, and had not spoken a single word to him. Yet her every gesture, her every solid, deliberate movement, had seemed threatening. Her eyes, watching him closely, seemed to advise him what everyone in the Secret Nation knew: that her brother was her life, that nothing and no one mattered but her brother, Royal Leader of the Secret Nation, and that her life and the lives of all of them counted as specks of dust in his light.

Eddie thought about the old man. His face, old as death but not a wrinkle on him; his skin stretched over the high cheekbones as smooth as purple fruit, his eyes as bright as beetles. Only the voice seemed old: not quavery-old, but so thin that you could hardly hear him. Yet when he stood before a meeting and spoke into those powerful microphones, his voice had a whispery sound that went right through your spine. Eddie thought about the crazy words—which he had never believed, not even for a moment, but which had a strange power over the auditorium filled with tense, silent, hopeful people.

"I am the living proof! I am the visible evidence before

94

your naked eyes!" The old man opened each meeting with the same recitation. "You are witness to the living proof and you see before you in my living body *nine thousand years of life* contained within this black and fleshless form. The flesh has been burned off through all the endless incarnations, but the inner fire [one long bone of a finger, held now to his forehead] has endured and remained and lasted through the succession of bodies, and the brain remembers how it was!"

The older people would begin now, softly, hesitantly, gradually becoming louder and surer: "Amen. Amen, brother! We have seen. We believe!"

Then the old man would seem to withdraw from them; his body would nearly disappear in the continuous chant of his words as he evoked the story: "This brain, this mind, this inner fire, remembers. Remembers the hot and steaming jungles of the beginning. [Oh, yes, amen. Remembers, remembers!] Remembers the great nation, hidden deep in the forests and the swamp. Remembers the blood vow and the blood promise, bought with blood, paid for with blood, renewed in blood, in blood everlasting, and my voice has spoken unto you, thick with the blood of the vow [Amen: blood of the vow!]. Thick with the blood, the voice speaks to you of the new generation of my children. From the blood and by the blood, this voice of nine thousand years, this voice, raised first over my people in the generation of their triumph in their eternal kingdom, speaks and tells you this: This nation shall prevail and this generation shall prevail and this black and beautiful skin, bound by the promise and the blood, shall prevail and shall avenge the destruction of our greatness. Shall not ask, but shall demand, the splendor and the glory and the power which is ours! [Demand! Shall not ask: shall demand! Amen!]"

By the time this weekly litany was finished, the old man had them, right in the palm of his bony hand. And when he demanded they give him their sons and their daughters, they gave him their sons and their daughters. But everyone over twenty-five was barred from the indoctrination courses that were run for the Youth Brigade and every member of the Youth Brigade took a blood oath—a small knife prick on the inner left wrist marked each of them—of silence on pain of death. The parents saw their sullen sons and restless daughters stand straighter, abandon their seemingly purposeless wanderings. They saw their sons crop their hair close and proud; they saw them abandoning wild colors in favor of dark suits and white shirts and dark ties. They saw their daughters become more modest and discreet about their bodies and their behavior and they were grateful, for—God be praised—the Saviour was here to take things in hand.

They never heard the first indoctrination talk the Royal Leader gave to their sons and their daughters, and no word of it was ever repeated anywhere outside the confines of the meeting place. The Royal Sister stood beside him, solid and unmoving as carved ebony, only her eyes alive and alerted, while the Royal Leader stood before them and told them their purpose in life.

"You are now the blood of the new generation of the Secret Nation, and as your blood flowed this night, so shall other blood flow. As you have been born tonight, so shall our enemies die. They shall feel the might of the Secret Nation in small ways at first: small mysterious terrifying ways that build and build until they are overwhelmed and defeated and leave us these streets and these rat tenements and these Jew stores and shops, and we shall rule our streets ourselves after driving them out, and we shall create from their ruins our triumph, and little by little we shall move outwards. Street by street, we shall take over until our boundaries pass the boundaries they have set for us, and they shall flee from their own great modern buildings in terror of their lives and their children's lives, and what they abandon in their fear, we shall occupy in our triumph!"

This part of it Eddie Champion believed. This part of it excited the lust and anger and emptiness within him. He could not believe in any nine-thousand-year-old memory any more than he believed in some glowing angel stopping the innocent Mary with great tidings. But the old man knew what he was about and he had a plan and the plan was working. Eddie could not conceive of how the Secret Nation thing had got started, but it was well entrenched and its membership was growing. Yet it was a select membership and Eddie was surprised at some of the people who carried the secret scar inside their left wrists: teachers, nurses, social workers, firemen, salesmen, two writers, some guy who did television commercials, and even six cops among the nearly six hundred assorted men and women who ranged from professional to semiprofessional to unskilled labor. The emphasis was upon personal upgrading. Snotty girls with teased hair and skirts tight across their rumps, who spent their days cleaning and sweeping and fetching and carrying for the white ladies, now spent their evenings learning to type and take shorthand and to file and to operate sewing machines. The boys were measured and tested and evaluated and steered to various city agencies where skilled training was offered, where in fact the city *paid* them to learn a trade.

But the real training for the boys and young men, the earnest secret training, was offered by the members of the Trained Brigade. Eddie Champion could kill a man with his hands in twenty-two ways with either one blow or a combination of blows and strategically located pressure. His training had been as precise and accurate and exacting as a medical education, and he became so proficient that he was appointed an instructor as soon as he completed his course.

Until he had been assigned as a member of the Royal Guards whose sole duty was to follow the direct commands of the Royal Leader, Eddie Champion taught ninety-three young men the art of bloodless, weaponless murder. Toward the end of the course, twenty students were selected to demonstrate the effectiveness of their education. One after another, over a period of weeks, each ventured into the streets and proved himself. Several had had some slight difficulty, some clumsiness, some hesitation, but each had been successful.

He felt honored by his elevation into the most elite body of the Nation, yet he felt some regret because he had truly loved his job as an instructor. Working closely around the body of the Royal Leader completely demolished any small shred of illusion, any superstitious hangovers. This was just a small dried-up old stick of a man who drank warm goat's milk and spooned in some kind of mashed-up vegetables six times a day and rubbed his thin belly under his robe and belched and rumbled. Eddie's assignment was to stand within the large office of the Royal Leader, his eyes fixed straight ahead, his body motionless: one of six invisible fixtures who silently opened doors as the Leader approached, fetched papers from one room to another, sharpened pencils and kept their eyes on anyone who came anywhere near the Royal Leader. Watched for a sudden motion of the Leader's finger, alerted to the silent command to destroy an enemy.

Though his face remained blank and vacant through the hours he was on duty, Eddie Champion's mind had come suddenly awake. In all his life Eddie Champion had never had an opportunity for prolonged independent thought; his childhood had been spent in memorizing those things his elders and betters told him he must memorize. His early days in New York had been spent mindlessly pushing racks of clothing through the streets and gutters without getting either smashed by some truck or yelled at by some pedestrian. As a new member of the Secret Nation, he had taken part in a crash course sponsored by one of the city's poverty programs and he had learned to operate a fairly complicated duplicating machine, which qualified him for a job that paid more money than he had ever held in his hand before.

But now Eddie Champion was a full-time employee of the Secret Nation, and though some small money came into his pocket each week, all his expenses were taken care of, his rent paid, his food provided, in exchange for his services and special assignments; and now, for the first time, Eddie Champion began wondering about the Secret Nation. He began noticing the procession of visitors. He began listening to the snatches of words and phrases, the quiet-spoken telephone conversations, and he began to wonder about money. His experience was too limited, his knowledge too confined and narrow, but little by little he began to realize that the Royal Leader seemed to have vast sums of money at his disposal. He knew that at each weekly meeting the elderly couples placed folded-up five-dollar bills in the contribution box, after first holding up the corner of the bill to the gatekeeper to assure him that it was the right denomination. That was a pretty good take, but the hall had to be rented, and the chairs. And there was this large apartment, where the Royal Leader and his sister lived and had the office. And there were the expenses of the Royal Guards, and the travel expenses of the Leader.

Since there was, for a long time, no action assignment to occupy his thoughts, Eddie found himself, more and more, alone in his small closet of a room, trying to calculate what sums of money came into the Royal Leader's possession. None of the special assignments involved robbery; they were terror attacks on white merchants in the area or on rent collectors; a few quick jobs on frozen-faced white social workers. The object had been to create terror: a feeling of directionless violence. Where did all the money come from?

And then one day it all became clear to Eddie Champion, and that was when he started his plan. The Royal Leader had a visitor Eddie had never seen before: a tall, thin, light-skinned man in a tan business suit who spoke in a high crackling voice. The man had carried a leather attaché case, like the white men downtown carried, all businesslike and professional. Eddie could not hear the Royal Leader's voice—it did not carry to the far corner of the room that was his post —but he could hear the other man, whose voice had a nervous, frightened sound.

"I had to come myself. There was no one else I could trust. Jed was busted and I had to come." There was an inaudible whispering sound and then the man had said, "Yes, yes. I will. Never again. I swear to you, never again." The man snapped open the case, and though his body hid his hands, Eddie had one quick glimpse of packets of money reaching the Leader's hand, then disappearing into the top drawer of his desk.

Eddie could not sleep that night for pondering the mystery of the money, and the walls of his small room in the tenement building two blocks from the Leader's apartment offered him no solution. He had got dressed, walked aimlessly along the nighttime streets, then stopped at a bar. It was a run-down place, flyspecked, with a sticky counter and a fat woman bartender. It was a place to stop and think, and Eddie was fingering the watery drink the woman had placed before him when the man in the tan suit came in. Eddie's first reaction was that the man had come into this place by mistake; he didn't fit here nohow. But the man walked purposefully through the bar, pushed opened a door marked PRIVATE and closed the door behind him. The woman bartender, a wet dirty towel rag in her hand, stared after him, her face angry. She turned, hit the no-cash key on the register, carefully counted out some tens, slammed the drawer shut, and followed to where the man was apparently waiting for her. After a few minutes the man came out, his face damp with perspiration, his eyes set straight ahead. He had noticed neither Eddie Champion nor, apparently, the low mutterings of the woman who stood watching him leave.

Eddie Champion took one more sip of his drink, pushed the glass away and strolled slowly out of the bar. That night he followed the man in the tan suit to six bars, and in each place the procedure he had observed was repeated. Then the man entered a tenement building. At first Eddie cautiously held back, but his curiosity got the better of him. From the outside the building was just another rotting stink hole, so that the interior hallway was a surprise. It was cleanly painted a bright light blue, it was well lit, and the doors were clearly and neatly numbered. There were no roaches scurrying along the walls, and a faint, tantalizing fragrance floated around Eddie's head. He heard the sound of high, light voices, laughing voices: female voices. Eddie turned his face quickly to the door marked 4 as the door behind him opened and the man in the tan suit emerged. A female voice called out to Eddie, "Hey, babyboy, don't take *her*. She nothin but an old bagga guts. What you want is something young and fierce!"

Eddie faced the young prostitute with a growing awareness of what he had learned. She taunted him, called things after him, hooted hilariously as he raced down the tenement's steps. The man in the tan suit was gone, but Eddie Champion knew now where the money came from. The Royal Leader was collecting payoffs. From bars, from whorehouses, probably from permanent and floating games of all kinds: numbers, dice, cards. It came to him in a flood of reality now, the answer to the things that had bothered him most. Not all of the chop victims had been whites. There had been some black men, too.

It was then that Eddie Champion broke the cardinal rule of the Secret Nation. He had gone to Bedford-Stuyvesant, in the heart of Brooklyn's black slum, and—no questions asked —he had bought his gun. It was the first step in his plan to take over the Secret Nation, the first step in the gathering of weapons. The no-weapons law never had made sense to him. The Leader spoke of blood, constantly drumming the word into them, yet no blood was shed. Necks were broken, bodies were paralyzed, but no blood flowed, and the deaths were not dramatic enough or frequent enough. There should be blood, because blood was terror and the terror should not be secret, it should be out in the open. The Royal Leader had lost his hold on Eddie Champion; there was nothing mystical or magical about him. He was not the Saviour and the Remnant; he was a shrewd little old bastard who was making a fortune, and they were doing the work and Eddie Champion wanted his share.

The plan to kill this Everett kid was pretty clever and it was carefully figured out by the old man. This kid was a moderate, an idol of all those slobbering do-good, do-right, you-are-my-brother-I-am-your-friend jerks. His death—at the hands of a cop—would be the fuse, and the members of the Secret Nation were to be the torch. Out on the streets, talking it up, but quietly, just setting it in motion, in the right direction, they would trigger the violence that would serve the Leader's purpose. Violence on the streets, open and declared warfare against the white police and the white merchants, and then the calming down and the cooling off. But the white men would want to get the hell out; some of them would be killed and some would be hurt and all of them would be scared to death and anxious to sell out. And the Royal Leader would have the cash and they would take whatever he offered and be glad to get it.

The thoughts seared across Eddie's brain: the old rotten bastard. It was all for him. But not any more. Eddie had laid his groundwork carefully, selecting those he could see were getting restless, tired of waiting, wondering what the hell it was all about and when the real action would occur. He had let them talk, encouraging them to express some signs; then he had added his voice: "Yeah, hell, we always hearing about the blood flowing. Only two ways to show blood: with a razor or a gun."

Then this goddam bastard Rafe Wheeler. Of all people, he was the last Eddie would have suspected of being a pigeon. He knew Rafe couldn't be trusted to go along with him—not like some of the others Eddie had cultivated until finally they were open with each other. He figured Rafe for a dumb Southboy who thought the whole deal was de Lawd come to them for sure—but never working for the cops. Eddie held his hand against his sweating forehead, remembering his report to the Royal Leader. The Everett execution had gone smooth as silk, nice as butter; it was just like they'd had it figured. No one believed anything but what the crowd had chanted: "The cop killed Billy."

Eddie tried to recall, exactly, what his Royal Whatsis had said when he'd given him the crap about Rafe Wheeler, but he could only remember the masklike expression, the small, unblinking eyes. "We was all shoving around, yelling about the cop. Rafe and I got splitted by the crowd and I fell down and crept real fast among all the legs and bodies, so no cop would get a hand on me. I never looked back, just kept moving steady until I was out of it, then just walked away fast. I figured Rafe did the same thing and thought surely he'd be here by now."

The Royal Sister's eyes had moved, slithered like snakes to her brother's face, then back to Eddie. Eddie forced himself to dinch his newly lit cigarette; the air was heavy with smoke and she'd notice and maybe wonder why he smoked so much. He just had to stay cool. He had pulled the labels out of Rafe's clothes, every scrap of paper from every pocket. Rafe would be some unknown dead colored boy found in a rooming house. The landlady would tell the cops just about what she had let them know she believed when they rented the room: two nigger queers shacking up. Probably had a falling-out.

The only cop who'd think different would look around and get himself another ten-buck stoolie. And that would be the end of it.

FOURTEEN:

The people in the County Clerk's office looked as though they never sweated. They all seemed old and powdery and slow-moving and unconcerned. Christie felt the impatience she always experienced when surrounded by people who were calm and serene and unexcited and positive that the information being sought would, sooner or later, in one massive volume or another, appear. It was just a matter of locating the right ledger.

Her eyes stung and itched and she raised her face from the endless lines of handwriting. She tried to match the various scripts to the various clerks who sat poking among papers. The contentedly plump woman with the yellowish-gray hair must be responsible for the round, thick entries; the thin, emaciated, birdlike little man, hunched over his paper container of coffee, must have authored the comments written in the fine spidery hand.

This was the part of her job Detective Opara hated, the research. The slow, tedious, laborious task of tracing some piece of information through the endless city agencies. Each office clung possessively to some small fragment of detail, considering that fragment an entity unto itself. Reardon had instructed her to begin her research with 1960. She took the precaution of starting a few years before that date, but he was right this time. Apparently, the Church of the Kingdom

Here and Now had not registered a certificate of incorporation prior to the sixties. In fact, the ledger before her was opened to a page dated October 1963 and still no registration was indicated.

They had listened to Reardon's tight rundown on this Secret Nation thing without comment, taking a few pertinent notes, asking a few questions, accepting his specific assignments. Stoner Martin had told them, in a low, hoarse voice, about Patrolman Rafe Wheeler. Christie had stared at the dead boy in the morgue and thought she was looking at the man who had shot Billy Everett. "That's how much alike Patrolman Wheeler and Eddie Champion are. Were," Stoney amended. Christie wanted to get out into the field with the men, mix with the college students, pick up some information about this Eddie Champion. But Reardon had listened to her request with a blank stare, then handed her his scrawled notes: Do a background on this church angle.

It was ridiculous. Time-consuming. Pointless. And useless to argue. Christie turned the pages, carefully running her finger along the lines. She felt some slight gratification when the words she had been seeking for several hours finally appeared. Laboriously, Christie copied every word from the ledger: "Church of the Kingdom Here and Now, 626 West 122nd Street, Manhattan, New York. Type of structure: storefront, room 20′ x 30′, lavatory and sink with running water in rear; owned by Wiselow Corporation; rental $75.00 per month; application in name of Church of the Kingdom Here and Now by Reverend Darrell Maxwell Littlejohn, Jr., pastor. Purpose: religious worship and instruction. Services: Sunday mornings 11:00–12 noon; Young Peoples' Instruction: Sunday mornings 9:00–11:00 A.M.; Tuesday and Thursday evenings 7:30–8:30 P.M. Date of incorporation: November 13, 1963." Christie added the ledger number and the page on which the information appeared. She closed her notebook with no sense of relief. This was only one task completed.

At the department of the Attorney General of the State of New York, Christie spent more time trying to locate the right office than she did in actual research. One after another, clerks referred her to different locations, different divisions, different assistants. Each assistant to an assistant attorney general in charge of some particular, singular legal technicality questioned her as to her exact purpose and Christie felt a bewildering lack of specific direction. She was surrounded by highly competent people who were ready, able and eager to answer her questions, but she was unable to frame any intelligent inquiry. Mr. Reardon should have given this assignment to old Detective MacDuff. A man in his early sixties, with a fringe of gray hair circling his balding head, and endless patience, MacDuff had a capacity to take all the various scraps of research information and pull them together into a dull but informative report on any organization or any individual. He spent eighty percent of his working time in these municipal buildings, culling and sorting through official records. The other twenty percent of the time, he prepared his reports. He was a researcher, not a cop. Fine. For MacDuff. But Christie Opara was a detective and . . .

The fifth official was a tall, heavyset young man with a lazy, good-natured expression and a soft voice. He motioned Christie into his cubicle of an office and proceeded to give her a rundown on the entire operation of the Attorney General's office. He was completely oblivious of her growing impatience. She lost the thread of his dissertation in the steaminess of the room, but the man, identified by a small metal plaque on the corner of his desk as Mr. Zakadarian, spoke with enthusiasm.

"So, Detective Opara, we can find the information you are seeking, which will be, of course, the following: Has the religious organization in question been certified as being legitimately entitled to tax exemptions under state law and has the religious organization in question ever sold any real property under its identification of incorporation? That would, of course, raise certain tax questions, depending on our findings. If you'll just wait here a minute or so, I'll run this down for you."

Mr. Zakadarian returned twenty minutes later and Christie gratefully copied down the information he had obtained and thanked him profusely. It had saved her some real effort. Mr. Zakadarian shrugged. That's what he was here for.

Christie rode the elevator up two floors, as directed by Mr. Zakadarian, and followed the signs that jutted from the wall until she located the Trust Estates Bureau of the Attorney General's office. This time, prepared to make specific inquiry, she found it easier to locate the information that was available. It was contained in a series of ledgers, and she copied every entry pertaining to the Church of the Kingdom Here and Now. Apparently, over the last two years, the corporation had sold several valuable pieces of real estate in the heart of Harlem. Christie's mind began to function again; if the church had sold property, it must first have purchased property, and that information would be located in the State Department of Real Estate.

At the State Department of Real Estate, a broad-faced, broad-hipped young Negro woman held one finger up at Christie to indicate that she would finish her telephone conversation in a minute. Her part of the conversation was more a series of small, annoyed sounds than words. She carefully replaced the receiver, then said to Christie, "Boy, they can be a pain, can't they?" Christie smiled noncommitally, identified herself and started to speak.

The woman glanced at her shield, then smiled. "For real? Hey, Sarah, take a look at this girl." Then to Christie, "Why, honey, you're just a baby. You ought to go on one of those TV guess shows; they'd never guess what you are. My, you're too little to be what that shield says. What's the minimum height? You don't look tall enough."

Christie's smile was stiff and automatic. Sarah, a morose blonde with a tiny red nose and thin lips, measured her with unimpressed eyes.

Christie followed the woman behind the typical municipal

rubber-topped counter into the office, through a wire-mesh partition and into a windowless, airless room that was filled with metal shelves of familiar blue ledgers.

"Arranged alphabetical," the young woman told her. "There's a stepladder over there, slides around. You be careful now, it moves pretty easy. Don't get your pretty dress dirty, honey. Everything covered with dust up there. There's a table over there, where Frank is working." Frank looked up without interest, and bent his head over his work again. "You make room for this little girl, Frank, when she needs it. And behave yourself, Frank. She's the Law!"

Her laughter filled the room for several seconds after she had departed. Christie warily looked about the room and determined that the volume she needed was on the top shelf. Just like every witness or complainant, she thought—always on the top floor. The ladder was wooden and splintery. Christie's shin was pierced by a sliver of wood: not enough to cause bleeding, just enough to send a narrow run up and down her stocking. The dirt from the ledger impressed itself against her light pink dress. She tried to brush it off and succeeded in smearing it in solidly.

For once, all pertinent information was in one place. A full page was devoted to each subject. Christie copied the information verbatim: a catalogue of real estate transactions conducted during the previous three years, during which time the corporate body of the Church of the Kingdom Here and Now had acquired and disposed of some four tenement buildings, three industrial sites (two laundromats, one wirebasket shop); acquired and apparently still held two tenement buildings that had been converted into furnished-room dwellings; seven bars and grills ("Check with State Liquor Authority," she noted in the margin of her notes); five grocery stores; one bowling alley.

Christie climbed the ladder and carefully replaced the ledger. As she was leaving the small wire-encased room, Frank raised his face, and his voice was amazingly deep and unexpected from so small a man. "Don't go locking up any innocent people," he said, and roared with great gulps of laughter. Christie smiled politely and thought someone really should let Frank out now and then.

At the Metropolitan Office of the Division of Taxation for the State Commission, Christie measured the value of the interested smile of the heavyset clerk, returned it full blast, and was able to obtain photostatic copies of the certification for tax-exemption purposes approved in the name of the Church of the Kingdom Here and Now.

"You tell your boss to send you around more often and not that old lady MacDuff. I could give *you* loads of valuable information," the clerk advised her, his eyes dancing over her body.

Christie whispered, "I bet you could." She tucked the photostats into her notebook and ticked off the Division of Taxation.

Back at the squad office, Christie resolved for the hundredth time that in the future she would take more careful notes. The cryptic little half-words, which had seemed so comprehensible as she wrote them, lost in the transcription. She never had to take notes when she interviewed someone; her mind could hold and fasten onto the substance of a conversation, her special insight could see through the welter of words and locate the true substance. But official documents, dryly stated in the morass of legal terminology, would have to be translated and evaluated by Mr. Reardon. His was the legal mind. She raised her hands from the typewriter, flexed her fingers and glanced around. Pat O'Hanlon was whispering on the telephone. Probably talking to his wife; his pad was filling with stars and triangles. Sam Farrell had left as Christie arrived, announcing he was heading up to the Bronx. Probably going home, Christie thought. Marty Ginsburg was making up a list of orders for hamburgers and coffee, so apparently everyone else was staying on. Christie had skipped lunch and had no appetite for supper.

Arthur Treadwell was bent over a stack of 3-by-5 index cards, and he looked at her with fatherly concern. "Christie, you have Marty get you something more than coffee. My God, girl, you're getting so thin you have to stand in the same place twice to cast one shadow."

"She's in training," Marty said. "We're going to get her so flat that when we got our eye on a place and can't risk a forced entry, we'll slide her right under the door." He cast a speculative eye over Christie's thin body. "Hell, I think she's ready now."

The fan on the wall near the ceiling had developed a hum that was interrupted periodically by a metallic click. The rhythm began to filter through the room, adding to the discomfort and irritation Christie felt. She found herself counting; at the count of six, the hum was interrupted by the click. Christie got up and yanked the plug from the wall.

O'Hanlon, finished with his telephone call and doodling, leaped to the fan. "Come on, Christie, put the fan back on. Stop acting like a woman."

"It just makes a racket and blows the hot air around. Pat, pull it out—it's giving me a headache."

Pat O'Hanlon hesitated for a moment, then pulled the plug. "Women. Women. They rule you from the moment you're born." He launched into his familiar recitation, which no one listened to. "They feed you and tell you what's good for you and what to do and what not to do. Then you get put into a classroom with them over you, telling you what to do. Then you lose your mind over some pretty face and next thing you know she's picking out a ring and telling you what date suits her and where she wants to go on *her* honeymoon. And where *she* wants to live and what *she* wants you to do. And then, God help us, you have kids and one of them turns out to be a girl and *she* begins telling you what to do from the first word out of her mouth. No justice. A man's job should be his refuge. But no. You've even invaded this part of the world. A woman has no right being a cop. A man can't even have a little cool air blowing on him, some *woman* has to tell him to pull the plug."

110

Casey Reardon came into the office at 7:00 P.M. The first thing he said was "For God's sake, somebody put the fan on in this room." Ginsburg and Treadwell, at Reardon's signal, followed him into his office, returned and informed Christie the boss wanted to see her.

The cold air made her feel chilled and light-headed. Her dress stuck to her back as she leaned into the green leather chair. Reardon, his jacket and tie off, glanced through her report, then reached for his glasses and went back to the first page. He frowned and squinted over the words, then searched in his desk for a pad and pen. He shook his head, began taking notes, then stopped and looked up at Christie.

"Is there something wrong, Mr. Reardon?"

"You're damn right there's something wrong. There's something *very* wrong." He waved his hand quickly. "Not with your work, Christie. You've done a good job. Look, you knock off for tonight. Be here tomorrow at around eleven. I guess you know everyone's on a twelve-hour day until further notice. I have a special assignment for you tomorrow evening, and in the meantime you can help Ginsburg and Treadwell." He pulled his glasses off, tossed them over the report on the desk. "Hold it a minute, Christie. I got something for you." He went to the clothing rack by the door, dug in his jacket pocket, then consulted a slip of paper. "You got a phone call this afternoon. From a Captain Gene O'Brien." He sounded as though he was accusing her of something.

"Gene called me here?" Immediately she thought of someone informing Reardon about a phone call intended for her, and impulsively she asked, "How do you know that?"

Reardon crumpled the paper into a small pellet which he tossed at the wastebasket across the room. It bounced against the wall, then fell to the floor. "Gee, Detective Opara, you see, there was no one in the outer office and I just happened to be passing the desk and the phone rang. I thought it would be all right if I answered it. I mean, it *was* all right, wasn't it?"

"I'm sorry, I didn't mean it that way. I just—"

Reardon's voice was hard. "Yeah, I know what you just. Who's Captain Gene O'Brien?"

"A friend of mine." She hesitated, but couldn't resist adding, "Why?"

"Personal friend, professional friend, family friend— what?"

Reardon could see the deliberation; the sharpening process, the careful calculation. Without saying it, she was telling him to mind his own business.

He broke the silence. "You see, when a member of my squad gets a call from any other member of the Police Department—particularly from a ranking officer who is not connected with this squad in any way—I have certain questions. Like what the hell is *this* all about?"

"Captain O'Brien is a *personal* friend," she said quietly. "He's never called me before at the office. He probably tried to get me at home and couldn't reach me."

"Yeah, he said something like that. Also that he'd call again tonight, at home. He works at the Communications Bureau?"

Christie met his eyes steadily. Reardon had checked Gene out. Probably knew the color of his eyes and how tall he was and what marks he got in math in the seventh grade.

"I'm sure you know, Mr. Reardon."

Reardon bit down hard on his back teeth and exhaled. He had known, of course, that this captain was a personal friend of Christie's. Her confirmation came as no surprise. What surprised him, or irritated him, was his reaction to her response. What the hell did it matter to him that Christie was seeing some goddam captain? Not a damn. It had nothing to do with him. Nothing. He had no reason to be bothered by the concerned, articulate deep masculine voice asking if Christie was all right. He just didn't like being a message taker, that's all.

"Go on home and get some sleep, Christie. Tomorrow is going to be another long day."

When she left, he snatched up the balled scrap of paper and flung it into the wastebasket and returned to his desk. He had enough problems without getting involved with Opara and her boyfriend.

He held the papers before him and said softly, "Something's wrong, all right." A hell of a lot of money was coming into this hokey Church of the Kingdom Here and Now. Too goddam much money: big money. Reardon sat hunched over his pad, making notes, and what it added up to was a great deal of wrong. He took out a small leather-bound notebook and thumbed through the indexed pages. He would have to be very, very careful on this. Only people he was absolutely sure of; they would be stepping on toes and maybe opening up a huge can of worms. He dialed the phone number next to the name of a lieutenant in charge of a narcotics squad in lower Manhattan.

A woman answered and asked him to wait for a moment; her husband was putting the children to bed. Then, after a series of household noises, a familiar voice said, "Hey, Casey, how's things?"

"Got something that might be very explosive. I'm going to need all the competent help I can get. Might involve a lot of people—*Department* people."

There was a momentary silence, then: "When shall we get together?"

By 11:00 P.M. Reardon had completed five similar phone calls. He put the small leather book back in his desk drawer, locked the desk and rubbed his eyes. He felt sick, and before this damn thing was over a lot of other people were going to feel a lot sicker.

FIFTEEN:

No one in his squad would have described Stoner Martin as a mean man. But then, no one in the squad had ever seen Stoner Martin exactly as he was being viewed by a massively fleshed individual known, appropriately, as Fat Man.

In the considered estimation of Fat Man, Stoner Martin was a mean man. Not a loud, grab-your-throat and crack-your-skull mean man, but even worse: the kind of mean man who purposely spoke so quietly that you had to hold your breath so as not to miss a word he whispered at you, because if you missed *one* word, it might mean you blew what it was he wanted. There was something so held-in about Stoner Martin, you just knew that if he let go, you would be a dead man.

Stoner Martin leaned both of his elbows on the polished bar and gazed into the drink he held between his palms. His eyes did not look at Fat Man, but his voice, soft and tight, was directed at him. Fat Man hunched his three-hundred-pound body as close to Stoner as he could get.

"You locate this boy for me and you do it real quiet, because I don't want anything to happen to him. Do it nice and easy with no alarms, Fat Man. You see, I got to get me this boy. You understand, of course, that if I don't get me *this* boy, why, then, I'll just have to get myself someone else. Maybe somebody big and fat, you know?" The detective sipped from his glass as he held it, rotating it slowly.

"Why, Stoner, my man," Fat Man began, then stopped and awkwardly removed his hand from the hard lean shoulder as the dark head turned slowly in his direction and regarded the fleshy touch with a withering look that traced its way up along the fat arm and clear into his eyes. This bastard could make your whole body shake just by blinking those mean black eyes once. "No offense, Detective Martin. Hell, man, I forgot you don't like to be touched." He settled uneasily on the stool. "Hell, let me tell you this. These young kids, they don't have nothing much to do with us older cats, like me. Why, man, they crazy little tiger cubs and they got a world of their own. Why, they crazy little cats, all the time howling how they going to take over everything and them learning how to chop people up with their hands and like that."

Stoner Martin held the cool glass against his chin, his mouth open slightly and his eyes smiling as if they could see right through Fat Man. Fat Man laughed but even he was aware that the laugh sounded scared. He would like to jam that glass right into the cop's throat, but the cop just kept on with that real cool stare and the fat man couldn't stop talking, like the cop was asking him questions, only the cop didn't say another word.

"You know how these young clowns are, Detective Martin. Hell, they don't consider me nothing like them. Why, God, they consider me a *white* man, compared to them. Can you buy that?" He leaned back against the bar, and the rolls of damp flesh, hot against his heavy sports shirt, spilled over the bar, and his loud, unhappy laugh filled the room, which was not as cool as the blueness reflected by the tinted mirrors suggested. The bartender, a fleshless man who shone purple in the glow, glanced at Fat Man, then at Stoner Martin. He moved to another section of the bar and became very busy polishing some glasses.

The detective spun about on his stool so that he didn't have to move his eyes. They just naturally rested on the heavy face before him. He put his glass down and reached out with an index finger, which was as cold and hard as steel.

The finger found some vulnerably painful spot right where a nerve was hidden beneath the heavy flesh. "You don't tell me any of your problems of alienation, man. You just find out where this boy Champion is. *You dig?*"

It didn't make any sense that the pain was so intense. Hell, he was just poking with one finger. Fat Man tried to lean back, to avoid the prodding. "It's going to be tough. You know that, don't you? Real tough."

"I got faith in you, baby."

Fat Man made a loud, gasping strangulating sound. "Why, you are just the end, Stoner. Having such faith in me. Why, God, I just old-time to these young ones, running around the streets and busting windows and beating up on cops and such. They don't talk to the likes of me."

Stoner Martin narrowed his eyes and carefully considered the quavering mass of humanity beside him. Fat Man, whose given name was Tomlin Carver, was fifty-one years old. He had been arrested fourteen times; convicted of various misdemeanors seven times; convicted, sentenced and served time on felony raps three times. One more felony conviction and Tomlin Carver would automatically be sent to prison for the rest of his natural life as a habitual criminal.

But Tomlin Carver was a man of varied and interesting accomplishments and value. He was not only a professional stool pigeon; he also supplied information to various members of his particular community relative to impending "showcase" cleanups on narcotics, prostitution, gambling and all other illegal operations well in advance of such actions. Those who were taken in such drives were those few remaining independents who were not incorporated into the unofficial tangle of threads that related certain elements of law enforcement to certain elements of the criminal community. Detective Martin was not certain—not *really* certain— of how deeply Carver was involved, but he was a good prospect for his purposes.

"Fat Man," the detective said quietly, "I'm going to lay it

116

right on you. Going to tell it to you like it is, just once, so listen real good."

Fat Man held himself so still, he could hear his own swallowing sounds.

"Now, you're going to tell me, by noon tomorrow, not a minute later, exactly where this Champion is. *That is a fact.* Now, here's another fact. I got me a little plastic bag, oh, about yea big." Stoner Martin separated his thumb and index finger, holding them about two inches apart, and Fat Man's eyes were fascinated by them. "Weighs maybe half a pound, ounce more, ounce less. Pure, untouched, uncut heroin. Collected, a speck at a time, over my sixteen years in the Police Department." The fingers closed inside a solid fist and the voice was still smooth and velvety, but his eyes were shining with a hard glow. "That would about do it for you, right?"

Fat Man felt a twitch alongside his left eye. He could feel the jerking but he had no control over it. "What? What's that got to do with me? Hell, I don't handle no junk. Never. Not stuff. Not this fat boy, indeed not." Stoner Martin just kept staring at him, and a flood of words began to gush from Fat Man's heavy lips. "Not since—oh, you know. Okay, so I handled stuff once, but that was long, long ago. Many long years past, when I was just a dumb punk in Chi. You know about that, huh? Sure, you know all about everything, I guess. But junk—now? Not me. Not once in all these many years. I'm not too bright, but I learned, yessir, learned the hard way." He wiped his forehead and his voice was low. "How's that little bag of stuff connect up with me, anyhow?"

"Where'd I get my little bag of stuff?" Stoner asked quietly. The effect of his words was incredible. The body before him oozed large beads of sweat; the material of the sports shirt was soaked through and the fat hands trembled as they smeared the moisture across his broad cheeks.

The laugh was nervous. "Oh, hell, Detective Martin, you'd never do that. I known you many years. I'd lay my life on one fact. You not the kind of cop plants something on somebody.

No, sir, not you. Why, you the one and only hundred-percent cop ever been around here. Everybody knows that."

Stoner's voice was as fine and deadly as a honed razor. "That's exactly why I could get away with it, Fat Man. Because of my reputation. No one would doubt I took it off you. Then it would be goodbye Fat Man. Life on a fourth felony."

Tomlin Carver no longer smiled or attempted to smile. There was an unaccustomed hardness in his voice. "All right, all right. I'll call you tomorrow. By noon. See what I can do."

He watched the tall lean figure move through the darkened bar and wished Stoner Martin had raised his arm over his eyes to protect himself from a rain of deadly bullets instead of from the sharp biting late afternoon sun that hit him as he reached the street. He finished his own drink, then picked up the remainder of the detective's drink and swallowed. He'd like to bury them all: Stoner Martin and all cops everywhere. And yes, those friggin' little dumb black boys with their secret army of choppers who really thought they were going to set up that Secret Nation.

And he'd like to bury Darrell Maxwell Littlejohn, too, for making it all so complicated. But now he'd have to go and see him.

SIXTEEN:

Detective Sam Farrell sipped the homemade wine and nodded his approval. The old woman noticed the red spot that was rapidly spreading into the grey gabardine fabric of his trousers, and despite his protests she dashed from the room, returned with a clean washcloth and dabbed at his trouser leg.

"No, no problem, Mrs. D'Angelo. It'll come out in the cleaners. Fine wine, real good."

Patrolman Nicholas Linelli waited until his mother-in-law left the room. He was a pale man with a worried expression. "Detective Farrell, no kidding, how do things look? I mean, you know, you guys are working on it."

Sam swallowed the rest of the wine and felt the warmth creep down into his chest. "Wow, that stuff's got strength. Well, look, Nick, we're working on various aspects of the case, you know? I know my part, another guy knows his part. I can't tell you too much, except that all our work is in your best interests. See, what I want to point out is that anything I find out, well, other people can find out too, you know?"

Linelli wiped his hand across his dry mouth. The large man sprawled on the couch regarded him with large, round candid blue eyes. "Like what?" he asked nervously.

Detective Farrell shrugged. "Well, like I wouldn't expect you to volunteer any detrimental information about yourself, like to the newspapers or anything. But on the other hand, you got to come clean with us, you know?"

Linelli glanced toward the kitchen. "Let's keep it low, okay? My wife and her mother been crying for two days now, since it happened." He sat beside Farrell and lit a cigarette. "What do you want to know, Detective Farrell?"

"Well, when I interviewed you right after the kid took one in the head—I mean, I know a lot of people were all talking at once and all, but remember, I asked you a couple of questions. Wait a minute." Farrell dug in his jacket pocket and there was a sudden flurry of small papers in the air. He leaned forward, collected them, sorted them out, then jammed them back into his pocket. "Now, see, you told me you didn't belong to no organizations but the VFW and the church and like that. But, see, Nick, you belong to a couple of organizations and signed a couple a petitions you never mentioned, you know?"

Linelli's face was bloodless. "Well, you know. Hell, they were busing those colored kids in, okay. I didn't say nothing. Then they were going to start busing our kids out. I mean, how the hell would you like it? The school two blocks away and they're planning to send my three little girls into the colored school twelve blocks from the house to even things up. Sure, I signed a protest thing against it. Sure, I belong to a property-owners association formed to fight it. It's legal isn't it?"

"Sure, kid, sure it's legal. I'm not questioning that. Just, see, you should have told me. Would have saved me some legwork, you know. Look, the reason I'm here is just that: to save me some additional work. Wait a minute." He dug into his shirt pocket, glanced at a scrap of paper. "The sergeant you worked with that day—Sergeant Frankel, TPF guy— said you made some wisecracks in the van, when he was briefing the men. Like you thought those demonstrators were going overboard or something?"

Linelli's face was blank. "Remarks? I don't know. We all—

120

everybody was cracking wise. You know how guys do. My God, is that sergeant trying to crucify me too?"

Sam patted his arm. "Naw, nothing like it. He just told me that he didn't know you, but that you and most of the other guys seemed unhappy about the assignment. Nothing to worry about—he had no official statement to make, this was just over a cup of java. Now, look, reason I'm here, as I said —anything else, anything at all, I should know. Because if there is, I'll find out, so save me the trouble."

Slowly and definitely, Linelli shook his head. Without realizing it, he raised his right hand. "I swear to God, on my mother's grave, on my children's lives: nothing. Just those protest things about them busing my kids out. And not even against the colored kids coming in. That was okay by me— hell, kids are kids. I just didn't want my kids going out." His voice broke and he covered his eyes. "What's all that got to do with it anyway? I didn't shoot that Everett kid. They *know* I didn't. The lab men know I didn't fire any weapon. And I'm left-handed. All my life I been left-handed, so what was the gun doing in my right hand? For God's sake, can't you people get this out into the open? This is killing me and my family. My kids are upstate at my sister's. They know something's wrong, but they don't know what. When will it get cleared up?"

Farrell felt clumsy and uneasy. He pounded the cop's shoulder and tried to sound reassuring. "It's a little more involved, Nick. See, we want to do a nice, round, complete job. It'll come out better for you in the long run. You'll see, kid, it'll all come out better."

The patrolman nodded but he did not feel reassured.

SEVENTEEN:

The Mayor had a handsome, boyish face suddenly gone old. The smile lines around his eyes were crumply as tissue paper and there were deep hollows in his cheeks. He didn't remember when he had slept last. He remembered a succession of hot and cold showers, meals taken standing up in corridors or behind his desk between meetings. The meetings all ran together in his mind: angry, frightened, concerned, indignant, righteous, saddened faces confronting him, all asking him "What's being done?"

He drained the remnants of cold coffee from the cardboard container, swallowed hard to keep from choking on some coffee grounds, then lifted a folder from his desk. He fingered the typewritten report, which he had previously read thoroughly, then leaned back in his swivel chair and dug his long bony fingers into his tired eyes. What was being done? A hell of a lot was being done, had been done, since Billy Everett was killed yesterday morning. God, had it only been yesterday? Reardon must be working his people to death. He tried to absorb the conflicting reports and come to the same conclusions the DA had reached. This whole notion of a Secret Nation; it was so ludicrous. And so explosive. Yet there were Police Department reports confirming a great number of senseless, profitless killings and other crimes of violence.

The Mayor reached a long arm across his desk and his fingers located the typewritten list of names submitted by his Commissioner of Equal Employment Opportunities. All these boys and girls had been recommended by the Church of the Kingdom Here and Now. They all had satisfactory performance records and good follow-through. Were they all potential assassins? No. That wasn't what Reardon had said. The Mayor tried to think calmly but he knew that exhaustion tended to increase his edginess (or, as the press liked to call it, his "snappishness"). Reardon maintained that the Church of the Kingdom Here and Now was a front and, like all fronts, to a certain extent it operated on a legitimate basis. The youngsters who were trained and employed through the various poverty programs were the "window dressing." They gave the church the respectability of community support and involvement, and behind that façade the Secret Nation operated. The Mayor had been skeptical of the whole thing last night. The Police Commissioner had accused him of being naïve.

And now this new development: the worst potential development of all. On the basis of information Reardon was collecting from his undercover people, he had come out flatly, not twenty minutes ago, with a completely new theory. Reardon stated that the Secret Nation was a front, just as the Church of the Kingdom Here and Now was a front. He spelled out a theory of corruption and double-dealing so intricate that the Mayor could scarcely follow him. But the PC had followed Reardon, and the two men had shouted across the room at each other. The PC demanded to know Reardon's sources of information. Reardon accused the PC of not having competent people around him to keep him apprised of the situation within his own Department.

The Mayor silenced both men, ordered Reardon to explain what he was talking about. Reardon stated that the members of the Secret Nation had been duped into believing that they were to be advance troops who would establish this Secret Nation, starting in Harlem and moving outward to all parts of the city, when they were, in effect, merely the instruments of a large crime syndicate, strong-arming hoods who wouldn't fall in line.

The Police Commissioner, dangerously red-faced, was furious at the implications of police involvement and insisted that, to the best of his knowledge, the Secret Nation thing was strictly on the level, dedicated to terror and violence for the sake of terror and violence.

"Now who's being naïve?" Reardon demanded. The Commissioner had insisted that Reardon be made to turn over any proof in the matter to his confidential squad, and Reardon's reply had been "Like hell I will. I have people working on it and when my case is ready I'll let you know!"

The Mayor did not know what to believe. However, there was the one real piece of information Reardon had presented: the fact that the Church of the Kingdom Here and Now had an incredible number of real estate dealings, all duly recorded.

The Mayor leaned back and closed his eyes and after a moment, with a sense of shock, he thought of Billy Everett. The death of Billy Everett seemed to be getting lost in all of this. He had conferred with the boy twice and had been tremendously impressed by him. He was an unusually intelligent and bright young man, calm and reasonable and articulate, and the Mayor had made a note about Billy Everett for future reference. He would have made an excellent addition to his staff of young people. But he had been killed Thursday morning and there had been two outbreaks of violence on the streets of Harlem and the city was on riot alert.

Reardon had presented him with a biography of Billy Everett, tracing his life from birth in a small private hospital in Brooklyn, through his elementary, junior-high, high-school, college and law-school education. There was a complete rundown on every organization Everett had ever joined and/or led; every petition he had ever signed or authored; every academic honor and award; notes on every speech he had ever made; transcripts of every television interview and public statement. The Mayor had accepted the report with a sudden angry resentment: "Is Billy Everett suspect? Why all this background information?"

Reardon had shrugged. It was the way his staff conducted an investigation: touch all bases.

And this patrolman, Nicholas Linelli. The rundown on him was just as complete but scarcely as favorable. No derelictions while in the Police Department; just an average police officer with an average record. The Mayor believed that Patrolman Linelli had not shot Everett. There was enough technical evidence to clear him of the charge. Yet he could not stand up to public scrutiny. This business of joining a protest group against his kids being bused out to another school.

Oh, hell. The Mayor wished he could call a press conference and state categorically that Patrolman Linelli was a member of CORE or at least of the NAACP, that he had been in the vanguard of a group of liberal white parents who voluntarily sent their children into a minority school. The Mayor tapped his fingers on the surface of his desk. That wasn't fair. Linelli was just an average guy with average personal problems and he was trying to cope with them. He had been set up. Yes, the Mayor believed that now; but he wished to God someone closer to a saint had been picked at random. It would have made things easier.

One of the most disturbing reports had been delivered to him less than an hour ago. The Bureau of Special Services of the Police Department, working with some of Reardon's people, had compiled a list of names: 106 city employees who were members of the Secret Nation organization. Transit Authority employees, civil service clerks in various departments, policemen, firemen, teachers, a librarian, an engineer in the Department of Public Works, and so on and so on and so on. The organization was not illegal. Membership—if it could be proved—would prove nothing. There had been city employees involved in other questionable organizations: far left, far right, lunatic fringe. Some very questionable rifle clubs, semimilitary organizations.

He glanced at his appointment calendar and wearily anticipated his first meeting Saturday morning. His special group of community representatives: twenty-eight people, who were well known and accepted by the Negro community. They were probably out working on the streets right now, through the night. He would keep the meeting brief.

The news-media people were scheduled for 10:00 A.M. The Mayor's jaw tightened. Those bastards, sharpened by their own exhaustion and the demands of their editors, had lost all restraint and all pretense of courtesy, demanding to know all those things they knew damn well he could not, under the present circumstances, reveal. Where was Patrolman Linelli? What direction was the Police Department's investigation taking? When would a presentation be made to the grand jury? Was he pressing for an indictment? Then they would refer to his refusal to answer as another example of his "snappishness" under pressure.

And what about all those eyewitnesses? That was what he heard constantly from the contingent of civil rights leaders. What more do you need for an indictment, Mr. Mayor? What are you waiting for? You have all those eyewitnesses.

Well, the Mayor would leave that to Reardon. That was his job—to break the solid wall of testimony. Reardon had his one witness: that girl, Detective Opara. She had always seemed competent. Let Reardon build his own case; that was up to him.

The next notation on the calendar was terse: "12:30—Everett body." The autopsy on the murdered boy would be completed by then and the body would be released to his parents. The Mayor had some fragment of information which indicated that the parents planned to have the body laid out in their own home. Seemed it was a family custom to mourn their dead within their own walls. He would have to pay a quick, unpublicized visit to the Everett home sometime tomorrow afternoon.

The notation following "9:00 P.M.—Saturday" was the one that threw the Police Commissioner into a near fit. But it was the one appointment that the Mayor intended to keep, come riot or uneasy peace. The Mayor was going to take to the streets. More specifically, 124th Street and Lenox Avenue. He was scheduled to be one of the speakers at the Freedom-for-All tribute to Billy Everett. It was going to be his one real opportunity to keep things cool. He and his colleagues and his community people were going to walk the streets, and talk, and listen, and show the Harlem community and the people of the City of New York that their Mayor was as concerned as they were.

Let the Police Commissioner worry about protecting the person of the Mayor of the City of New York. That was his problem.

EIGHTEEN:

Fat Man Tomlin Carver tried to settle into the hard straight chair with as little commotion as possible, yet it seemed as though his very presence broke the silence of the room. It was a damned spooky room, dark heavy drapes on every wall, shutting out the streetlights and holding in the coldness that some hidden and soundless air conditioner produced in chilling waves. Fat Man felt the perspiration down his neck and along his body but it had nothing to do with heat.

He had been in this room several times before and yet the same tenseness filled him that he had experienced on his first visit. It was all a put-on; hell, he knew that more than anyone else. Like the big Catholic churches he and Darrell used to go to in the old days in Chicago, creeping along behind the large dark shining pews on their empty bellies, reaching up with hands quick as candle flickers, grabbing the pocketbooks of those mumbling old white ladies. Even then, Darrell had told him that the dimness and the statues and the eeriness were just a put-on to scare the people into doing whatever the priests told them. They had been just little guys—nine, maybe ten, years old—yet Darrell had always seemed the older. Not physically, because Tomlin was Fat Boy even then, yet Darrell, wiry and small and hard, had a way of talking, of controlling things, of taking charge, and not Tomlin or anybody else would think of challenging him.

There was something desperate and terrible born in Darrell, and even when he was a little kid you knew.

Fat Man tried to rest against the ladderback chair, but a low creaking sound stopped him. He leaned his elbows heavily on his knees and tried to see through the gimmicks in the room. There were two dim spotlights aimed at the large deep plush-upholstered chair: the throne of the Royal Leader. Fat Man wiped the backs of his large fleshy hands over his heavy cheeks, then wiped the moisture along the sides of his trousers. It was a put-on all right, but it worked. And, damn it, it shouldn't work on him, because he had known all about it right from the very start.

Some twenty years ago they were doing seven and a half to ten on a narcotics thing, each determined to be real careful and get the minimum. Fat Man kept cool, as he had done in all the other Illinois institutions: the home for delinquent and neglected boys (Darrell neglected, Tomlin delinquent); reform school (both caught on a mugging job); prison (narcotics). But Darrell had paced around like a tight little bundle of dynamite, whispering things to himself, his mind leaping and figuring and scheming. Then suddenly he got interested in the prison library, and every time you saw Darrell he was bent over a book or taking notes or writing letters. Even got himself transferred to the library and took to seeing the prison chaplain, and they were always talking about the Bible and the chaplain was only too glad to see him. Fat Man had expected Darrell to look up, as so many other prisoners before him had, eyes shining and lips dry, voice wild and shouting, "I done seen my Lord! Oh Jesus, I done seen my Lord!"

But not Darrell. No, not little smart something-else Darrell. He hadn't done any shouting but he had whispered all through one long cold winter night when Fat Man lay shivering on the hard bunk beneath him. His soft voice was so scary that Fat Man had shivered from its sound more than from the cold as Darrell told him, "I knew there was an angle. It will take time, and it will have to be done slowly and carefully, but we can wrap ourselves around with the holy protection of religion, and from behind that untouchable position we can take what we want." And then the quiet icy laugh, followed by the not so crazy words: "Going to have it both ways, Fat Man. Nice and respectable, and nice and rich!"

Fat Man had visualized Darrell addressing a howl-and-confess meeting, the women all fighting each other to come forth and tell their sins and begging for forgiveness, and the men smiling and watching and remembering each woman's weakness for future reference. But when they were released, he followed Darrell to Detroit where some mumbo-jumbo creep was waiting for Darrell with a small congregation of nicely dressed, respectable, middle-aged Negroes. Darrell spoke real slow and easy and said things Fat Man could not quite follow: about dignity, and self-reliance and responsibility and pride. *Pride.* Pride—that was the key word at each meeting, and when he invited the folks to send their youngsters to him, they did. Fat Man had surveyed the surly group of young punks and wondered what the hell Darrell was going to do with them. But Darrell knew exactly what to do with them; he spoke a language they wanted to hear.

Detroit was a warm-up. By the time Darrell left Michigan, they had some cash and some introductions. They moved about the country hitting big city after big city, and in each place Fat Man did what he was fitted for. He recruited. He haunted the bars and cellars and crap games and whorehouses and alleys and watched and selected what Darrell wanted: young, intelligent, physically fit; no junkies and above all no criminal records. How Fat Man got them was his own secret, but once he delivered them Darrell held them, and that was always a surprise to Fat Man. They hadn't come to New York cold; the way had been prepared for them, but how and by whom Fat Man never knew. Through the years Darrell had told him less and less. In fact, Fat Man rarely saw Darrell. As long as he kept up his end, supervising collections and payoffs, he was given his cut, and that was all Darrell wanted to do with him. It hadn't bothered Fat Man. He lived the way he wanted.

This Secret Nation stuff was pure crud. Sure, Darrell let them chop a few necks, but Darrell didn't want open warfare. The way he kept his punks in line was a puzzlement, but that was Darrell's concern. Let him promise whatever he wanted; his troops seemed content with promises and occasional action. The one thing Fat Man Tomlin Carver knew for sure and positive was that Darrell Maxwell Littlejohn, Jr., while talking from both sides of his face, was, at the same time, making one hell of a haul; and he wasn't doing too bad himself.

There was a rush of cold air from behind him, and instinctively Fat Man stood up and turned. The door, which had been opened momentarily, soundlessly closed into the wall and Darrell glided into the room, his soft slippers padding over the heavy dark carpeting. Without glancing at his visitor, he passed him, then whirled about; and in one graceful motion he was seated in his chair. His body was almost enveloped by the soft cushions under and behind him, and his hands, small and dark, rested motionless against the white fabric of his clothing. His outfit reminded Fat Man of the uniform of a busboy: narrow trousers and a short jacket buttoned right up to the chin. The box-shaped little hat that rested across Darrell's forehead was black and decorated with gold braid, and from the center of the ornate design gleamed a stone which Fat Man knew was a real diamond.

One small hand moved slightly, yet it was a stark command; and Fat Man, unable to resist, accepted the command and resumed his seat. The dark eyes watched him curiously but without recognition, two black olives, shining and demanding. The small head moved to one side, and the diamond picked up a sharp glitter of light that blinded Fat Man for a moment.

"Why did you request this meeting?"

Fat Man's voice was low and foolishly deferential to the stranger. He felt strangled in the tightness of his flesh against

131

his damp clothing, and in the eerie darkness, with some surprise, he heard his own nervous laughter. "Wanted to pass something on to you."

Fat Man wished desperately for some sign that Darrell was present in the room with him, but it was the stony Royal Leader who sat before him, frozen and questioning him wordlessly. One raised eyebrow, hitting the stiffness of the little cap, demanding that he speak.

"Some cop been around asking some things."

The Royal Leader moved just slightly, as though he were tightening some muscles. The taut skin over his face revealed high cheekbones and a pulsating at his temples. "Tell me."

Fat Man shifted and leaned forward. It was hard to see clearly in this damn light. "Well, man said to me, Who is this *Eddie Champion?*" His narrowed eyes could see no change of expression in the face before him. "Man said to me, You know a cat named *Rafe Wheeler?* Because if you do, man said, you don't no more. Because this here Rafe Wheeler, he got himself shot through the head in this here hotel downtown and going to be buried back in old Carolina."

That did it; Fat Man wanted to roar with relief. He glanced around the room quickly, wanting to tell the Royal Leader's Royal Guards to look now, because here was old Darrell, but the Royal Guards had been sent out of the room before the conversation began. Old Darrell's mouth opened and he gasped, actually made a human sound, and his hands jumped on his lap because for once there was something he had thought was under his control, and whatever the hell it was all about, something had gone wrong for Darrell.

Fat Man rubbed his wet hands on his rounded knees and smiled. "Something important?"

"Were you told to come to *me* about this?" he asked, ignoring the question put to him.

"Man said, ask around. So I thought of you first. No one told ask—where—just around."

"You've asked," the cold small voice told him. Old Darrell

was gone, as suddenly as he had appeared. He was gone and the old statue, hard and inhuman, was there again and Fat Man was wary once more.

"Seems this man wants this Eddie Champion. Real bad. Bad enough to make some hard talk."

"You've delivered your message."

The Royal Leader was on his feet and Fat Man rose, towering above him, looking down upon the crown of the box hat. He could have lifted his two huge arms and enfolded the small twig body and crushed the life from it, but the Royal Leader floated past him and the door in the wall opened as he approached it without changing his pace, and Fat Man knew that there were small holes in the walls and that cold, wary eyes were watching his every move.

He waited, calculating the time, which seemed endless in the coldness of the room. Silently a man appeared and motioned to him and he was led from the room of the Royal Leader, through a series of small rooms, onto an elevator, which he entered alone. He pushed the button marked "L" for lobby. He walked through the lobby of the building without admiring the shining cleanness of the marble floors and walls and kept going until he was through the door, which was opened for him by a dark-suited young Negro who was not a doorman.

Fat Man inhaled the heavy night air and wondered what was so important about somebody named Eddie Champion and somebody named Rafe Wheeler who had a bullet in his skull.

The Royal Leader sat behind his huge glass desk and closed his eyes for a moment. He needed glasses; he must remember to make an appointment with an ophthalmologist and see about contact lenses. He put his cold fingers lightly over each lid and massaged gently. Then he slid his hands flatly on the surface of the desk. That fat mass of human flesh —something like Tomlin sooner or later could ruin things.

He still served a useful purpose, but just how long or how successfully he would continue to serve a useful purpose was the question.

No, that wasn't the question at all. He would have had Fat Man Tomlin disposed of many years ago if it had been that simple. The real question was how to *safely* get rid of Tomlin and get his hands on the collection of facts and evidence which Tomlin had carefully collected through the long years of their association.

Darrell's fingers twitched on the smooth glass surface, leaving damp imprints. He pressed one hand over the other tightly, filled with anger at his own mistake. He had equated Tomlin's grossness with stupidity, but Tomlin Carver was not a stupid man. Not in the matter of survival, at any rate. His mentality could never have conceived of anything as complicated as the Secret Nation, but he was smart enough to have figured out the operation and to realize that at a certain point—two years ago—he was no longer needed.

"You are no longer useful." That was what Darrell had told him.

Tomlin, fat and sweating, aware of what happened to individuals so designated by the Royal Leader, had shaken his head ponderously and his voice was a hoarse thick whisper. "I got papers, Darrell, with names and places and numbers. I got all I need to send you to hell and you got no way of finding out where I got my papers, but I got 'em Darrell. When I die, brother, you die."

Fat Man Tomlin was the living evidence of Darrell's greatest mistake. He would never again underestimate those around him.

What bothered him now was that the police had gone to Fat Man with a question about his people; that was bad. The small dark eyes moved slowly from side to side, straining at the exercise. So Rafe Wheeler was dead. In the hotel room. Of a bullet wound. And Eddie Champion had said he lost Rafe at the construction site. He had only one reason to lie: He had killed Rafe. That wasn't even important. What was important was that Eddie Champion had a gun. That couldn't be permitted.

The Royal Leader stabbed the button beneath his desk with the tip of his slipper. There was a soft, deferential tap and he slid his toe to another button and there was a buzzing sound, followed by the click of a lock being released. His sister, huge, powerful, strong, came forward, alertly waiting for him to speak.

"Eddie Champion. I'm afraid we made a mistake with him."

Instead of the single sure nod, his sister's eyes widened and he felt a wave of sickness grinding inside his stomach.

"He's gone," the Royal Sister said.

"Gone? Gone? When? Where?" His voice rose to a shriek and she offered him no comfort.

Her arms lifted in an empty gesture. "I don't know. He said he wanted some fresh air. He wasn't being held. Brother, you didn't tell me he was to be held."

He felt limp and nauseated and powerless and it was good to hear her voice become hard and controlled and reassuring.

"Don't worry, brother. They will find him. And when they do?" It wasn't really a question and she nodded when he responded, "Kill him."

NINETEEN:

Marty Ginsburg felt the stubble on his cheeks and chin. Though he had shaved less than three hours ago, he was already beginning to feel and look seedy. Right now, at this very minute, he should be jumping into the pool, roaring in his seallike howl that always broke up his kids. Except David, his oldest. Sometimes Marty wondered what the hell was the matter with that kid. Just because he was fifteen years old, all of a sudden his old man wasn't funny any more. But his other three sons, ranging in age from five to eleven, still thought it was funny when he took a flying leap and entered the pool backside first, and so did all the other people up at Valley Dale Cottage Colony High-in-the-Berkshires. Marty had postponed his vacation to wind up the meter investigation, and now he was stuck with this whole Secret Nation *megillah* and didn't know when he'd get a chance to cleanse his lungs with mountain air.

There wasn't any air of any kind in this little room. Marty loosened his tie and opened the top button of his shirt. Damn it, he didn't even have a clean summer shirt in the apartment, and the heavy oxford cloth was strangling him. Just his luck, he had to draw one of these sweatless little college bastards who had everything about him cool as frost. The kid—he couldn't have been more than twenty—took off his glasses and polished them carefully with a fresh handkerchief before replacing them and studying the subpoena Marty handed him. Even the subpoena looked seedy, crushed from being in Marty's jacket pocket which was filled with candy—which was a hell of a way to stick to his diet.

"Look, sonny," he told the boy, "there's the paper, so you just be a good kid and give me the list of names. It's as hot as hell in here and worse outside, and I got about five more stops after here."

"I'm only the recording secretary," the student told him. "I doubt if I have the authority to answer this subpoena. In fact, I question the legality of your attempting to appropriate membership records of our chapter of the FFA."

"You a law student?" Marty asked. Always there was a law student and always Marty had to come across him.

The student stiffened and jutted out his chin as though he had been insulted.

Marty put his hand heavily on the boy's shoulder and moved close to him, his eyes darting about the small room as though someone might be hidden under a desk, listening. "Let me give you some advice, kiddo. You *have* the authority. *Take* the authority, know what I mean? You're in charge here, right? Who the hell works on a Saturday? Nobody's around, you're top man. Look, that's a legal document signed by a judge and everything, you know? Don't go checking it out with anybody; you're covered by the piece of paper."

The student—a tall, slender boy with neatly cropped and parted brown hair, and small dark eyes magnified by his glasses—drew back from Marty's touch and words and regarded him with growing caution.

Marty nudged him. "What the hell, kid, you got a professor here knows more about law than you or me? Listen, I know more about legal law than all your book lawyers put together. This here's a legal document and you been served, so give me your membership list, and you got that legal document to back you up."

As he spoke, Marty Ginsburg shifted from one foot to the other and his eyes kept sliding toward the door of the small frosted-glass and metal-partitioned office. Suddenly he reached out and snatched the document from the student's hand.

"On second thought, you don't need to keep this. You been served, nice and legal-like, so I'll hang onto it for my files and you give me my information."

The student removed his glasses and extended his arm stiffly. "Officer, let me have that subpoena."

Marty shrugged, jammed his hand into his jacket pocket and removed the wrinkled paper. "Look, it's okay. Like if I presented this to my wife, she'd have to give me the membership of her PTA, you know? What's the big deal?"

The student held the subpoena flat against the desk and smoothed it with his palm. His right hand reached out slowly and he lifted the receiver of the telephone. As he started to dial, Marty Ginsburg pressed his thumb on the button, cutting off the dial tone. His face turned toward the door, Marty spoke rapidly. "Listen, kid, you don't got to do that. It's legal, it's legal."

The young man replaced the receiver and stepped back, regarding Marty Ginsburg with controlled but obvious indignation. His voice was surprisingly resonant. "Officer, I consider you and this—this document—highly suspect. I am going to check this out with Dean Alexander, the faculty adviser to our group, before I release any information to you."

Marty shrugged and pulled at his face. "Hey listen, answer me one thing first, will you? Look, if someone who isn't a college student wanted to be a member of the FFA—you know, some civilian or something—could he? Or do you hafta be a student? Or something?"

The question was carefully weighed and considered, then found to be harmless. "Our organization is based and led on university and college campuses throughout the city. However, our membership is open to all sincerely in tune with our aims. Our aims and goals—"

"Yeah, yeah," Marty said. "But you people keep membership lists of non-students, too?"

At the words "membership lists," the student stopped

138

speaking and warily regarded the detective. "I will be back shortly."

Marty sank into a gray metal chair beside the desk. "Make it quick, kid. I'm in a hurry."

"Yes. So it would seem."

Marty watched the tall figure hurry out of the office, and his eyes traced the shadowy silhouette along the smoked-glass upper half of the wall along the hallway. Facing the door, so that he could catch any trace of shadow, Marty quickly searched the top drawer, then thumbed through a small box of index cards placed on the large gray metal file cabinet. He tried the file cabinet. The second drawer seemed to be stuck; then Marty realized that he had to open the top drawer first, to release the other drawers. Deftly he ran his fingers through manila files, stopping at one identified by the words: "FFA-Manhattan." There were approximately ten onionskin copies of the membership list. Marty carefully removed a legible copy and folded it into a small, compact square, which he slipped into his right trouser pocket. He slumped back into the chair and wondered what the owner of the slow, heavy footsteps would look like. Probably old and tired.

Marty was wrong. Dean Alexander was young and alert with a red face and a nearly bald head fringed with pale yellow fluff that matched his heavy eyebrows. His eyes were light gray and angry, and the student stood back to allow him to enter first.

"Now see here, Detective—" He turned to the student. "What's his name?"

"He *said* Ginsburg."

"Yeah, how do you do? I'm Detective Ginsburg from the DA's squad and that document is a subpoena. There's nothing wrong with the kid giving me your membership list. I don't know why he went and bothered you about it—it's legal."

"You seemed very anxious to have Richard hand over the list. Well, Richard has no authority to do so, nor do I. We'll have our legal adviser go over this document and we'll advise the District Attorney of his decision. It seems rather odd to me that you people are culling names of the members of the FFA. For what purpose, may I ask?"

"Sure, you can ask. But you know how it goes, Mr. Dean. I just do what I'm told, you know. You could make my job easier by cooperating but"—Marty stood up, his words fading under the cold stares of the two young men—"well, I guess you got your procedures to follow, like I got mine, but it would help. So, okay. Do what you feel you got to."

Marty slipped his necktie from around his neck, bunched it up into a ball and stuffed it into his pocket. "Nice school you got here. Columbia is very famous, you know."

Marty reached out and grasped the dean's hand and pumped it roughly, then took the student's hand. It was damp and limp and that made Marty feel good. "Nice to meet you, Mr. Dean, and you too, Richard. You'll make a real good mouthpiece out of this kid someday."

Marty walked down the cool corridor of the university building and had a terrific urge to run at top speed and give a flying leap, but instead of landing in the nice green pool, he'd end up with his ass on polished marble.

TWENTY:

Casey Reardon pressed his knees against the metal seat in front of him, the way he used to when he was a kid at the Saturday matinee, but this was the first time he had ever occupied an entire theater by himself. Actually, it was a small screening room, and more luxurious than any West Side scratch house of Reardon's boyhood. There were six rows of pinkish-beige upholstered chairs ranged across the wide room at spacious intervals. Every seat afforded a perfect view of the large screen. Reardon was uncomfortable with his knees against the metal; the distance was too great for comfort. He shifted, crossed one ankle over a knee and rested his chin over his locked hands as he intently studied the screen.

The engineer, at his request, had turned off the sound at the fifth or sixth showing of the brief piece of television tape so that he could concentrate on the action, but the silent figures moved exactly as before. Billy Everett, his face startled and imploring, his lips moving over unheard words. Then a quick scanning glimpse of faces around him. Then the damn camera seemed to spin and the next shot was of Billy Everett's fallen body. Son of a bitch. The cameraman had missed the shooting.

The engineer stopped each frame as Reardon requested but the pictures were smeary and indistinct. At one point Reardon spotted what looked like his daughter's forehead, partially blocked by what was probably the back of Christie Opara's head. Reardon moved his finger and the engineer adjusted some dials over his gleaming panel of equipment and the film played itself out. The guy was very cooperative and helpful and Reardon thanked him. He absently massaged the back of his stiff neck and walked down the carpeted corridor to the door marked JOHN EDWARD TELLER, NEWS DIRECTOR.

Little John Teller really had it made, which just proves that you shouldn't make predictions based on a guy's performance in school. Hell, Johnnie Teller, mealymouthed and squeaky-voiced and argumentative, had grown up to be one successful boy: probably highest-paid in the graduating class. Reardon looked around the office: a Hollywood set, only all for real. Teller told him to make himself at home. Reardon poured a stiff shot of Scotch from the bar. It hit him too fast and he closed his eyes. What the hell did this guy make—sixty, seventy thousand a year?

He glanced at the cordless square glass clock on Teller's desk. Twelve-thirty. He wondered how Stoney was making out. His fat informant had called at noon sharp, but had no information except that Champion had dropped out of sight and that he would keep after it. Reardon smiled grimly. He wondered what pressure Stoney was exerting. He had known Stoner Martin for a long time and had never underestimated his toughness. He was working some other angles and would keep checking with the office for his message. Reardon dialed his office number.

"District Attorney's Special Investigations Squad. Detective Ferranti speaking."

Bill Ferranti was the only guy in the squad who answered the phone properly. "Reardon here. What's doing?"

"Nothing new, sir. No further word from Detective Martin. The rest of us are still working on the cards and lists. No one else has called since you checked before."

"Any matches between FFA people and Secret Nation people?"

There was a pause, some background conversation, then

Ferranti. "We've got three possibles, Mr. Reardon. Marty's checking them out."

"Right. Detective Opara in yet?"

"Yes, sir. She's been here since before eleven."

Reardon smiled, but his voice gave no indication that he was pleased by or aware of Ferranti's protection of Christie. "Right. I'm on my way in. See you in a little while."

He depressed the button on the phone, then lifted his finger, heard the dial tone and called his home number. "Barbara, it's me, Dad. Have you thought it all over? It's going to be a rough experience."

He could see her white-faced determination as she said, "No change of mind, Dad. I feel exactly the same."

"Okay. Christie Opara will pick you up in a cab by seven-thirty the latest. You're not to leave the house until she comes. That's definite, right?"

"Yes, Dad. I understand."

"Okay. See ya."

Reardon hung up and walked toward the bar, stopped and turned away. He needed some food. He'd been drinking too much and it was going to be a very, very long day.

TWENTY-ONE:

Eddie Champion lay on his back and felt the sun hot on his face and the stickly grass cool through the thin fabric of his white shirt. The crazy chant those creeps were singing was starting to get on his nerves. There were some pretty weird people around. Eddie thought he had seen it all, but this East Village deal was the end. It was a good scene for a quick switch job: black or white, male or female. Nobody seemed to care how you did it, or if you did it, or if you preferred not to do it. These creeps were strictly removed.

Eddie rolled onto his stomach and placed his folded jacket under his chin and looked at the groups of people around him. He tried to guess which were male, which female. It was hard. He looked up at the iron railing that encircled them, at the faces gazing down into the grassy circle, and Eddie felt anger tighten across his chest.

A string of vile words emerged soundlessly from his mouth. The seamy old Italian men and women, the high-cheekboned, small-eyed Slavs, the big brawny Irish guys, smirked or made disgusted faces and called out nasty remarks to the young people. Fine, let it all bounce off the hippies. It didn't touch them, but Eddie let it touch him, *deliberately* let it touch him; let it sink deep inside himself, into the center of his being, where it roiled around and bit into his guts.

It was a familiar feeling, bone-deep and as old as his mem-

144

ory: hatred. Eddie rolled onto his back again and closed his eyes. The tense feeling of anger gave way to a slowly building sense of excitement. Man, His Highness Old Mumbo-jumbo must be having ulcer attacks. He must be looking under his carpets, wondering who he could trust and who he couldn't trust. The old bastard. Forty-two of your best, old man. I got me forty-two of your best and we all got us guns and we are going to blast open tonight. And tomorrow—you are out! And all that crappy double-talk is out after tonight, you nine-thousand, nine-million-year-old phony.

Eddie moved onto his side, propped his chin up on the palm of his hand and watched a young uniformed cop outside the iron fence. The cop pushed his cap off his forehead, blotted his face with a white handkerchief. His eyes stopped at Eddie for a moment, then slid on.

Here I am, fuzz. But you're not looking for me, are you? You don't know nothing about nothing about nobody. Eddie almost wished he could stand right up and tell that cop, tell everyone. Hell, not one hour ago, cop, not one mile from here, buster, I got me a big fat man.

Eddie pressed his forehead against his arm and in the darkness, with pleasure and joy, he recalled the scene. The fat man: the Royal Leader's fat bastard. Jesus. Tailing *him*, tailing *Eddie Champion*. Waddling along, quivering along the side street behind him, never even thinking Eddie might know him. But Eddie knew who he was all right and what he was up to.

Eddie had turned into a black pit of a bar, a real deadbeat joint, stinking of cheap booze and beer and bums. He leaned against a stool and ordered beer and the bleary old slob behind the bar took his money and shoved the dirty glass at him without looking up. And the fat man. Eddie's fingers tightened as he thought of him. That elephant, so sure Eddie was as dumb as the rest of the brotherhood, just rolled into the bar after him, walked to the back of the joint and jammed himself into an old-fashioned metal telephone booth. Eddie had glanced around. Everyone in the dump was dead, gone in his own world. He had moved real easy, quiet, slow. Just leaned into that telephone booth and smiled at the fat man.

The fat man's hand fell from the dial and Eddie heard the dial tone and he leaned his face real close and told him, "Fat Man, you not gonna call up nobody nomore." It was comical, really funny, the way that big tub of flesh tried to squirm; hell, he was *wedged* in that booth so tight that when Eddie slashed him with the edge of his right hand across the throat, that fat man just kept sitting there, all pressed into the phone booth, just like he was still alive.

And nobody had noticed a thing; all those bums with their faces in their beers, the bartender with his head down. Nobody saw nothing and Eddie had just moved out, nice and easy, and never stopped until he got to this crazy park with all these crazy weirdoes.

He would stay right where he was, do just what he planned tonight, in front of them all. And the brothers who were looking for him would meet themselves coming and going, because the brothers who were with him had tipped him and had agreed to make the move with him tonight.

The whole deal: mine. I won't run it the way the old screw did. It will be the real thing—the real *Secret Nation*—and the streets will run red with blood. Eddie thought of money. Not nice new even stacks of bills, but crumply handfuls of green fives and tens and twenties, uncounted and endless. And not just for him—for all of them, all the brothers. All the other crap, the buildings and businesses and stuff—who needs it? Just the cash, collected every week, stuffed into the black bag and then divided up.

They had discussed it last night in Claude Davis's room and Claude had that scared look on his face. He was the only one asking any questions and finally Eddie had told him to just shut up and leave all the details to him. Eddie wasn't exactly sure himself how to set up that end of things, but with the men and the talent and the guns he'd work it out.

Eddie stretched his body and tried to get loose. He needed

146

to sleep a little. Tonight: they would show their strength and their power and the white bastards would bleed and die all over the streets. The Secret Nation would be whispered about and written about and it would be a fact. A real, true thing, not like the swindle the old man had pulled off.

He wished the sun would move real fast, sink, die, turn black. Come night. But before everything else, he had to go through with this FFA crap. He had to show up with them, mingle with them, be seen by them, just one of the nice kids sorrowing after young Billy. He didn't want to call attention to himself in any way; he could get lost in the crowd easy enough when the time came.

Eddie Champion frowned and tried to catch the elusive wave of panic, the sensation of weightlessness, of falling. His hands pressed flat against the grass beside his body; his fingers dug into the earth and tightened, but he could not hold on or reach out to whatever it was that was taunting him. Some feeling, some warning, something he had to remember. Something from the moment he had shot Billy Everett. Something. . . .

He forced his hands to relax, to relinquish the small bits of grass and dirt. He was determined to sleep. He had to sleep, to be prepared for tonight.

After all, it wasn't every night in your life that you got to shoot the Mayor of the City of New York.

TWENTY-TWO:

Christie Opara kept a close watch on Barbara Reardon. The girl had been tense and silent during their ride to the Everett home, her face a sick white, her eyes large and glazed. A policeman and a law student, Gerald Friedman, lifelong friend and neighbor and classmate and confident of Billy Everett, stood just outside the house and asked identification of everyone who sought entry. The curious, the sensation seekers, the hostile, the slummers, were kept a full city block away from the house, yet their voices reached from behind the police barricades from time to time. Barbara displayed her FFA membership card and didn't notice Christie flash her shield. The girl's face was set into a stony resolve but she couldn't have been any more prepared than was Christie for the terribleness of the mourning room.

The coldness generated by the powerful rented air conditioners was no more incongruous than the gay flowered wallpaper—all cheerful red roses and pink daisies rising up from behind the coffin which was set against the one wall. The coffin seemed huge in the smallness of the room, and rows of folding chairs were lined up facing it. In one corner was a large, comfortable high-back plush chair of bright green; it was the only piece of furniture that had not been shifted to another part of the house. Banks of flowers surrounded the coffin and young people moved uncertainly, fingering the cards of the donors. There was a soft, hushed murmur of voices in every corner of the room but there was an island of absolute silence radiating around the large, stiff, straight, middle-aged Negro who sat bolt-upright on a wooden chair directly in line with the open end of the coffin.

A lean, light-skinned Negro in black suit and clerical collar nodded at Christie, then saw Barbara Reardon's face and reached for her elbow and wordlessly led the girls to the coffin. Barbara knelt, crossed herself, her eyes wide and unseeing, her lips moving. Then she crossed herself again and rose unsteadily, her eyes on the dead face. She shook her head, then turned her face away and was steered by the minister to Billy's father. Her hand was pressed and released by his, but their eyes never met.

"Mrs. Everett is in the kitchen, my dear. She would take it kindly if you would have some coffee she has prepared," the minister told Barbara.

Christie looked down at the small, large-eyed woman whose hands twisted in the lap of her black crepe dress and found her hand going out and being reached for and held for one brief, tight second by a cold hand that quickly retreated. Christie heard herself whisper some words, some senseless words, which were accepted with a small, sad, devastatingly sympathetic smile. She was offered some coffee, which she accepted and tried to drink, but her hand trembled as she lifted the cup from the saucer to her mouth. She couldn't control the tilt of the cup, and a large unanticipated swallow of hot coffee flowed down the back of her throat and Christie had to clench her teeth to keep from choking. Barbara had moved to a corner of the kitchen and was speaking to some students. The girl looked sick: as sick with shock and disbelief as she had at the moment of the shooting.

Christie tried to concentrate on the coffee, on the small piece of cake that had been placed on a plate and handed to her, but it was as though the pores of her body had been opened and she could not stop absorbing the room in which she stood. Here, in this room, in this house, Billy Everett had existed in all the many facets of his life. Christie's eyes were drawn to the shining Formica table, beige with a marble pattern, where Billy had eaten his meals. To the large glass jar, half filled with chocolate-chip cookies, to the stove where his mother prepared his meals, to the small metal-topped cardboard box where offerings were made for the benefit of some Southern Baptist church, to the large calendar hung on the yellow-papered wall, with careful red circles drawn around significant dates. There was a collection of notebooks tossed carelessly on a counter top next to aluminum canisters of tea, coffee, flour and sugar. Christie put the cup and saucer down beside her cake plate. Her fingers slid over the notebooks and she opened one and saw lines of cramped notes, and in the margins were inked doodles of flowers and stars.

Against her will, she looked at Mrs. Everett and something far more terrible than sympathy welled up in Christie: the ultimate grief, the ultimate disaster, the one unacceptable, unbearable loss that she had never allowed herself to envision. Death of her father had been hard; death of her husband had been torment, the worst kind, the most terrible. But not really, for Christie had survived even that. But Mrs. Everett, holding herself quietly, concerned with her guests, had not yet been encompassed by the most unbelievable loss: death of her son. Fear welled up inside of Christie Opara, terror, and she could no longer look upon Mrs. Everett.

Barbara Reardon finished her coffee, placed the cup in the sink, and her eyes met Christie's and answered the unasked question: yes. She wanted to leave now.

The hallway just outside the parlor was filled with young people and though their voices were low and hushed, they were intent upon their conversation. Barbara lingered and Christie waited, standing back, not really looking at any of the faces. The light in the hallway was dim, and all the faces, brown and tan and white, seemed the same. Facing Christie was a small, thin, wiry white boy with large dark eyes and black circles of grief and exhaustion extending down his pale cheeks. It was Gerald Friedman, now temporary leader of the FFA. He was a tense boy, filled with quick nervous movements of his hands and arms and facial muscles.

"We have to go," Gerald was saying, "all of us. We have to present a united front. It is more important than anything we've ever done, to show ourselves together: black and white. To show people how it is and that Billy must not be used as a trigger for violence. To show the community that violence is not the way." His thin hand reached out and grasped the shoulder of a heavyset young Negro to his left. "Don't tell me about the mood of the crowd. We have to change that mood. To get out there and back the Mayor and make this an interracial meeting, on the streets. We have to, or we will have lost our last opportunity."

Barbara Reardon stood transfixed now, not taking part in the discussion, but standing close inside the circle of white and black boys and girls, just needing to be there for the moment. Christie was tired and her eyes smarted from the bad air, filled with smoke and human bodies and heavy flower scent and yellowish light. She stood impatiently behind Barbara, waiting for the girl to turn away. Christie followed the gist of the conversation but the words were blurred and hazy, as indistinct as the half circle of faces confronting her, as featureless and empty as she herself felt. She glanced at her watch, determined that they would leave now. She drew in her breath heavily, wearily, and the breath stuck in her throat and her eyes cleared and sharpened. Directly opposite her, a young man had edged his way into the circle, nodding politely as room was made for him. His eyes did not meet Christie's; they were intent upon Gerald Friedman and he was nodding in solemn approval of Gerald's words. His eyes, a clear, bright yellow, strayed about and Christie turned her face from Eddie Champion's.

She didn't know if he had just joined the group or had been standing there motionless in the semidarkness all along. But there he was, three feet away from her, and Christie didn't know what the devil to do about him. There was a telephone on the hall table directly behind her: call the office, check with Reardon. She forced herself to slow down; she couldn't possibly use the phone here.

Christie was startled by the pressure on her arm. Barbara Reardon was ready to go home. Christie glanced over Barbara's shoulder. Champion was saying something. Something about leaving now. Something about . . .

"Barbara, listen to me." The girl's face was expressionless and Christie whispered sharply, "For God's sake, listen to me. Something has come up." Champion was moving toward the door. "Barbara, I can't take you home. Listen, tell the cop at the door who you are. Ask him to get you a cab." The girl blinked, her mouth opened slightly, but she said nothing. "Please, Barbara. I can't explain. Promise. Promise you'll go straight home."

Barbara Reardon nodded, but Christie wasn't sure the girl had even heard one word she had said. She couldn't think about that now. She left the house quickly, then stopped on the small cement patio. Eddie Champion was standing on the sidewalk, his back to her, his head bent over a flickering flame, lighting a cigarette.

Christie stood beside the patrolman, her eyes on Champion. "Officer, I'm Detective Opara of the District Attorney's squad and . . ."

The cop, young and tall in his new uniform, squinted and said, "Huh?"

Christie looked at him, just one quick glance, and her insides felt like heavy plaster. She looked back at Eddie Champion. He was moving now. She paced herself to his stride, her eyes fastened on the figure as it moved in and out of the shadows. There was nothing else she could do: just stick with him.

TWENTY-THREE:

Detective Stoner Martin crossed his fingers before he asked Ferranti his question. It was the eighth time that day —the second time that night—that he had called the office. It was the first time he had spoken to Detective Ferranti.

"Any calls for me, Bill?"

Ferranti, always so calm, always so careful, hesitated. "Hang on, Stoney. I think you got one message. Let me check."

Stoner Martin's fingers pressed together so hard they felt numb. It was a stupid gesture, without meaning, but he was exhausted and desperate. He heard Bill's voice, quiet, polite, refined. Then, in the background, Marty Ginsburg, then, in his ear again, Ferranti. "You got one call about an hour ago."

"Right, right."

"Marty's scrawl is hard to—here. A Mr. Richard C. Jackson. He called about an hour ago, five-thirty P.M."

For a moment, just a bare moment, Stoner held his breath. It could be. It could be Tomlin.

"There's two numbers for you to call, Stoney. He said you should call him anytime. I checked the numbers he left—one for his office and one for his home. He's listed in the directory as an insurance agent. Home address is on Staten Island."

Stoner Martin uncrossed his fingers and his hand clenched into a tight fist which he tapped lightly against the metal shelf inside the phone booth.

"Nothing else? No other calls, just this one guy?" he asked.

"That's it. Oh, he did say it was important. Said feel free to call anytime."

"Great. That's what I need. An insurance man. Okay. I'll be ringing in periodically."

Stoney's fist lightly and rapidly continued to tap the metal shelf in time to his low, hoarse, continuous flow of words. That fat bastard. That dirty rotten stinking . . . that . . . His fist smashed the metal shelf with a thunderous painful blow. Fat Man's face; Fat Man's lying rotten mouth. Called my bluff. Called my bluff but it was no bluff. Not now. You're in, you slob; if I have to perjure myself into hell, you're in. He closed his eyes and stood rigid. Okay. Okay, now slow it down. There are other lines out. Fat Man later. Much later.

He dug into his back pocket and extracted a small index card from a dog-eared notebook. There was a coded series of marks against each of five names, based on thorough background reports on each of the individuals. He would call the office back and leave relay instructions for each of the four men assigned to work with him. Give each man a name: he'd take the top name himself. It was one of the alternatives that had been discussed.

He interrupted Ferranti's long recitation of identification. "Yeah, it's me again, Bill. Listen—"

"That Mr. Jackson called again."

"Forget it. Look, you know those men I got working with me? They due to check in again soon—like within the next thirty minutes?"

"Yes, they've been prompt with every ring."

"Okay. We're going to start a relay. As each man calls, assign him to one of these names: top to bottom." Stoney read off four names. "Note which man has which subject. Tell them I got Claude Davis. Instructions are they stay close, stay loose, and call whenever they can—most important, they are to stay with subject, right?"

"Okay, Stoner. Good luck."

Stoner replaced the receiver, glanced down at the card of names. "Okay, buddy," he said to the name before his eyes. "You lead me to my boy. Then I'm going to find Fat Man all by myself."

TWENTY-FOUR:

Christie watched Eddie Champion through the smudged glass of the telephone booth as she inserted a dime and heard the buzz of the dial tone. Carefully, her finger began to spin out the DA's number. She glanced from Champion to the dial, then back to Champion. She smashed the receiver back into place the moment the incisive busy signal began. She immediately reinserted the dime and began dialing the second office number. Everyone was calling in. The whole squad was calling in to say they couldn't find Eddie Champion. Get off the phones—get off the phones, damn it, *answer*.

Champion removed a brown paper bag from the locker and held it in the palm of his hand. His face was averted from her and there were a lot of people moving about the vast arcade: tourists heading to or from the Central; passengers taking the shuttle to Times Square or searching for the IRT trains. The small fan inside the booth was blowing something that felt like tepid water directly on Christie's face. There was a noise from within the receiver, a clicking of gears falling into place, then a split second of silence. The phone rang.

Champion moved into the crowd and Christie hung up and darted into the stream of bodies. Champion followed a series of lights that directed passengers to the uptown IRT. He kept pace with the tide of human beings who shuffled along. Christie kept to his right and slackened her pace. She was close enough to reach out and touch him. To arrest him. But for what? Killing Billy Everett? No proof, no proof. The words pounded in her brain in time with her steps. Reardon hadn't instructed her about Champion; the possibility of her coming upon him was so remote. But here he was. She could reach out and grasp him. New laws, new statutes, new penal code, new. I should keep up with these things, Christie thought; if I take him now, it might mess everything up. Might violate his rights. What are his rights? My God, if only someone had answered the phone. Patrolman Wheeler? Grab him for suspicion of murder? Too loose, no good. Stay with him; just stay with him.

I don't have a subway token.

The thought filled her with panic. There were always at least two tokens in her pocketbook, but she had switched pocketbooks this morning. The IRT control gate was so complicated. In order to be admitted she would have to approach the booth, show her shield to the agent, and return to the small iron gate, which could not be released until the agent pressed a buzzer unlatching the gate. The exit doors were turnstiles, rotating in reverse. Her fingers dug into her small change purse, identifying pennies, nickels, dimes. She couldn't move ahead of Champion and enter the controls before him; he might spot her. Maybe there wouldn't be a long line at the booth; she'd buy a token.

There were two long straggling lines before the booth. Champion moved toward the turnstile. He had a token. For a split second Christie thought of crouching under or leaping over, but that would attract too much attention. She pushed her way to the agent's window, slammed her shield against the iron grillwork and instructed the woman. "Gate. Hurry, please."

She moved quickly to the gate and pushed against it as the buzzer sounded. She was through the controls, but Eddie Champion was gone.

Christie forced herself to think logically. He must be heading uptown, to 125th Street. That was what the group had been planning. Apparently he had just been killing time, but now he was heading in a definite direction.

Christie moved resolutely toward the uptown express platform and systematically sifted the crowd. Professionally, her eyes moved among the hundreds of bodies milling about the platform. She was looking for one man; therefore, she could dismiss everyone else. If his objective was 125th Street, Champion would probably head for the first car. Christie moved rapidly, but deliberately. She ignored the local side of the platform, assuming he would take an express train.

The crowd moved toward the edge of the express side as a train rumbled far down the tunnel. Christie stepped back across to the local side for better perspective. She ignored the dry choking sensation in her throat and the squeezing and pressing inside her stomach. She concentrated on the absolute necessity of finding Eddie Champion in that crowd which was hardening, tightening, to jam onto the express train. She scanned the people about to enter the first car. He wasn't there.

As she moved toward the second car, there was an explosion of tumultuous movement. Faces came toward her as people exited from the newly arrived train, bringing with them a blast of human heat and a resolve not to be forced back onto the train.

Eddie Champion entered the first door of the second car and Christie Opara drew in one great breath of relief and forced herself into the second door of the second car.

Champion leaned against the closed door and was visible to Christie from the waist up. He stared vacantly at the subway advertisements and Christie observed him without looking directly at him. At the 86th Street station, he stepped out of the car to allow other passengers to detrain, then moved inside the car and resumed his leaning position at the door. Christie hadn't moved from her place in the center of the car. The warm enamel post was filled with hands clutching for balance and she managed to hold on with three fingers. She kept her head low, for Champion was glancing around, then his face settled into a mask of subway staring.

Christie felt moisture running down her back. Her dark dress clung damply to her back and shoulders. She licked beads of sweat from her upper lip but the heat didn't really bother her. She was too intensely aware of her own uncertainty. That brown paper bag. Was there a gun in that bag? The gun he used to kill Patrolman Wheeler? The possibility was so strong that she had stood momentarily poised at the 86th Street station, her fingers moving inside her pocketbook, touching her own revolver. She should have taken him then, when he backed off the train, her gun jammed into his stomach, quietly, effortlessly. She should have. But what if he didn't have a gun? What if he had a sandwich or a pair of socks in the bag? Or anything but a gun. At this very minute, maybe Stoner Martin or Bill Ferranti or someone had just located Champion's gun. If she grabbed him now, could she make the arrest stick? Christie thought of the squad bulletin board and the endless sheets of mimeographed papers tacked up haphazardly for their information. She never read them—not all of them; she never had time.

If she lost him now. He has a gun. I know he has a gun in that bag. I'll stick with him and play it from here. There's nothing else to do. If only Stoney were here, or Ferranti, or Ginsburg. Or Casey Reardon. Or somebody. *Anybody.* She steeled herself against a wave of panic and forced herself to listen to a strong, familiar, inner voice, devoid of all emotion: Handle it. However it turns out, it's yours. Handle it.

The train stopped at 125th Street and just as she knew he would, Eddie Champion detrained. As she walked, Christie tied a navy blue kerchief over her light hair, even though it wouldn't be much help. She was emerging into a world of darkness and that kerchief wasn't going to do much good.

TWENTY-FIVE:

Stoner Martin muttered an obscenity into the telephone. "If he calls again, hang up. I don't want any insurance. You won't hear from me again for a while."

There were four other detectives in the vicinity and each of them was in visual contact with one of the four other closest friends of Eddie Champion.

Stoner Martin watched Claude Davis play with the glass of beer on the bar before him. It was a cinch this kid didn't care much for beer. He was a big boy, slow-moving and deliberate, and his mind seemed far away. He looked at his watch for the third time in fifteen minutes; then, satisfied that it was time for whatever it was he had in mind, Claude Davis, without looking behind him, left the bar.

Detective Stoner Martin followed right after him.

TWENTY-SIX:

Christie was relieved and surprised by the number of white faces she spotted in and out along the swarming streets. All youth workers and case workers and members of the Mayor's various community groups had been mobilized and they were out: mingling, speaking good-naturedly, jostling among the kids, gossiping, easing things to a climate she hadn't anticipated. It was like some huge neighborhood festival with everyone converging on the spot where a platform truck had been set up at the intersection of 125th Street and Lenox Avenue.

All traffic had been diverted and small children were taking advantage of the vast, soft, tar gutter free for once of vehicles. They darted in and out, behind legs and bodies, grinning and shouting, excited by the strange things that were happening around them. Technicians were testing loudspeakers and amplifiers. All over, voices shrieked, and sudden sharp piercing electronic sounds were echoed by whistles and hoots and shouts from the children.

Members of the FFA stood around the platform, earnestly speaking with groups of people who threw questions at them. Units of TPF men stood near the platform, directed by a captain. They moved police barricades into place and worked quickly. The Mayor and his aides were expected momentarily.

On the surface, it was a friendly gathering, yet Christie

161

felt the undercurrents: strong, sullen, dangerous. She spotted some detectives moving among the crowd, but she didn't know them. She could tell that they were cops: wary, tense, alert. If she could just find one familiar face, anyone from the squad, anyone she knew. She was close to Champion and he was standing close to Gerald Friedman and the other FFA people.

Here? Now? What if he resisted? Fought, managed to get his gun out? One wrong move and this false gaiety could turn ugly and savage, could explode into uncontrolled and uncontrollable disaster. She could not risk setting it off.

There was a loud, steady scream of sirens and the policemen stiffened. A deputy inspector came from behind the platform and scanned the nearby rooftops; his troops were in place to guard against any hurled missiles. His face was drawn and tired.

Television cameramen pulled at cables, admonished a group of teen-agers to stop yanking at the lines in exchange for a promise that they would be included in a shot. Familiar faces appeared on the platform: civil rights leaders, moderate and fiery; a Negro Congressman; some sweaty, red-faced commissioners; Gerald Friedman; and a well-known liberal TV commentator, who looked hot and somewhat bored.

The young Mayor emerged from his shiny black limousine, his famous smile encompassing them all. He acknowledged both the cheers and the hoots with a large, friendly wave of his arm. He ran his fingers through his light hair and the resultant disorder added to his youthfulness. He loosened his tie, then tossed his jacket back into the car and rolled his sleeves up as he walked. As he moved into the crowd, his hands trailed in back of him, grasped and touched and clung to an excited group of young children. Someone bumped into his leg and there was a wail. A detective moved quickly between the Mayor and a crying child. The Mayor moved to one side and grinned at the lump of chocolate ice cream that trickled down his trouser leg.

162

"Hey, son, I should cry, not you. I don't even like chocolate."

The child grinned shyly and accepted a coin which the Mayor put into his damp hand. He bounded up the wooden steps of the platform, his manner outwardly as relaxed and casual as the stance of his police officers was stiff and tense. He shook hands with various people on the platform, scanned the faces before him and noted with satisfaction that all his neighborhood liaison people were out in force and seemed to have established a good climate.

The crowd around the platform had tightened into an unyielding wedge of bodies and the air was filled with calls and yells and hoots and jokes. The Mayor fielded whatever comments reached him and his responses drew both laughter and cheers, and Christie saw mostly smiling faces around her. But Eddie Champion wasn't smiling and, in profile, his face was frozen and strange and frightening.

The Mayor walked to the front of the platform and held up his arms. The noise subsided somewhat and he introduced a tall, dignified, familiar Negro minister. The deep, resonant voice did not need the assistance of the microphones as solemnly he recalled to them the reason they were here. His heavy sad words seemed a rebuke to the cheerfulness of the Mayor, whose face became serious and unmoving.

The minister intoned a prayer and there was a hushed quietness now interrupted by a calling out: *Amen, amen to that.* "And bless the soul of our beloved Billy Everett." The minister's voice caressed the name; he paused for a moment and then continued. "He was the bravest of our youth, the finest of our progeny." (*Amen. Yes, sir, amen.*)

Slowly at first, then periodically and insistently, there was a loud, ugly calling out of words, first from one direction, then from another: young voices, hard and ugly. Christie felt the climate change swiftly and the change was reflected on the faces of the policemen, white and black, in a narrowing of their eyes and in the rigidity of their posture.

163

"Whatcha going to do there, Mr. White Man, about that black boy killed by your Gestapo? Huh? Huh? Whatcha going to do?"

The minister ignored the intrusions as though they had not occurred and finished his prayer. Commissioner of Human Relations Philip Moreley, a tall, powerful, handsome, light-skinned man with startlingly gray eyes, spoke next. He spoke with great emotion, but the catcalls had some effect on him and his speech was short and brusque. When he sat down, his eyes raked the faces before him, stopping and exchanging signals with his people in the crowd, instructing them with quick glances, and it seemed to work. They moved out, male and female, white and black, all experienced, all known on these streets, mingled with one group, another, spoke softly in the vernacular, telling the noisy parts of the crowd, "Let the man talk, we're with you, baby, that's what it's all about."

The captain in charge of the police detail silently mouthed a Hail Mary and vowed a Rosary tonight if this damn thing would just get over and done with. It could blow. Oh Christ, how easy it could blow. That goddam idiot of a Mayor making out like this was one great big friendly little meeting with his community staff circulating around giving out handbills. Jesus, after the meeting the Mayor was planning to stay on and listen to a five-piece combo made up of neighborhood boys and there would be dancing on the streets. Dancing on the streets, for God's sake.

The Chief Inspector, the gold gleaming on his shoulders, explained in flat, official tones that the Police Department was in the middle of a very intensive investigation and was preparing a case in the matter of Billy Everett and he knew that the community would be satisfied with their complete and thorough and fair investigation. He continued speaking right through the growing catcalls and obscenities that greeted his words.

The Commissioner of Human Relations then introduced Gerald Friedman, and Gerry, pale and trembling, began to speak about Billy Everett, whom he had known all his life.

Christie kept her eyes on Champion; he was motionless, but a small smile pulled at the corners of his lips. The faces around her, beside her, were strange and unknown.

"He one of your *best friends,* honkey?" a voice called out. The insult was followed by a roar of laughter and was repeated several times. Christie's eyes were drawn irresistibly by the passion in Gerald Friedman's voice.

"Billy Everett was the best friend I ever had or ever will have. He was also the best friend any of you could ever have and *you better believe it!*"

There was a surprising instant of almost complete silence. Something about the ragged nakedness of the white boy's feelings reached out and touched nearly everyone in the crowd and they stood, for one bare moment, electrified by his emotion. Even the hecklers needed time before they began again.

But they did begin again and Gerry controlled himself and forced himself to remember that he was not facing a group of demonstrators. There was no bond of understanding and communication uniting them to him. They were hostile and considered him an enemy. He tried. He tried harder than he had ever tried anything in his life, but he could not make it. He ended in the middle of a sentence that could not be heard over the loud jeering sounds.

The Mayor of the City of New York stood beside the sobbing boy and turned him toward the row of chairs. He used an old trick. He spoke very softly, almost whispering into the microphone so that the crowd, more curious than courteous, settled down, hushed and leaned forward.

Christie heard the Mayor's voice, uninterrupted, begin to explain about the investigation that was under way, but her eyes were not on the man on the platform. Eddie Champion had moved. Some part of him had moved, was moving. There was a jostling next to her, then something hit her foot and she looked down. It was a brown paper bag and it had been kicked toward her by a youth standing next to Champion. Christie's fingers dug into her opened pocketbook and located her gun and undid the snap that held the gun inside the holster. There was a sudden surging of bodies, and instead of moving closer to Champion she was shoved back and away but she had a clear view.

Champion brought his right arm up, unnoticed in the crowd. He aimed the black revolver at the Mayor and as the loud blast shattered the air, several things, a million things, happened. Someone pounced on the Mayor, knocking him flat on his face. There was a surging and lunging and press and pull of bodies. There were cries and screams and curses, and shots and bottles and pieces of chain sailed through the air. There were hard muscular bodies forcing through the pliant, directionless mass of humanity.

But Christie Opara saw none of these things. She was intent on pulling herself upright and flinging herself into the small circle of space that appeared around Eddie Champion. Still, no one seemed directed toward him and Christie's main objective was to wrench the gun from his hand, which dangled loosely at his side, hidden and unseen. Champion turned his face; then his eyes, glazed and yellow, fastened on Christie Opara and he blinked and his mouth fell open in recognition. As though in a dream, there it was: that one haunting something from the Everett shooting. Those green eyes in that white face. He raised his revolver directly at Christie and pulled the trigger.

Champion's revolver misfired, but Christie Opara's did not. She held her revolver steadily in her hand and squeezed the trigger. The shock of the explosion raced up her arm, wrenched at her shoulder. Champion disappeared beneath the sudden press of bodies. Christie felt a heavy arm locked around her throat and chest, pulling her backwards. Her gun was no longer in her hand. She saw a face—thought she saw a face—Stoner Martin's; then her head was forced back and she could see only the black sky pierced by pinpoints of stars.

She thought of two things: her pocketbook containing her shield, and her missing gun. She dug her feet into the tar of the gutter and tried desperately to resist whoever was dragging her, but the hands and arms that held her were too powerful and her voice was held back inside her throat and she could scarcely breathe.

The sounds of gunfire and screaming howling terror came from all sides. Christie felt weightless as a doll as she was spun about and thrust against a police sergeant who shoved her into a squad car. She tried to rise from the floor of the car, to identify herself, but a man scrambled over her, stepping on her hand. Then another man got into the back of the car and held her down, but she lifted her head and through the window of the car Christie saw the sergeant. His face was chalk-white as he instructed the uniformed patrolman in the front seat.

"Make it quick, for Christ's sake. Get her out of here!"

TWENTY-SEVEN:

Lieutenant Godfrey, the squad commander of the precinct detectives, was a thin man who looked too small to meet Police Department minimum requirements. He had a rise of wavy yellow-gray hair which gave his head a slightly lopsided appearance. His eyes were small beads, half covered by heavy lids. Everything about him seemed slightly out of kilter. His lips did not quite close over long yellow protruding front teeth; his ears were too large and stuck at right angles to his skull. The lobes were bright pink. He constantly hitched at his trousers with his elbows.

As he spoke to Christie Opara, he seemed fascinated by his own reflection in the mirror directly over her head. "Now, let's get this story straight. You admit that the .38 detective special is yours?"

"Call my command, Lieutenant," Christie said for the fourth time.

"Oh, well, I'm not disputing your assertion that you're a member of the Department. But the fact remains that you are under my jurisdiction at the moment. And you have committed a homicide—justifiable or not remains to be seen. I want to get a few things straightened out before any DA people come into my command." His fingers played for a moment with the neat knot in his dark tie; then his eyes met Christie's. His mouth twitched at the hostility confronting him.

168

Christie was glad for this lieutenant. She could think straight because of him, because of what he was: an uncertain little martinet. That was all she had to think about and she could handle him. She touched the open cut near her mouth without looking at her fingers; they were warm with blood. She could taste the saltiness inside her mouth and wondered if any of her teeth were loose. Her hands trembled and she clenched them into fists and kept her voice as steady as she could. "Lieutenant, you had better call my office. You also better notify the communications bureau at Headquarters that my shield and pocketbook are missing. I notified you to that effect approximately thirty minutes ago. It was your responsibility to make the notification and you still haven't."

Lieutenant Godfrey swallowed. His Adam's apple bobbed and his face was a dull, unhealthy red. His eyes signaled one of the two men who had brought her in. The detective needed a shave. His eyes were large and watery and his voice was a growl.

He placed his hand heavily on Christie's shoulder. "Look, kid, don't be telling the lieutenant here what to do. You know, you're in some pretty hot water right now yourself and you ought to cooperate."

Christie glared at the man and moved free of his touch. Her voice was as clear and cold as ice. "Take your hands off me."

The detective scratched at a thick cluster of curly light hair that poked through the two opened buttons of his sports shirt. He looked at the lieutenant, who hitched up his trousers and told Christie not to get excited. The lieutenant glanced toward the Negro detective, who was speaking into the telephone, then back at Christie and leaned close to her.

"Detective Reilly here saved your life. Those niggers would have torn you apart. Now, you're just upset and that's understandable. You'll see I'm right when you just calm down." He dug in his back pocket, handed her a crisp linen handkerchief. "We have a sink over here, and some soap. Just wash up and you'll feel better."

Christie pushed his hand away, saw a box of tissues on a desk, took a wad and soaked them in cold water to make a compress. She rinsed her mouth and felt the soreness inside her cheek. Her face, looking back at her in the mirror, was a mess. Her right eye was bruised and beginning to close. The cut, extending about an inch from the left corner of her mouth, wasn't too bad; not deep, but bleeding. She applied pressure for a moment.

"Let's sit down and discuss this over some coffee. Here we go." The lieutenant carefully placed a paper napkin under a mug of coffee, but Christie didn't touch it. His voice changed, went higher. "Look, I want to know how you came to be up here in *my* precinct. What are you people from the DA's office up to? What are you looking for? Why were you after this guy Champion? What's going on anyway?"

Christie's voice was sweet and innocent. "Why, Lieutenant, don't *you* know what's going on in your own precinct?"

A flush, like a flicker of flame, touched his cheeks. The lieutenant fingered his tie. Detective Reilly seemed to surround her, his stubby legs wide apart, his hairy chest close to her face. "Look, girlie, don't go giving the lieutenant no hard time. He can be a dangerous enemy, know what I mean?"

Her cold contemptuous stare was not lost on the man and he seemed to press against her; the heavy smell of him reminded her of the ride to the precinct. She stood up, her voice strained but still controlled. "Listen, you, back off. Lieutenant, tell your trained ape here to back off. You're talking to a *first-grade detective,* flunky, and don't you forget it!"

Reilly intoned a long string of four-letter words, then stopped, snapped his fingers and pointed at her. "Hell, that's who you are. That little hotshot *O-per-uh.*" He exaggerated the correct pronunciation of Christie's last name, then leaned forward as though accusing her. "Only seems to me *O'Para* is a good enough name. What are you, lace-curtain Irish?"

The lieutenant motioned Reilly away. He tried a smile. It

looked more like a grimace. "Detective Opara, of course I know what's going on in my own precinct. I'd just like to confirm certain information of my own so that—"

Christie smiled. "Lieutenant, you want confirmation of something? There's the phone. Call my office. Ask Casey Reardon whatever you want to know."

The lieutenant's voice was shrill. "I'm asking you! What the hell are you people digging into? There's nothing up here that concerns the DA. Why were you sent up here?"

Christie closed her eyes. There was a commotion in the hall, the sound of heavy feet running up the iron stairs, echoing through the dirty, dark corridor. Christie squinted; her right eye was almost closed. Casey Reardon, Stoner Martin and Tom Dell filled the room. Stoner crossed the office and came directly to Christie's side.

"Come on, little one. Up and away."

The lieutenant's voice rose in protest. "Look here, Reardon, this is *my* command and you can't—"

Reardon stood directly in front of the lieutenant, his solid body lithe and threatening, his eyes burning nearly red. "I'll see you again, Godfrey. I surely will."

"Don't you dare remove her from this office. She is technically a prisoner. You tell your men to—"

Reardon stared at the rapidly blinking watery blue eyes, caught the nervous hitching gesture and smiled, then said simply, "Screw you."

Tom Dell measured himself against Detective Reilly, who watched his boss for some signal.

"Let's move," Reardon said.

Stoney pulled at Christie's arm, leading her out the door. They were followed by Reardon and backed up by Tom Dell.

Christie felt giddy and slightly hysterical. It was crazy. It was all so absolutely crazy. *She* had been in *police custody.* And now Reardon and Stoney and Tom Dell were *abducting* her. She was one of five first-grade women detectives in the entire city of New York and . . . She felt like laughing, but her mouth hurt now and she felt like crying, but her eyes seemed unable to produce tears. If she completely lost her grip on herself now . . . She wouldn't.

She leaned back against the seat of the Pontiac and Reardon turned from the front seat and called to her, then tossed something at her. Her hands went up reflexively; then her fingers closed around her pocketbook. Before asking any questions she checked for her shield. It was there. Reardon turned again from the front seat, but this time he carefully handed her something. Her gun.

"Put this back in your holster and hang onto it."

"But—how?" Then she remembered something: some vague impression. "Stoney, were you there?"

He nodded. "I was there."

"But—but my gun. The lieutenant had my gun. How?"

"*I* didn't get your gun, just your pocketbook, and that was sheer dumb luck," Stoney told her.

Reardon, still turned to her, said, "Dell copped your gun from the desk when we copped you."

"Wow."

Reardon was frowning, his eyes narrowed. "My God, how the hell did you get all messed up like that? Did those bastards—"

"It was wild out there. I really don't know." She stopped speaking, then her hand went to her mouth. "Champion? The lieutenant said he was dead. That I killed him."

Reardon reached back and pressed a folded handkerchief against her mouth. "Hold this. Real tight. Don't worry about Champion. You didn't kill anybody. We'll tell you all about it later. Just relax."

Then Christie remembered something else. She leaned forward, touched Reardon's arm. He studied her for a moment; then his face relaxed and he nodded. "It's okay. Barbara's home."

TWENTY-EIGHT:

The minute Reardon pushed the door to the squad room open, Christie knew there was something wrong. There was an unnatural silence, a tenseness surrounding Art Treadwell and Bill Ferranti. Neither of the men looked up or seemed aware that anyone had come into the office. Christie turned to ask Stoner why the men were still here; they must have been on duty since early morning.

But Stoner Martin was standing against the closed door, his face close to Reardon's. Reardon said something, reached out and pressed Stoner's shoulder, then turned and looked at Christie. "Go into my office, Christie, and wait there," he said.

Christie tried to catch some message from Ferranti, but he glanced from her to Reardon, then back to the paper work before him. Christie walked down the connecting corridor and caught her breath at the assault of air-conditioned coolness. She sat on the chair in front of Reardon's desk, stretched her legs in front of her and waited, but Reardon didn't come. She touched the swelling under her eye lightly and settled into the chair, her face upturned, and fell into a dead sleep.

Reardon glanced in, walked lightly behind the chair. Good. He closed the door carefully behind him and returned to the squad office where Marty Ginsburg was waiting for him.

"Well?" Reardon asked him.

Marty shrugged heavily. "Not a goddam word out of him."

"Okay," Reardon said, "forget it. Just forget it. You other men"—Treadwell and Ferranti looked up—"you saw nothing, you know nothing, right?"

"About what, Mr. Reardon?" Ferranti asked quietly.

"All I know is the telephone's been ringing and I been taking messages, Mr. Reardon," Treadwell said.

Reardon nodded briskly and the men continued with their work. He crossed the office and carefully fingered the edge of the chrome-bordered squad bulletin board. Silently, the bulletin board swung back on hidden hinges and Reardon pressed his face close to the rectangles cut into the wooden backing of the two-way mirror. Claude Davis sat stiffly in a chair in the middle of the room and Stoner Martin was speaking to him, but Reardon couldn't hear anything. He watched for a moment, then pressed the panel back into place and said a short, fervent prayer.

Stoner Martin lit a new cigarette from the stub of his old one and his head was enveloped by the mist of smoke that curled from his mouth as he spoke.

"Champion's dead. You know that, don't you?"

"Who's Champion?"

"How old are you, Claude?"

The boy pressed his lips together firmly. Any answer would be cooperation and he intended nothing of the sort.

Stoney straddled a chair, his long hands resting on the gray metal frame. He put his head down for a moment and rubbed the back of his hands against his eyes. Without looking up, he began to speak, softly, without expression. "Claude Davis, age twenty, born April 2, 1947. Second child of Audra Johnson, eighteen years old, and her common-law husband, Frank Davis, twenty years old. Lived two years in Liberty, North Carolina, with grandmother, Sarah Johnson, and grandfather, Farley Johnson. Returned to New York at age twelve, attended Junior High School 42 until age fourteen. Dropped out of high school in 1963 at age sixteen; in

174

October of 1963, admitted to Harlem Hospital with a broken leg as a result of skylarking accident aboard southbound IRT local."

The detective raised his face, held his hands palms up and shrugged. "Want me to continue? I got it all—every day of your life right up to and including the present." In response to the silence before him, Stoney's voice sounded almost gentle, as though he had some terrible information to reveal and was trying to be kind about it. "You are third lieutenant in command of the Young Men's Karate Group and you hold training sessions every Tuesday and Thursday evening between eight and ten P.M. and Saturday mornings between nine and eleven A.M. Students are limited to those approved by the Royal Leader."

Claude's smile was stiff and mechanical and he wasn't sure how it looked. He wasn't sure if it hid the sudden waves of shock that were stinging his chest. "You're just a bundle of information, aren't you?" he asked, not sure if he should say anything.

Stoner Martin looked toward the tan drapes that covered the steel-meshed window, his eyes fixed as though on a landscape, then turned back to Claude. "Son, you are in a mess of trouble. I *saw* you give it to Eddie Champion."

"Who's Eddie Champion?"

Davis's voice was taunting but he didn't expect the explosive reaction from the detective. Stoner rose swiftly and grasped the chair he had been sitting on and flung it across the room. It hit the wall and bounced across the floor, but the detective stood with his back to Claude. Claude caught his breath but didn't move.

"You know what's happening out there, son? You know what's happening on those streets? People are being killed and injured and maimed and worse. Something so much worse. They are being *set back!*" Stoner turned slowly and the softness with which he spoke contrasted with the burning anger in his eyes. "One night of letting loose, cutting up and smashing and shooting and yelling and looting. That's all this whole goddam night adds up to and I want to know why. *Why?*"

Claude Davis hesitated, then underestimated the anger of the detective. "*You* want to know why? Hell, man, don't you never look in a mirror? You're blacker than me, so that's pretty funny, coming from you, really pretty funny. They make you see yourself white when they give you that tin badge?"

Deliberately, almost dispassionately, Stoner Martin slashed the back of his hand across Davis's mouth, then stepped back, legs apart, not breathing. His anger was soft-spoken. "Try, Davis. Come on, you're a karate expert: *try.*"

Davis's eyes lingered on the detective's throat and his right hand stiffened, his fingers ready and strong as steel, aching, just aching, to slash at one vulnerable spot after the other, but he didn't move. "You think I'm crazy?" he asked in a thick voice. "You not gonna shoot me through the head. What the hell you want anyway?"

Stoner Martin counted silently. When he reached ten, he blinked, inhaled, righted the chair, straddled it again. His voice was reasonable, friendly. "Here's what I want, and here's what you're going to give me. Your confession, first that you killed Eddie Champion on direct orders from the Royal Leader; second, a statement relative to your role in the Secret Nation; third, a statement relative to the real purpose of the Secret Nation."

"That's all you want?"

"Yeah. That's it."

Claude debated for a moment, then decided against the two-word answer. He could taste blood inside his mouth and he remained silent, waiting. He watched warily as the detective rose from the chair, carefully pushed it back and suddenly yanked Claude Davis to his feet. They were about the same height and their faces were inches apart. "Okay, kid. Listen real good. You see that door?" Stoney pointed to the metal door leading into the squad room. "You go through that door, through the squad room and right on out. I'm going to give you one minute to leave the building and five to leave the neighborhood. If I find you anywhere in the vicinity, I'm going to put a bullet right here." Stoney dug a finger into Claude's forehead, then shoved him across the room.

The boy stood, uncertain. Was this guy setting him up: prisoner shot while escaping? What the hell was he up to? Claude shook his head. "Hey, man, you nuts? I walk in there, you got a whole office of cops ready to blast me. I'm not moving."

Reardon closed the hidden two-way mirror for the third time and turned in time to see Christie Opara crossing the office, greeting Marty Ginsburg.

"Hey, Marty, you still here?" she asked in a sleep-heavy voice.

Reardon barreled across the office toward her at the instant the door from the interrogation room was flung open. His shoulder hit against her face, blocking her view, but she heard Stoner's voice, loud and angry, not like Stoner at all: "This bum is leaving. I want him out. He shows his face around here again, kick him out."

Christie couldn't see Reardon's face, for he spun her around and his fingers dug into her arm as he pushed her. "God damn it," he said, his voice furious in her ear, "I told you to stay in my office. Now do what I told you!" He pulled the door closed behind her and Christie stood, stunned, inside the cool office. She turned and stared at the closed door and it all caught up with her: anger, humiliation, pain, pain all over her, in her mouth, her eyes, her knees, her elbows. She kicked the metal door as hard as she could; then her foot hurt and she threw herself on the green leather couch, face down. God damn Reardon. Damn him. She could get killed doing her job, knocking herself out, doing her best—better than the rest of them even. *She* found Champion. She was the one who . . . Christie pressed her clenched fists into the leather and let the tears come. She felt great sobs forming deep inside her and for one quick moment wanted to let them come, take over, but if that happened she would fall apart and that was one thing Reardon wasn't going to see. She ground her teeth together, pulled herself up and walked to the window, her back to the door.

Stoner Martin hadn't seen Christie; he saw only Claude Davis, moving uncertainly into the dark corridor. The boy looked around at the shadows, searching for a stairway or a trap.

"Take the elevator," the detective told him, stabbing the down button, waiting with him.

Claude felt dizzy and sick, expecting someone to pounce on him from the darkness, someone invisible, but his eyes stayed on Stoner. The detective's face was calm, all traces of anger gone. He dug into his back pocket, removed a scrap of paper, frowned over it for a moment, then held it up for Claude to see in the dim light over the elevator door. There was a telephone number written on the paper. In green ink.

"Before you leave, son, verify this for me, will you?"

Claude narrowed his eyes, and to help him Stoney read the number. "MElrose 8–6174. That's the right number, isn't it? That's the Royal Leader's direct line, isn't it?"

The threat no longer seemed from some invisible, unseen enemy lurking somewhere behind him. Claude Davis felt a sickening chill along his spine. "What do you mean?" he asked.

Stoner jabbed at the button again. "Damn thing never seems to come this time of night." He glanced up, saw the red light shining. "Good, here it comes. Five minutes, Claude. You be gone, because I'm going to come looking."

The elevator door slid open and Claude faced the small cubicle. It was dimly lit by a fluorescent light, and small and square as a box. Stoner Martin hit the flat of his hand against the rubber that lined the door, and with his other hand he pushed Claude forward, but Claude's feet dug into the floor and he didn't move. "What you going to do?"

"What do you think I'm going to do?"

Stoner Martin turned abruptly and headed back toward his office. Without breaking stride, he shrugged off Claude's hand, which clutched at his shoulder, and seemed not to hear the voice, hoarse and frightened. "But I didn't say nothing. You know I didn't say nothing, Detective Martin."

Stoner whirled about and pushed Davis against the corridor wall. The hardness was in his voice as well as in his eyes. "You try and tell *them*. When I get finished with my phone call, you're a dead man and you know it." Claude's head rocked back and forth, denying, but Stoner's hand reached up and grasped his chin and held his face immobile. "Whatever I know about the Secret Nation—and, baby, I know what there is to know—that's what I'm going to tell his Royal Bastard. And then I'm going to tell him I got all my information from *you*."

Claude's knees seemed to dissolve. His legs bent sideways and he swayed, his hands sliding against the wall. There was a sound in his voice that was unknown to him, yet it was his voice. "Jesus, Detective Martin. You know what they'd do to me. Jesus, Detective Martin. Don't do that, you can't."

Stoner felt no triumph, not even relief. All he felt was a cold and sickening disgust. He turned his back and walked into the squad office, followed by Claude Davis, who slumped into a chair Stoner indicated with a jerk of his thumb. No one was even set to guard him. He just sat there, ignored by the detectives. Reardon glanced at him once, then signaled Stoner Martin into his office.

TWENTY-NINE:

Christie turned from the window and stared at Casey Reardon. She tried to arrange her features into a glare but it was difficult. Her mouth was numb and her eye was swollen. Actually it was a waste of effort because Reardon was too busy talking to Stoney to even notice her.

"It worked," Reardon said to Stoney.

"It worked," Stoney affirmed.

Reardon glanced at his watch, but the time—1 A.M.—didn't convey anything to him. He ran his hand over his face, dug at his eyes. "Well, buddy, we better start touching some bases and real fast. We have been treading on some very dangerous ground. You know that, don't you?"

Stoner nodded, then his eyes moved to Christie and Reardon turned. He pulled at his mouth, grimaced. "Christie, come over here." He motioned toward the couch. "Sit down and listen. You have been in here since you arrived, right? You didn't see anything and you're not hearing anything. You got that?"

And you don't see anything either, Mr. Reardon, do you? Not my cuts and lumps and . . . Her voice was acid. "Yes, Mr. Reardon. *Right.*"

There was a slight flicker in his eyes, which lingered on her for the barest instant, but it was impossible to know if he was getting any message from her. He turned back to Stoner,

180

his hand guiding him across the room, but Christie could hear his words.

"Send Davis out the back way. Tell him to walk around the block and come in the night entrance. He is to sign in at the elevator, present himself to us. He wants to make a statement. We read him his rights, tell him he's entitled to remain mute until he has legal representation—et cetera."

"Right, Casey."

"See if there are any cleaning people in the building—any civilians at all. Get someone in the office, tell the night man downstairs we spilled some coffee or something and want it cleaned up." Stoner nodded, understanding Reardon's request for a witness. Then to Christie: "Opara, you never saw Davis, right?"

Christie frowned. "Who?"

Sharp, terse: "Forget it. You don't know anything."

Christie searched his words for the insult, but Reardon waved at her to relax. "Stoney, we never laid eyes on Davis in this office, right?"

"Right. I saw him uptown when he chopped Champion, so I recognize him when he walks in."

Reardon stood for a moment, his eyes closed, his breath a tired sighing sound. His voice was softer now, concerned. "Buddy, we could all hang on this. You know that, don't you?"

Stoner Martin smiled. "I'm not looking to hang, boss."

"Neither am I. Let's get going."

Reardon looked down onto the darkened street and watched the two figures: Claude Davis, uncertain, moving cautiously yet without choice. The second figure, Tom Dell, was almost invisible and would remain so. Davis would never know he had been followed, except of course if he changed his mind and decided to run. Then Dell would help him to think clearly. He turned from the window and looked at Christie Opara.

"Christie, Christie." His voice was a mixture of annoyance and concern. "Come over here. Let me get a good look at you."

Christie lifted her chin, tried to hold onto her anger, but Reardon's concern seemed genuine. He moved toward her. "My God, you are one hell of a mess. How'd you get the eye and the cut lip?"

Christie shrugged, her fingers automatically touching the wounds. "During the melee—I'm not sure. Maybe when I was taken into custody."

Reardon's voice tightened. "Did those bastards—"

Christie spoke quickly. "I don't know, really. The whole thing was rough and—"

"They give you any first aid? Put anything on the cuts?" She shook her head and Reardon went to the metal locker where he kept a first-aid kit. "Come on, sit down on the couch. This will sting a little but that cut by your mouth looks dirty." He held her chin and dabbed antiseptic on her cut with a wad of cotton. The sting brought tears to her eyes. "You want a shot of Scotch, Christie?" She shook her head again. "How do you feel?"

"Tired."

She leaned her head back and closed her eyes. She wanted to sleep. Just to sleep. She heard Reardon's voice on the intercom. "Ginsburg, you there? Good. Listen, go around the corner to that all-night greasy spoon and bring in hot coffee. A lot of it." The button clicked off and Reardon's voice was crisp again. "Come on, Opara. You can sleep another time. We got a lot of work to do."

THIRTY:

Stoner Martin looked up from his typewriter, his face a blank mask.

"My name is Claude Davis and I want to make a statement," the tall, dark young man told him in a monotone.

The statement was not made immediately, however. Claude Davis was advised by Supervising Assistant District Attorney Casey Reardon, in the presence of Detectives Stoner Martin, Marty Ginsburg, Arthur Treadwell, Bill Ferranti and Christie Opara, and in the presence of Mrs. Mary Bathgate, a sixty-two-year-old cleaning woman, that he was entitled to legal representation. When he learned that Claude Davis had no funds for such representation, Reardon earnestly advised him to request the services of a Legal Aid attorney.

The Legal Aid attorney, a small young Negro honor graduate from St. John's, with odd rimless glasses, appeared forty minutes later, spoke quietly with Davis, then asked Reardon to provide a stenotypist. The stenotypist arrived nearly an hour later.

In the intervening time, Casey Reardon received two telephone calls from the Mayor's office, one call from the Police Commissioner, six calls from permanent and temporary members of his squad. He made four telephone calls, relaying his collection of up-to-date information. Five armed members of the Secret Nation had been arrested by his people, in addition to fourteen armed suspects arrested by other Police Department personnel. Yes, his people were preparing reports of the night's events; yes, he would arrive at the Police Commissioner's office with his statements before morning. Reardon stared at the telephone for a moment, then pressed the intercom. "Detective Opara."

She was chalk-white and Reardon carefully kept any sympathy from his voice. "How you doing on that report?"

"The best I can," she answered shortly.

"Well, hurry it up because we're going over to the PC's office in about an hour. The Mayor will be there and . . ." He stopped speaking. She looked so exhausted and battered and vulnerable; he didn't know how the hell she would get through the rest of the night. "When was the last time you ate?"

Christie shrugged. That wasn't important. There was something else, and she stood there, deciding. Reardon told her, "All right, let's have it. What's the problem?"

Christie laughed shortly. It was a bitter, harsh sound. "*The problem?* Mr. Reardon, you have to be kidding."

Reardon leaned back in his chair. "Sit down and say it and make it fast."

"All right: Will you please bring me up to date? I'm walking around in a fog. *Is Eddie Champion dead? Did I kill him? Who's Davis? What's happening? How did you and Stoney know where I was? What—*"

Reardon held his hand up. "You want me to answer, then keep quiet for a minute. Champion isn't dead. So you didn't kill him. Stoney was tailing Davis, hoping Davis would lead him to Champion—and he did. Champion is in Harlem Hospital with a shattered vocal cord—"

"I shot him in the shoulder," Christie interrupted.

"Yeah, but Davis chopped him in the throat, as he went down from your bullet and . . . "

Christie felt the words whirling around inside her head; questions, responses leading to deeper confusion. She saw Reardon through a haze of weariness. His voice receded into a meaningless hum. Her head felt so heavy. Then Reardon's voice cracked into her consciousness.

"Detective Opara, *I* have some pertinent questions to ask *you*."

Christie's head jerked up in surprise. "What?"

"You shot Champion in the shoulder?"

His voice came through very clearly. "Yes, I told you that."

"Where the hell were you ever taught to aim for a shoulder?" She started to protest but Reardon continued coldly, his words reaching into her. "As far as I know, the only reason a police officer draws a revolver is with full intent to shoot and the only intention in shooting is to kill the person you're aiming at. If you're not justified in killing a person, you have no justification to pull the trigger in the first place. Didn't you know that?"

It was like ice water, hitting her in the face, alerting her, shocking her back into the moment. Her hands tightened around the armrest and the voice was controlled but angry. "I did exactly what I set out to do. Under the circumstances, I had to use my best judgment and . . ."

Reardon stood up and raised his clenched hand. "One," he said, straightening his index finger, "your assignment was to escort Barbara Reardon to the wake and back to her home. Don't interrupt; just listen, Opara. You spotted Champion, left your assignment and took off after Champion. You stayed with him all the way from Brooklyn up to 125th Street. Wasn't there any opportunity, anywhere along the line, of bagging him before he got uptown?"

All the tiredness disappeared; Christie felt new energy flow through her body, quickening her, sharpening her. She tried to interrupt, but Reardon continued, counting her mistakes on his fingers as she breathed in short, furious breaths of cool air.

"Don't interrupt, just follow what I'm saying. Assuming there had been no opportunity, once you got to the site of the rally—there were uniformed men all over the place— couldn't you have contacted one of them? Okay: assuming the opportunity didn't present itself—and I will have to assume that—when it finally came down to your taking a shot at Champion, why the hell didn't you shoot to kill?"

The silence was so unexpected that Christie hesitated for a moment, waiting for him to continue. This time he waited for her answer and it was clear and a little louder than she intended. "There was no need to kill him; I knew you'd want him alive."

"If this other guy inside, this Davis, hadn't shown up and chopped Champion down, what makes you so sure Champion couldn't have gotten off a few more shots?"

Quickly, she told him, "Champion fired at me and his gun misfired."

Reardon's mouth opened. He hadn't known that, but he latched onto the information immediately. "If he had had the opportunity to keep pumping, his gun *could* have fired. Christ, you were lucky."

She started to say something more, but she stopped. Reardon was right. Champion might have been able to get a bullet off. She couldn't quite grasp the possibility, not fully, not yet. She shrugged. "But he didn't."

"Christie—" Reardon sat down again, rubbed his eyes, then looked at her. "Another thing. Why the hell were you so surprised that Stoney and Tom and I were uptown? You think the rest of us have been sitting around on our tails all day while you've been carrying the ball for us?"

"I wouldn't know," she said coldly.

"Well, you know now. Go on and type up your report and, for God's sake, wash your face and comb your hair before we leave for the Commissioner's office. You look like hell."

She slammed the door behind her and Reardon felt a hollow thud inside his stomach. She was okay now, she'd make it through the night and for however many hours into the day, but—Christ—he hadn't known about Champion firing at her. He didn't even want to think about it.

THIRTY-ONE:

It was past three in the morning and Christie, finished with her report and waiting for Reardon to take her to the Police Commissioner's office, was relieving Art Treadwell on the telephone. She glanced through the logbook which they had started keeping some twenty-four hours ago, then told the elevator man, "Hang on a minute, John, I'll check it out." She pushed the hold button and took the log with her.

She tapped twice on Reardon's door and Stoner Martin opened it. "Excuse me," she said quietly, "but John downstairs is on the phone. There's a Mr. Richard C. Jackson to see Stoney. Says its important. According to the log, he's been calling pretty steadily since about four P.M. yesterday. Or today, or whatever it is."

Stoney shook his head in response to Reardon's question. "Never heard of him."

"What the hell, tell him to come up. Find out what his beef is, Stoney, then get rid of him. I told Tom to bring the car around. Opara, you ready to leave?"

She resisted the impulse to tell him she'd been ready to leave for the last few hours. "Yes, sir."

She relayed the message to the man on the phone and pushed the log aside. Whatever they had been hoping to learn from Claude Davis, apparently, had not come through. She overheard Stoner telling Reardon that "the dumb bastard thinks it's strictly on the level; he was trying to assassinate Champion as a threat to the Nation." Well, that was their problem. Christie had done all she could. And more.

He stood in the doorway, an elderly, drawn, tired Negro in a neat dark suit. The edges of his starched collar bit into his thin neck and he clutched a soft leather portfolio to his chest.

"Can I help you?" Christie asked.

"Yes. I don't know. My name is Richard C. Jackson. I'm looking for Detective Stoner Martin—I was told it would be all right for me to come up."

Christie nodded, indicated a chair and buzzed Reardon's office. "Mr. Jackson is here to see Detective Martin."

Stoner's face indicated no recognition, just a weary resolve. He shook the hand offered to him with some impatience. Mr. Jackson's voice was thin and wavery. "I've been trying to reach you all day, Detective Martin, all day and all night. Since the moment I was notified, but—"

"Notified? About what?" Stoner's question was mechanical.

"Why, about Tomlin Carver's death."

Stoner's arm encircled Mr. Jackson, pulling him more than guiding him into Casey Reardon's office. Reardon's voice blasted into the Squad Room. "Detective Opara, you there?"

"Yes, sir."

"Call the Commissioner's office—tell him we'll be delayed, that something just came up and I'll call him as soon as I can."

Christie relayed the message to the Commissioner's secretary but could give no further information to the sharp voice questioning her. "That's all Mr. Reardon told me. He'll be in touch with the Commissioner."

Christie rested her head on the surface of the desk and wished the whole thing was over and done with.

THIRTY-TWO:

Christie Opara sat on a bench in the mirrored outer office of the Police Commissioner's domain and regarded her image in dizzying repetition. Fatigue weighed so heavily on her that she was no longer disturbed by her appearance. So she had a black eye and a swollen cut mouth. So what? All she wanted to do was sleep. But she knew that she had to force herself awake; more than that, she had to force herself to be alert. She crossed the room and threw the damp container, with remnants of tea, into the wastebasket beside the desk of the uniformed patrolman. He did not look up. In fact, he had been bent over a large ledger for over an hour, laboriously making entries, not even raising his eyes as the parade of visitors entered and departed. Yet as each person stopped at his desk, he added a name, time of arrival and time of departure to his journal.

"Where's the ladies' room?" Christie asked.

The patrolman raised his left hand but didn't look up. "Next flight up, turn left at top of the stairs. Wait a minute. You'll need the key." He dug in the top drawer, then handed her an oblong block of wood with a key dangling from a large metal circle.

There was an eeriness in the large, dark old building. Not just because of the emptiness and the echoing of her every step, but it seemed that suddenly, at any moment, people would emerge from behind all the locked doors, that the building would come to life and be filled with sound and movement. Christie ran cold water over her wrists for a moment, then cupped come water in her hands and held it to her cheeks and forehead. It had no stimulant effect at all and she *had* to shake off the terrible dead weariness. She dug in her pocketbook and found a small shiny smooth green capsule. Marty Ginsburg had slipped it into her hand before she left the office. He had told her it was one of his reducing capsules—an amphetamine. It would get her through. She put the slippery capsule in her mouth, then scooped up a mouthful of water and swallowed. She returned to the Commissioner's waiting room, vaguely disappointed at her continuing exhaustion.

The first effect of the capsule, some fifteen minutes later, was an urgent nausea. Her image in the succession of mirrors seemed to be floating around in a circle. Christie closed her eyes and clamped down on her back teeth, then found some gum in her pocketbook and chewed hard. The sick feeling subsided and she began to feel better. She began to feel good. She stood up, stretched, and paced around the large, circular, windowless room. The patrolman looked up from his ledger, finally, curious.

"Mind if I put your transistor on?"

The patrolman shrugged. "You won't get the news for another fifteen minutes." He glanced at his watch. "It's four-fifteen."

"Maybe some music, then. What's happening, anyway?"

"In there—or where?"

Christie turned the radio on. The music was soft and dreamy. "Anywhere—in there—uptown, downtown, anywhere."

The patrolman clicked his ball-point and stretched his arms across his desk. Apparently he had finished his work for the time being.

"Well, the local citizenry marched on the Twenty-Third Precinct in force. We rushed troops up there and it's under control, but there's been some bad injuries: them and us.

190

We're sealing off streets and reinforcing barricades. Some looting; some shooting. Earlier, of course, we locked up about twenty-eight of those Secret Nation guys—all armed with firearms. We're really geared and it's been blowing in a few places but no fatalities so far." He sounded like a general in complete command of the situation, cool, uninvolved, but on top of it all. "Oh, and his Honor the Mayor is on his way— got a blast on the phone when you went upstairs."

His Honor the Mayor arrived exactly five minutes later. Christie was surprised at how tall he was and how quickly he moved. He strode across the carpeted expanse in a rapid, gliding motion and she instinctively came to her feet. The patrolman leaped to attention and the Mayor tossed him a casual, friendly salute. The patrolman must have buzzed a signal somewhere, for the heavy door leading into the Commissioner's office opened as his Honor approached. Christie caught one quick glimpse of light before the door silently closed.

The door opened again some thirty minutes later, and Casey Reardon stepped out. Christie stood up, meeting him in the center of the room.

"So far, so good," he said slowly, not looking at her. "The Mayor has skimmed over our reports and the medical reports confirm that Champion was hit across the throat, so that lends credence to Davis's tale of woe. Now, you're just going to answer some questions. Nothing too detailed. He was impressed by your work." Reardon sat down and looked up at Christie. "Sit down for a minute. This is important."

Christie sat on the edge of the cushioned bench. Reardon looked terrible. There were deep lines across his forehead and his eyes were narrowed to slits. He was speaking rapidly. "Very briefly, a touchy area relates to your appearance at the precinct. Listen carefully. You *knew* the men were detectives when you got into the car with them, right? As soon as you got to the precinct, you called our office and asked that we send someone for you. Tom and I picked you up. Got that?"

Christie nodded briskly and stood up. "Okay, got it. Let's go."

Reardon pulled her back onto the bench and studied her face. "Christie, what's wrong with you?"

"Me? Nothing. I feel great. Anything else?"

He studied her for a moment, not releasing her arm. "Yes, something else. You'll be asked about the Everett shooting—about why you were on the scene and . . ."

She nodded. "Right. I was on a special assignment at the building site and was right up against Everett when I saw Champion pull the gun from Patrolman Linelli and—"

Reardon's fingers tightened about her arm. "Christie, take it easy. You didn't see Champion take the gun, you—"

Christie snapped her fingers. "That's right—I meant that I saw him transfer the gun into Linelli's hand. Listen, Mr. Reardon, don't worry about me. Really. I'm fine. But you look awful. Gee, you look tired. Are you all right?"

She started to stand up again, but Reardon held onto her arm. "Christie, did you take something? Don't look blank; this is important. What the hell is the matter with you? You act like you're hopped up or something."

Christie grinned. "Just got my second wind, that's all."

"All right, we'll talk about that later. Right now, listen to me. If you are asked for specifics about your assignment at the building site—"

She interrupted, her voice earnest. "Listen, Mr. Reardon, don't worry about a thing. A confidential assignment is confidential. I won't tell them a thing."

"My God, Opara, shut up and listen. If they ask for specifics, you are to tell them *exactly*. You got that—exactly. That you were assigned to tail my daughter—tell it exactly the way it was."

"I don't see why . . ."

Reardon felt a terrific urge to belt her. He knew how to stimulate her through her exhaustion but he hadn't the slightest idea how to calm her down. Particularly when he didn't know what she had taken. He spoke quietly, trying to carry her along with him. "Christie, that is the Mayor of the City of New York and the Police Commissioner of the City of New York in that room. Answer every question they ask and we'll all be fine, okay?"

"Right."

Reardon released his breath slowly between his teeth. "That's my girl," he said.

Detective Christie Opara was completely at ease during the fifteen minutes she spent inside the Police Commissioner's office. She was bright, alert, rapid and articulate. A little too articulate, Reardon thought, watching her closely. But the Mayor, his eyes slightly glassy and his color bad, seemed favorably impressed, and the Police Commissioner, with a more serious problem before him, paid cursory attention to her statement.

The Mayor rose and everyone in the room stood up, ignoring the brief wave of his long hand that indicated informality. "Almost five A.M.," the Mayor said, sounding surprised.

"The night sure flew by, didn't it?" Christie asked brightly, not seeing Casey Reardon's face.

"It seemed very long to me," the Mayor said. The clearness of his light gray eyes surprised Christie; he seemed to be rallying somehow. "You know, Detective Opara, I had a slightly different impression of what happened uptown. When we all hit the deck, I raised my head for a moment and it seemed to me that you were grappling with a uniformed patrolman. Was there a uniformed man there, near you?"

Christie shook her head. "No, sir, just the two detectives. And we weren't grappling. They were assisting me to get out of there, as I told you before."

The Mayor clicked his tongue against his teeth, and he said thoughtfully, "A matter of perspective, I guess. Commissioner Moreley was lying right next to me and he was under the impression that a uniformed policeman collared this fellow Claude Davis."

Christie started to speak, but Reardon moved suddenly

and spoke before she could. "No, sir, apparently no one even saw Davis until he presented himself at our office. Seems he found himself caught in the middle of the two factions of the Secret Nation people and decided to seek our protection."

"That's right," Christie added; "he just popped up in our office and—"

Reardon's hand grasped her wrist, pulling it around in back of her. "It's interesting how things appear in retrospect, Mr. Mayor," Reardon said, and the Mayor nodded in agreement.

The Mayor turned to the Police Commissioner. "This other matter—this information from this man Tomlin Carver—we'll have to discuss it at length. You realize what seems to be involved?"

The Police Commissioner's face was pale and his voice was thin. "I realize fully what seems to be involved."

The Mayor said, "I'm going to shoot uptown. Detective Opara is, I think, entitled to some rest. Mr. Reardon, I'll leave that to you. You also have the rather tricky matter of the Grand Jury presentation relative to the Everett shooting. You still have your twenty-five witnesses. Well, sleep on it and we'll see what we come up with after some rest."

Reardon, still holding Christie's wrist, agreed with the Mayor and he watched Christie in amazement. A sudden light glowed on her face; an idea seemed to flow through her and she seemed about to reach out for the Mayor's arm as he walked past them. Reardon wrenched her closer to him and in a hoarse whisper, right into her ear, he told her, "Christie, keep quiet or I'll murder you!"

Christie sat in the back seat of the Pontiac and didn't answer Reardon. She didn't know what he was so angry about; she had handled her part well and, besides, she had a great plan, if only Reardon would shut up for a minute.

He was turned from the front seat and his voice was a steady, continuous blast at her. "I don't know what the hell you took or where you got it, but we're going to drop you off at your house and you take a hot shower and get a few hours' sleep and drink lots of coffee. I want you back in the office by two P.M. at the latest and I expect you to be quieted down and—" He leaned toward the back seat. "Christie, are you listening to me?"

She shook her head thoughtfully. "No, not really, because I'm thinking about something else."

Tom Dell stared straight ahead and concentrated on the black and empty streets. Reardon's voice was like a razor. "*You're thinking about something else?*"

Dell thought Christie had gone off the deep end: probably too many hours without food or sleep. The poor kid just went on, completely unaware of the boss's mood.

"Mr. Reardon, I've got a great plan—really great. About the twenty-five witnesses." Christie laughed. "Wow! Even the Mayor of the City of New York and his Commissioner of Human Relations didn't know what they saw. Can you imagine—they were eyewitnesses and they don't know what they were witnessing. It's great. It's perfect."

Instead of an explosion, which is what Dell was prepared for, there was a silence, and then there was Mr. Reardon's voice, quiet and controlled, almost interested. "All right, Christie. We'll go back to the office and you tell me about your idea." The threat implied by his next words didn't bother her. "It better be good."

She knew it was good and she wasn't worried.

THIRTY-THREE:

It rained on Monday morning: not a cool, refreshing, relieving rain, but a steady hot steamy relentless outpouring of liquefied heat. The room on the fifth floor of the Criminal Courts Building shimmered with moisture. The dim yellow light that radiated in glowing circles from the antiquated chandeliers across the ceiling added to the gloom. Slashes of rain streaked and tapped at the narrow windows, which had been opened for a moment, then hurriedly closed when the direction of the wind shifted and poured warm water onto the tiled floor.

It was a small courtroom, used for various purposes: conferences, briefings, meetings. At various times when court calendars were desperately overloaded, it was used for arraignments of juveniles, family court proceedings, Night Court, Women's Court; and on this particular Monday morning it was being used by Casey Reardon.

The students sat in uneasy groups along the shiny wooden benches, as subdued and hushed as though they were aligned in pews. The darkness added to the churchlike atmosphere, the altar being a high, unoccupied magistrate's desk in the front of the room. Several men appeared, then disappeared, across the front of the courtroom; yet no one addressed them or gave any indication as to why they had been requested to appear here. They had all received subpoenas to appear before the Grand Jury on Tuesday, relative to the matter of Billy Everett, and had been requested by telegram, received late Sunday afternoon, to present them-selves in this room at 9:30 A.M. They weren't quite sure if this was proper legal procedure, but they had all shown up. Well, this was the District Attorney's show and they waited, miserable, clammy, despondent, in the depressing room.

Casey Reardon lit a cigarette and noted with some sur-prise that his hand trembled.

"How about offering me one, Dad? I could use it."

Reardon extended a cigarette to his daughter Barbara. "I keep forgetting that you're grown up." He held the match to the cigarette, noting that the girl didn't inhale. She blew smoke directly into her eyes and blinked furiously.

"I don't really enjoy it—I'm just very jumpy. And sur-prised, I guess."

Reardon shrugged. "We can't just brush facts away, can we? You were there; you feel a moral obligation to see this thing through. Well, okay. Let's just say that after an unbe-lievably busy weekend I found a minute or two to think about you—about your point of view—and that I feel I don't have the right to make this decision for you, right?"

Barbara nodded, crushed out the cigarette and studied her father. She raised her hand and touched Reardon's cheek. "Dad, you look so tired. Have you been eating—sleeping?"

Reardon laughed sharply and pressed her hand in his, turning her toward the door. "Listen, kiddo, I'm letting you make your own decision this morning, but I'm not reversing roles. Don't start mothering me."

It was the needling, tough, in-charge Casey, and Barbara smiled, reassured. She had spent a long, miserable, disturb-ing weekend at her aunt's cottage upstate and had come to several unpleasant, unacceptable conclusions. The chief con-clusion was the one that pained the most: that her father was, basically, a coward; that he would advocate standing up for what you believe in only as long as you weren't in danger. She had dissected her father completely, going back through the years. Incidents long forgotten came back to her. He had

197

always insisted that she and her sister be willing to take the consequences of their actions, good or bad. Yet when something really important, not just an object lesson but the *real* thing, came up, he surrounded her with a wall of protection and negated everything he had ever taught them. She had been surprised by his phone call last night. All the way from upstate, she sat staring out the train window, wondering what it was all about. He greeted her at his office with a professional remoteness and quietly asked if she wished to make a statement relative to what she had witnessed at the building site on the morning of Billy Everett's death. A stenotypist arrived, Casey asked her questions, made no comments, and the stenotypist moved his fingers steadily over the keys, and the odd narrow tape unwound, filled with cryptic letters. Her statement was typed, Barbara signed it, and it was witnessed by a woman clerk. And that was that.

"Go up to the fifth floor, Room 594, and find a seat. The other witnesses are there. I'll see you in a little while."

"Dad, what's going on this morning?"

Reardon grinned. "That would be telling, wouldn't it? Go on, you'll find out soon enough."

In the small office just off the courtroom, Christie handed her revolver to Stoner, who examined it carefully and gave it back to her. Marty sang softly, the words to his song lost between bites of a Danish.

"Marty, I thought you were on a diet. Besides, how do you have any appetite, with those diet capsules?" Christie asked him.

Marty swallowed. "Cheese Danish is allowed. Besides, I don't take those pills—they ruin your appetite."

Christie shook her head, and looked around at the other men. They seemed so calm. She wondered if she was the only tense person in the room. Casey Reardon looked calm; a little tight, a little quick-moving, but then he always seemed to be holding back some deep driving energy. He was smiling, cracking tough jokes at them, but he seemed at ease, sure of himself. Christie felt an aching weariness beneath the surface tension, and at the pit of her being she felt a terrible dread. The plan—*her* plan—had seemed so great at first telling; everything had seemed so great. But when the damn diet pill wore off, she felt burned out, more empty than she had ever felt in her life. She took a tissue from her pocketbook and wiped her sunglasses, turned at a touch on her shoulder to face Reardon.

"Hey, the eye looks better—you heal fast."

"Yes, it's pretty good. But I need the dark glasses—the doctor said for a day or two. Mr. Reardon, I wanted to talk to you a minute."

"Go ahead."

"Well, this—this whole thing—I . . ." She shrugged, her hand moving emptily in the air. Reardon's fingers tightened around her arm and he pulled her to a quiet corner of the room, leaned against a desk.

"All right, what's the problem?"

"Well—the whole thing. I mean, all of a sudden, the whole thing seems . . . pretty risky."

Reardon's eyes flickered beyond her, then darkened and focused on Christie. "Listen, Opara. Let's get something straight, right now. When you first discussed this plan—you remember, the night you were so goddam high you thought everything was one big joke? Well, I heard you out, right? What did we do all day yesterday? *All of us?*"

"We kicked it around and—"

"We kicked it around and we argued it out and we changed it around and we discussed all the various angles and aspects, right? Seems to me we worked—what was it, eight, nine hours? A lot of people were involved, not just you. We're set now and we're going to let it roll, so you just hang on tight and do just what we planned and you'll be fine."

"But—I feel so *responsible*. I mean, if this thing backfires . . ."

Reardon's face stiffened and he moved so close to her that Christie took a step back. His voice was low and tight. "*You* feel responsible? Well, then let me straighten you out, De-

199

tective Opara. You're looking at the guy who's responsible. This is *my* show. No matter how it falls, I'm the guy holding it. If it works, it works. If it blows up, it blows up in *my* face. It was *my* decision. You got that?"

He walked past her, signaled Stoner, then leaned over a desk, his finger pointing at various names, his voice low, asking questions. Christie heard Stoney comment, "I don't like the Mayor's boys, boss. They seem very edgy. They've been asking a lot of questions."

"The hell with them," Reardon said tersely. "Is Patrolman Linelli all set?"

O'Hanlon jerked his thumb over his shoulder. "Got him in the little interrogation room next door. Boy, he looks like hell."

"He's in uniform, isn't he?"

"Yes sir. Boy, that guy must have lost twenty pounds. The uniform hangs on him."

"Yeah? I wonder what his diet is. I'd like Marty to try it." Again Reardon's voice was bright, sharp and needling. He rested his hand on Marty's shoulder, looked him over. "Ginsburg, you must have gained ten pounds since you started your diet."

There was some quick wisecracking, a final briefing. Then Reardon walked past Christie, turned for a moment, his eyes scanning her briefly. "You look good in blue, Christie. Ought to wear it more often." It was not offered as a compliment, just a statement of fact. Then, the smile tight on his lips, Reardon inhaled. "Okay, fellas. I'm going in. Stay loose."

Casey Reardon stood inside the wooden railing that separated the magistrate's desk from the rows of benches in the courtroom. He held his hands over his head and signaled those in the rear to move forward. "I'm going to ask for your complete attention and cooperation. Would you kindly move to the first three rows so that I can be heard?"

There was a heavy brushing, scuffling of feet, a subdued

sound of voices and bodies as the rows directly in front of Reardon were filled. He waited until the noise faded, then spoke quietly, his voice pleasant and friendly.

"I'd like to thank you all for coming here this morning in response to my telegrams—I believe you all know who I am —Assistant Supervising District Attorney Casey Reardon. I'm responsible for the investigation and preparation of the case involving the death of William Everett, Jr. You have all signed sworn depositions relative to what you witnessed on the day in question and I'd like to brief you relative to what the procedure will be tomorrow morning."

Reardon's voice was that of an instructor: clear, certain, professional. "Now, I assume that most of you know the function of a Grand Jury. It is to hear information, take testimony from witnesses and anyone having direct knowledge relative to a matter under investigation. Before any witnesses are heard, I—as the District Attorney in charge of the case— will make an opening statement, spelling out in detail what the findings of my own investigation—"

The door in the paneled wall to the right of Reardon opened suddenly and two men lurched across the front of the room. The interruption was so startling that for an instant there was complete silence. The first man, a frightened Negro youth dressed in dirty tan denims, was pursued by Stoner Martin who quietly locked his arm over the fugitive's chest and throat.

"For Christ's sake, Stoney, I told you to keep him out of here!" Reardon's voice was harsh and angry.

As the detective tried to pull the boy back, Reardon moved toward them and somehow the boy wrenched free. He turned, stunned by the rows of faces confronting him. He grasped the railing, his fingers curled tightly, and leaned forward. His voice was a ragged scream. "They keeping me in there! They holding me prisoner. For God's sake, somebody get help! Get me outta there—they going to kill me!"

As the boy was shouting, the door opened again and Gins-

201

burg and O'Hanlon raced across the room and joined in a wild struggle, assisting Stoner Martin to pry the boy from the railing.

A voice cracked across the courtroom. "That's Eddie Champion's brother! That's Champion's brother—let him talk! Why you holding him?"

The youth, his arms held in back of him, stared into the courtroom, searching for the person who seemed to have recognized him. "They framed Eddie," he called out. "You seen the papers this morning—they holding him. They saying *he* shot Billy. They trying to frame me, too. Don't let them— don't." An arm was forced across the boy's mouth and his voice was held back.

A tall blond boy leaped from one of the benches and vaulted the railing. He pulled at the detectives, shouting. Reardon's voice called out and the door in the wall opened again and a uniformed police officer, gun drawn and held toward the ceiling, faced the rows of benches. His face was sick and his hand trembled but his voice was strong. "Everybody stay put! No one move. Stay in your seats!"

The Negro prisoner disappeared beneath the shoulders and backs of the detectives; the blond boy fell, pulled a detective down with him, climbed up, was down again. A tall, thin, light-skinned, middle-aged Negro woman burst across the room from the door, dragging Christie Opara with her.

"That's my son!" she screamed. "What are they doing to my son? Help us, please, somebody help us! Dear Jesus, they killing my boy."

"They killed him!" a voice from the benches called out, and his shout was interrupted by a burst of gunfire and a loud, piercing, animal scream. The woman fell on the boy who lay crumpled and silent. She began to wail. Everyone on the benches was shouting and one voice reached over the others, strong and steady. "Reardon shot him! Reardon shot him!"

Barbara Reardon, in the second row, limp against the smooth wooden bench, shook her head slowly, as if she were in a trance. Her voice was a whisper behind her clenched hands. "He didn't. No, he didn't. My father didn't. He didn't."

The Mayor's aides, two young men not quite thirty, chalk-faced and glassy-eyed, moved to the railing, not sure of their authority over the stone-faced patrolman who stood, legs apart, revolver leveled. "Mr. Reardon! Mr. Reardon, we're representatives of his Honor the Mayor."

From the back of the courtroom came a long, shrill, unbelievably loud whistle. All the spectators turned, their mouths open. A tall slender Negro youth stood in the center aisle, his fingers in his mouth. He emitted the whistling sound twice more; then, all eyes on him, the young man took a silver shield from his back pocket and pinned it to his jacket and walked down the aisle. "I am Patrolman Ralph Jenkins. Everyone will please sit down and remain seated."

Casey Reardon yanked a heavy chair from beside the long smooth table inside the railed area and centered it, then stood on it. "There will be no talking." The rows of heads spun from the patrolman to Reardon. "Knock it off. I want absolute silence in this room!"

They obeyed. Shocked, stunned, leaderless, they listened to Reardon. Four young men seated among the witnesses rose, carefully pinned silver patrolmen's shields to their shirts and walked to the front of the room. They reached over the railing and took lined white papers from Stoner Martin, then distributed the papers to everyone on the benches.

"What you have just witnessed," Reardon said carefully, "was all planned. Every word, gesture, action was carefully rehearsed by all participants."

There was a slow, indignant hum within the room, the fear and shock turning now to anger. Reardon silenced them swiftly. "Knock it off—I told you there would be silence in this room. Okay. The 'prisoner' who called out for your help is a patrolman." Reardon gestured and the young man stood up, his eyes on his audience. He nodded solemnly. "The woman who claimed to be his mother is a policewoman." The policewoman, rubbing a wrenched elbow, smiled slightly. "All the people you saw and heard—with the exception of me—are police officers."

A stocky young man waved the sheet of paper over his head to gain Reardon's attention. He stood up and his voice was deep, his words clear. "Mr. Reardon, I am Victor Callum," he said briskly, "third-year law student at St. John's."

Reardon nodded, acknowleging the introduction. He was impressed by the poise and self-assurance of the student.

"Before we go any further with this 'experiment,' I would like to ask just one very pertinent question."

He waited politely for Reardon to consider his request, then continued at Reardon's nod. "Sir, it is apparent at this point that you intend to test our reliability as witnesses. My question is this: What is the authenticity of this test? How do we know that you won't change things to suit your intent?"

What had occurred to Victor Callum so quickly now occurred to the others and they began to call out their demands and protests. Reardon moved his hand, and a familiar figure, the large, easy-moving Commissioner of Human Relations, who had been seated in the rear of the courtroom, came forward.

"You all know me, I believe?" Reardon jumped from the chair and shoved it aside, making room for the Commissioner. "I was with Mr. Reardon and all the people involved in this for several hours last night. They performed what you have seen according to an exact script—exactly as you saw it reenacted here this morning. Mr. Gerald Friedman was also present." He nodded and Gerry came from his seat among the students.

The boy was very pale and his face was damp. His voice trembled when he spoke. "It was all according to an exact script. I can verify that. The Reverend Morse was present last night as was the Commissioner, and Dean Lockwood of the Columbia School of Law. I will assist these gentlemen in evaluating the papers you are going to fill out. We are the control in the experiment."

Reardon brusquely waved down any further comments. "Now, I want your complete cooperation. There is a procedure you are to follow. First, no conversation of any kind. Second, will you kindly seat yourselves throughout the courtroom so that you are not sitting in close proximity to anyone else." There was the noise of feet and bodies, but no words. "Fine. Thank you. Now, you've all been provided with paper and something to lean on. Don't put your name on the paper. In response to my questions"—Reardon held a typed list before him—"you are to answer according to what you witnessed here this morning. First, I would like you to put down, in narrative form—take as long as you want—exactly what happened from the moment I first began addressing you. Naturally, you are to assume that everyone was who he or she claimed to be. Then I will ask you specific questions."

The two young men from the Mayor's office looked about them uncertainly, then looked at Casey Reardon nervously. They decided not to speak, and bent over their papers.

A girl near the back of the room stood up unexpectedly. Her voice, high-pitched and nearly hysterical, declared, "Mr. Reardon, this whole thing is incredible. You staged the whole thing—for what? To prove what? We were entirely unprepared for this and—"

Reardon's voice cut through her words. *"Were any of you prepared to witness the murder of Billy Everett?"*

He kept them as closely guarded as a jury in a first-degree-murder trial. They could smoke, relax, talk, order sandwiches and coffee, leave the room—escorted—for the washroom. They could not leave the building or make phone calls.

Afterwards, it took an hour for the papers to be marked and catalogued and witnessed. The students were restless and irritable and started to protest when Reardon emerged, followed by his control group, and once again distributed papers. His instructions were identical to those he had previously given; they wrote their narratives, then answered his list of specific questions.

The grading of the second papers took less then half an hour. When Reardon approached with papers for the third time, several of the students folded their arms and shook their heads.

"Last time," Reardon said cheerfully. He forced the papers on them, waited for them to finish their narratives. Reardon scanned the serious young faces and he felt a great wave of sympathy and understanding. They were all so young and untouched and earnest. His daughter's face had a stricken look and she never once met his eyes. Some of them, he noticed, seemed to hesitate, to search behind closed eyes for accuracy of recall. He knew their answers would be carefully and honestly given.

He read the list of familiar questions to them. Then, very quietly and unexpectedly, he inserted a new question. "What is the name and shield number of the uniformed police officer?"

There was a gasp somewhere in the center of the room, a startled realization. Reardon's voice was firm. "Not one word. No talking! If you can't answer the question, draw a line through that number."

The final evaluation took nearly an hour. The results of the tests were carefully noted and the Commissioner of Human Relations, flanked by Gerry Friedman and Reardon, addressed them.

"Twenty-seven of you—including the two gentlemen from the Mayor's office, witnessed what occurred here this morning. Relative to the use of revolvers, there were two main points of contention: who drew revolvers, who fired revolvers. In the first statement, in narrative and in response to specific questions, seventeen people stated that Mr. Reardon drew a revolver from his back trouser pocket and fired three shots at the body of the victim, whom twenty-two of you

206

identified as Eddie Champion's brother. One of you stated that the uniformed patrolman fired two shots directly at the victim. Seven stated that each of three detectives drew revolvers and fired one shot each.

"Relative to the uniformed patrolman: in the first go-round, eighteen people stated he drew his revolver when the melee started; five stated he drew his revolver after the shooting had occurred; three stated he did not have a revolver in his hand at any time. All persons who stated the uniformed patrolmen had a revolver in his hand at any time stated it was in his right hand."

The Commissioner's voice rolled over the collection of statements; he did not look up at his audience. Their silence was enough to assure him of their rapt attention. "Nineteen people stated that the alleged prisoner's alleged mother was thrown to the floor by the female detective. Three people stated that the woman forced herself into the middle of the struggle with the prisoner and was violently hurled back by the detectives. One person stated that the woman leaped to a chair and was knocked off the chair by Mr. Reardon. One of you never mentioned her presence. Three people stated she entered the room after the shooting.

"Relative to the words spoken by the prisoner—" The Commissioner shuffled his papers, stopped, then resumed. "Yes. We have *twenty-seven* versions of what the prisoner said. Four are reasonably accurate; the remainder are very disparate and bear no relation to what was actually said.

"Now, before Mr. Reardon and his staff have a reenactment for you, I want to point out one very disturbing factor. In the first statements taken, seventeen people stated that Mr. Reardon drew and fired a revolver at the prisoner. In the second statement, taken one hour later, twenty-four of you stated that he fired at the prisoner. In the third and final statement"—the Commissioner's eyes slowly circled the room—"*twenty-six* people stated that Mr. Reardon fired at the prisoner. Mr. Reardon will now have a step-by-step enactment of the original scene which you witnessed. I will vouch for the authenticity of what you saw earlier and are about to see now."

Once again, Reardon stood before them. Once again, he addressed them, was interrupted by the eruption of violence and sounds and confusion. This time, however, the movements were slowed, the words carefully stated, the speakers easily identified. At crucial points throughout the reenactment, the Commissioner asked them to pause. Then he consulted his papers and read out significant inaccuracies. Then, his eyes on the students, he asked the police officers to continue.

Finally it was over. The shrill whistle hung in the air; the young patrolman, his shield pinned once more to his jacket, stood at the front of the room.

The Commissioner dropped his hands to his sides and his voice was sad. "At no time, as you have observed, did Mr. Reardon *touch* any revolver. Three shots were fired: one by Detective Martin, one by Detective Christie Opara, and one by Policewoman Nielsen, the supposed mother in our little drama, or melodrama. I believe you do not need to have the implications pointed out to you. More than half of you accused Mr. Reardon of the shooting; then, after a few hours of free conversation, *all but one of you named him as a murderer.*"

Reardon's eyes moved irresistibly to Barbara, but she did not raise her face. She was very pale and her hands were clenched tightly in her lap.

Then Reardon addressed them. "Tomorrow morning you are all going to appear before the Grand Jury. As I started to explain to you before, prior to your appearance I will apprise the Grand Jury of the findings of my squad. We have been conducting a very intensive investigation and have uncovered some very pertinent information. I am not at liberty, of course, to disclose any of this to you—nor would I if I could. I will make certain recommendations to the Grand Jury. What action they decide on will be their prerogative. All I ask you to do is to turn over in your minds the events that transpired here this morning. And more importantly, what transpired on the morning that Billy Everett was killed. Bear in mind that the patrolman whom you have accused of the shooting stood unnoticed and unrecognized by any of you for several hours this morning. Bear in mind that this officer is left-handed and that without exception, in your statements this morning, those of you who stated he held or fired a revolver claimed that he used his right hand. In our reenactment, you learned he held the gun in his left hand." Reardon hesitated, shook his head. "I want to thank you all for your cooperation and your time. There is nothing further I can say to you at this time." He turned and walked through the opened door into the small office.

They were waiting for him: his people and the members of the Department he had borrowed on the basis of age, race, appearance, ability. They stopped speaking when he entered the room, but he had caught the note of excitement. The young patrolmen, two of them still at the Academy, were grinning; this had been something new for them—something *real.*

His own people knew better: Stoner, solemn, dark, drawn and exhausted by his total immersion in the case; Ginsburg, eating nervously, compulsively gathering up crumbs of cake; O'Hanlon, whistling mindlessly between his teeth, doodling shapeless little stars on a scrap of paper.

And Christie Opara. Her bruised face was half covered again by the huge sunglasses. The small cut by her lip looked sore. She stood with the motherly policewoman and nodded politely over some gossip, but Reardon knew she wasn't listening. Her thin body looked so vulnerable. Absently, she cradled one elbow in the palm of a hand. Her knees, beneath the short blue dress, were covered with scabs. Her short dark blond hair, cut for a month at the beach, clung damply to the nape of her neck. Reardon's fingers flexed and he had a strong desire to caress those thick, short, damp spikes of hair, to turn her toward him, to handle her, gently—tell her, gently.

The two aides from the Mayor's office were admitted to the room in response to a somewhat hesitant tap on the door.

"Mr. Reardon?" He offered a clammy, limp hand. "I'm Roger Harris and this is Fred Randall. We—er—I guess you know that we weren't briefed at all as to what was going to transpire here today."

There was a definite note of complaint, slightly peevish and annoyed. Reardon snapped at them, "Right. Worked out pretty good that way, didn't it?" What had been an oversight now became an advantage. "We figured we wanted you people from the Mayor's office to be right in the middle of it. No preconceived notions, you know? Well, now you can both give his Honor a completely objective report."

The second aide nodded quickly. "Yes, that was really a good idea. We appreciate your thoughtfulness, Mr. Reardon. Don't you agree, Roger?"

Roger agreed and as he was agreeing, Reardon led them through a door, down a corridor, to a bank of elevators. He jabbed the down button, patted both men on the back, sent his regards to the Mayor with them. When the doors slid closed, Reardon stepped back and said aloud, "Dumb little bastards."

Bill Ferranti and Arthur Treadwell were on the phones when Reardon arrived at the Squad office. They each indicated a series of messages and Reardon scooped them up, reading as he moved toward his own office. He was behind his desk, his finger dialing, before he looked up and saw his daughter. He replaced the receiver.

"Well, now you know what was up this morning. You okay, Barbara? You look sick."

She shook her head. "I'm not sick. I know you're terribly busy, Dad. I think I really understand now how very busy you've been with all this. But, can I have a minute—just a minute?"

Reardon sensed that this was important; he leaned back but he worked at looking casual. "A minute, that's about all."

She clenched her hands, one over the other, then looked

210

up at him. "Dad, I was the one witness who said that you didn't shoot the prisoner."

Reardon shrugged. "Well, then you were the only one who was accurate on that score."

"No. That isn't it." She raised her face toward the ceiling, her eyes closed tightly. "You see, I thought you *did* fire the shots. At least one of them." Her eyes were wide open now and seemed to be pleading with him. "I really thought you did. But when it came to putting it on paper, I just couldn't. Even though I knew it was a test, I couldn't write that you had shot someone."

Reardon didn't move. "Okay, Barbara. You thought I was guilty and you tried to protect me. That's natural enough under the circumstances, isn't it?"

"That isn't the point," she said impatiently.

"*I* know it isn't the point. *But do you?*"

For a moment she was surprised by her father's sharpness, then reassured. It was, after all, the most familiar thing about him. She stood, walked to the front of his desk, and her voice was very soft but certain. "Yes, Dad. The point is—I was not a reliable witness. I really did think I saw you shoot that man. With Billy—with Billy that morning . . ." She faltered, but Reardon didn't help, just waited. "With Billy, there was so much emotionalism involved. In trying to reconstruct it now—after what I learned in that courtroom today—I don't think my statement has any validity. I don't think I should go before the Grand Jury tomorrow and—"

Reardon stood up and his voice was harsh. "*You* don't think you should? Well, you just listen to me, baby. You've been subpoenaed. Weren't you served in the courtroom?" She nodded, fumbled in her pocketbook and held up the document. "Damn right you'll appear."

"But—what will I say?"

"You will respond to the questions put to you. Just like every other witness will do. You'll tell the truth, exactly as you know it. I won't rehearse you any more than I will any other witness. That's the way you want it, isn't it?"

Barbara Reardon carefully folded the subpoena and put it back into her pocketbook. "Yes. That's how I want it."

"Okay, your minute's up. Get out of here and let me get back to work."

"Dad, one more thing."

Impatiently, Reardon smashed the phone back into place. "Now what?"

"Dad, when you can, and try to make it soon, have a talk with Ellen. She has something she wants to discuss with you. It's very important."

"Like what?"

Barbara smiled, pressed two fingertips to her lips. "You've got work to do. Dad, thanks. I really mean it."

Reardon dialed, waited for an answer. He felt a sudden new surge of energy. No matter how this damn thing turned out, at least he had this.

THIRTY-FOUR:

The presentation took three full days. Reardon's opening statement and collection of evidence relating to the Secret Nation took the first full day. He carefully laid the groundwork for his case and backed up each of his accusations with evidence collected by members of his squad. He impatiently answered questions submitted by members of the Grand Jury; they were anticipating him and he refused to be sidetracked. He would present everything he knew in good time.

The Police Commissioner was his first witness and he established the identity and assignment of Patrolman Rafe Wheeler. Stoner Martin continued the narrative of Rafe's short life as a member of the Police Department. A coroner's report was submitted, citing cause of Rafe's death. A ballistics report was introduced relative to the bullet that had caused the death and relative to the gun removed from the hand of one Eddie Champion.

What had been the crux of the matter, in the minds of the Grand Jurors, now became secondary. They listened with interest to the testimony of Detective Christie Opara, interrupted with two or three questions to which she responded quietly. Reardon felt a warm pride; he had seen many normally confident, reliable police officers quake under the scrutiny of the Grand Jury, whose members ranged around the large room, seated on raised chairs. The witness was in the position of a victim in an amphitheater. The chairman of the Grand Jury, a retired industrialist, complimented Christie on her performance and testimony.

The young student-witnesses appeared. One after the other, briefly, they answered Reardon's questions. One after the other, they could no longer swear to their previous statements. When the fourth witness, Gerald Friedman, negated his sworn affidavit, the chairman, indignant, perplexed, demanded an explanation.

Gerry raised his thin face, his eyes bright and steady, his voice firm and clear. "Sir, I am appearing here today in good conscience. My emotional involvement in the entire situation interfered with my good judgment at the time of my original statement. I have had an opportunity to reflect on everything, calmly and unemotionally."

The chairman shot a cold glare at Reardon, then back to Gerry. "Did anyone tell you what to say this morning? Anyone prompt you in any way?"

"Absolutely not!"

One member of the jury mentioned the word "perjury"; he whispered loudly to a man seated beside him and Gerald Friedman raised his eyes, intent on the whisperer. "Sir, if there is any element of perjury involved in my statement here today, or in my written statement made on the day of the shooting, I am unaware of it. It would be perjury for me to stand by my original affidavit. It was made in error. I am correcting that error right here and now."

After he had left the room, the chairman, smiling, asked Reardon, "Law student, no doubt?"

"Third year—Columbia."

Barbara Reardon's words were almost identical to Gerald Friedman's. They were spoken honestly, in a nervous voice that shook with determination. The chairman motioned to Reardon and whispered, "Any relation?"

"My daughter," Reardon said.

"Good girl, good girl," the chairman said.

Only two of the witnesses adhered to their original state-

214

ments. Reardon did not question them beyond their direct testimony and no one had any questions for them.

On the third day, three of Reardon's men carried in a large collection of evidence. Evidence which described the involvement of segments of the Police Department with the Royal Leader of the Secret Nation. The material included a thick manila folder of information carefully prepared by one Tomlin Carver and held in safekeeping for him by one Mr. Richard C. Jackson.

Mr. Jackson nervously glanced past Reardon's head, his eyes seeking the many faces that watched his every move. Reardon leaned close to him. "Mr. Jackson, please speak in a loud clear voice, and talk directly to me. I am the only person who will question you at this time."

Carefully, Reardon led him through a series of identification questions: Yes, he was Mr. Richard C. Jackson. He spelled out his home address, stated his office address; he was an insurance broker.

"When did you first meet a Mr. Tomlin Carver?"

Mr. Jackson pursed his lips, then nodded. "It was two years ago, come next October."

"Would you describe that meeting?"

"Yes. Yes, it was very unusual. I was at my office, which as I said is located on Staten Island. And it was just before lunchtime and this very—large, fat man came into my office and asked if I was Mr. Richard C. Jackson and I said that I was. He sat down on the chair next to my desk—and I remember this so well because—well—the chair collapsed under him."

The Grand Jurors appreciated the predicament of the insurance broker, but Reardon cut through their laughter. "Go on, Mr. Jackson. Did Mr. Carver purchase any insurance from you?"

"Yes. In fact, I didn't even make any suggestions about it to him. He took out a slip of paper, said he wanted to buy twenty thousand dollars' worth of life insurance on his own life. He wanted the beneficiary to be his son, a Mr. Randall Carver, in Chicago."

"Did you prepare the policy for Mr. Carver?"

"Yes. He came to my office a week or so later and paid cash for the policy. Paid up in full for two years, which is unusual, of course."

"Did anything else unusual transpire?"

"Well, yes. Something I didn't like, too much. Mr. Carver —I mean, after all, I had never seen the man before in my life—he gave me a large manila folder, all bound around with string." Mr. Jackson craned his neck, trying to see behind Reardon to where the envelope was on the table.

"What did he tell you about the envelope?"

"Well, he said that it was some very personal documents that he wanted me to keep for him. Said that in the event of his death, from whatever causes, I would be notified. He kept a little card in his wallet with my name and phone number on it, as the person to be notified, which I was of course, as you know and—"

Reardon cut him short. "The envelope. What were your instructions from Carver?"

"Oh. Yes. That I immediately contact Detective Stoner Martin and deliver the envelope to him upon hearing of Mr. Carver's death."

"Mr. Jackson, do you know now, or have you ever known, the contents of that envelope that you kept for Mr. Carver?"

The man shook his head. "No, sir. Don't know. Don't want to know."

"When it was put in your keeping, what did you say to Mr. Carver?"

"Well, I told him I didn't think I was the proper person to have it. I suggested an attorney, but he said he didn't trust lawyers. I suggested a safe-deposit box, but he said that would be too involved and the material would not get to Detective Martin fast enough that way."

Reardon held the envelope before Mr. Jackson. "To the

best of your knowledge, is this the material you held for Mr. Carver?"

Mr. Jackson pushed his glasses against the bridge of his nose, frowned and nodded. "Yes, sir, that's it."

Reardon stepped back, turned to the jurors. The chairman had a question. "Mr. Jackson, have you any idea why this Mr. Carver selected you to safeguard this material?"

Mr. Jackson flicked his tongue over his dry lips. "Well, sir, Mr. Carver, when I asked him that, I thought maybe someone had recommended me, but he said that he picked up the Staten Island phone book, flipped through the yellow pages and picked my name out. Just like that." There was a degree of hurt professional pride in his voice and the chairman told him kindly, "Well, sir, I think he made a wise choice."

At the end of the third day, Reardon's presentation was completed and he went home and slept for twelve uninterrupted hours. The fourth morning, the Grand Jury acted. They moved to indict Eddie Champion for the fatal shooting of Patrolman Rafe Wheeler; further moved to indict Champion for the fatal shooting of William C. Everett, Jr., based on the testimony of Detective Christie Opara. The matter of the attempted assassination of the Mayor of the City of New York would be held pending, as would the homicide death of Tomlin Carver which had been accomplished unwitnessed.

The chairman then read a long list of tentative charges against Darrell Maxwell Littlejohn, also known as the Royal Leader of the Secret Nation, and declared that the jury had settled on one charge of first-degree murder, pending continuation of current investigations. The charge was based on the sworn and witnessed statement of Eddie Champion, made suddenly and unexpectedly and in full knowledge of his grave condition and impending demise. The statement covered some fifteen typed pages and cited twenty-two homicides ordered directly by the Royal Leader and executed by his Royal Guards. The homicide for which Littlejohn had been indicted had been committed by Claude Davis and wit-

217

nessed by Eddie Champion. Davis had not been able to resist a beautiful ruby ring his victim had worn on his right pinky and, acting against all orders, he had wrenched the ring (which bore its owner's intials) from the dead finger, and placed it on his own.

Claude Davis was indicted on a charge of murder-one, based on the statement of Eddie Champion and on a charge of felonious assault against Eddie Champion, based on his own legal confession.

Reardon strode through the squad room, his eyes scanning the activity of his people. He switched on the radio in his own office, jiggled the switch on the air conditioner, hit the machine with the flat of his hand. There was a low growl and a blast of lukewarm air hit his face. He listened to the news report. The commentator had an ominous voice, but his words were more encouraging than anything he'd had to report in many days. The anticipated riot had not occurred. All incidents were under control. Reardon had heard the taped voice of the Mayor several times on television and radio last night. He listened again, with admiration for the quiet guts of the guy. Carefully, calmly, effectively, he reported to the people of his city that the complete facts of the Everett case were in and that the solution was an honest one. To prevent anticipated reaction to his announcement, he had moved quickly. In a clockwork-precision operation, the Mayor appeared, with startling rapidity, surrounded by his aides, on various street corners in various parts of the city. He took along a large group of students: the eyewitnesses, who stood with him, telling the people that it was true: the cop hadn't shot Billy after all.

Reardon didn't know how many people accepted the explanation, but it seemed to have worked. All violence in the city was contained. All the members of the Secret Nation who had been found armed had been arrested and were being held pending bail.

The other part of the city's trouble—that part was being

kept quiet. Reardon switched stations, tuned in soft music. Well, it couldn't be kept quiet for very long. He thought of the Police Commissioner's face: white and waxy, like that of a man who had just been kicked in the stomach. It was rough on him, being brought back into the Grand Jury. The chairman demanded to know why Reardon's people weren't going to continue with the investigation; they were the ones who had uncovered it.

Reardon had replied, "The Commissioner is entirely capable of cleaning up his own house. I have turned all pertinent information over to the Commissioner. It is his responsibility and I have the utmost confidence in his ability to handle the matter properly. If I were in his position, I would insist on this as my right."

The Commissioner had thanked him with one small nod and Reardon was certain he would do a good job. He wanted no part of it himself.

He turned from the radio, grimaced at the disorder of papers and folders and books and reports scattered across his desk. He picked up his calendar, puzzled over the circle around next Friday's date; then, remembering, he swore out loud. He had to prepare that goddam address for that goddam convention: all those out-of-towners. Great. Terrific. Just what he was geared up to do. Maybe he ought to tell the yokels— The soft tap on the door distracted him. "Come on in."

Christie Opara stepped in tentatively. He motioned her to a chair. "I just wanted to tell you that I'm leaving, Mr. Reardon. Stoney said you told him I could when I finished that report for him."

"Going out to the island, huh?"

"Well, for two weeks. I'll save the other two weeks for Christmas, if it's all right with you."

"It's okay with me. You could use a little sun on you. How are all your cuts and bruises and trick knees and things?"

Christie smiled. "A little stiff, but all in all, I'm in good shape."

219

Reardon smiled. His eyes moved slowly over her. "You certainly are."

"Well, I guess everything worked out all right."

"Oh, I think we'll be able to manage without you for a few weeks. I mean, I think there are a few capable people left." Reardon stopped. He hadn't intended to be sarcastic. He didn't even realize he had been until he saw his words register in her eyes: the green deepened and glittered. "Christie, before you leave, I want to tell you that you did one hell of a job. I really mean it."

She watched him suspiciously, waiting for his wisecrack. Reardon laughed. "Hell, put your guard down. I'm not needling you. You were good. Out in the field; with Barbara; before the jury. You really earned your vacation."

"Thanks, Mr. Reardon. I can use it all right. Oh, by the way, Barbara told me about her sister—Ellen."

"Yeah," Reardon said reflectively, "how about that kid? Leaving school to join the Peace Corps. Last kid in the world you'd expect to do something like that. But apparently it was a well-thought-out decision. She convinced me, anyway."

"You sound proud. You should be."

Reardon's mind wasn't on his daughters. He sat down on the couch, arms folded across his chest, his eyes on Christie. "Stand up and let me take a good look at you. Face looks okay, cut pretty well healed. Your legs are still pretty messy. Pretty, but messy. It's a little ridiculous for a grown-up lady to have scabs on her knees. Only little boys and girls are supposed to have scabby knees. Opara, you will have to learn to take better care of yourself."

"I manage."

"What did O'Brien say about you? About the way you got yourself all cut up?"

"I haven't seen him." Christie stopped, bit her lip. That was exactly what Reardon wanted to know. She knew that much, but she didn't know why.

Reardon slapped his hand on the arm of the couch and

220

stood up. "Well, Jesus, how come he didn't see you? If I was a guy crazy about a girl—"

"Gene isn't. Not really. At least, I'm not. We're . . ."

As he spoke, Reardon moved closer to her. He spoke softly, rapidly, ignoring her interruptions. "Hell, I wouldn't let any girl of mine work at a job where she could get herself all—"

"He has nothing to say about my—"

"I'd be goddam sure that she wouldn't be mixed up in all this mess."

"I don't see where you can say . . ."

His eyes were on her lips and Christie lost the sense of what she was saying and what he was saying, and all she knew was that Reardon was kissing her. And that she was kissing him. And that it felt warm and natural and good and—

And Casey Reardon stepped back abruptly and gestured impatiently at the door. "Detective Opara, will you get the hell out of here? You're supposed to be starting on vacation, right?"

"Yes."

"Well, get going. Unless you want to type up a speech for me. Hey, I've got loads of work for you, if you're going to hang around." He faced her again and shook his head. His voice lost the sharp, bantering tone. It was quiet and serious. "Christie, Christie. Look, do me a favor. Do *yourself* a favor. Find some nice available guy who sells shoes or something and get married and stay home and have lots of kids and take care of them and a house and . . ." He rubbed the back of his neck, his hand lingering against the bristles. "Christie, why don't you quit the job? Or—I'll tell you what: This squad is no good for you. You're getting too pushed around. While you're away, I'll arrange a transfer for you. You name it, you got it. Any spot in the Department. How about it? All you have to do is say the word."

His eyes were intent on her.

"Do you really want me to request a transfer?"

221

"I'm asking what *you* want."

Slowly, Christie shook her head. "I like it where I am."

Reardon released his breath, touched her arm, then turned and began moving papers on his desk. He looked up, his face set into an expression of mock annoyance. His voice was too tough, too impatient. "What are you waiting for, Opara? You're on vacation, right? Get going—out!"

Christie Opara smiled, then came stiffly to attention and saluted. "Yes, sir, Mr. Reardon. See you in two weeks, *sir!*"

"Don't be so fresh."

Reardon watched her move across the office. He anticipated the quick turn, the quick smile, the quick wave. He picked up his calendar, counted off the days, then drew a circle around the date when she would return. It seemed a long time off.

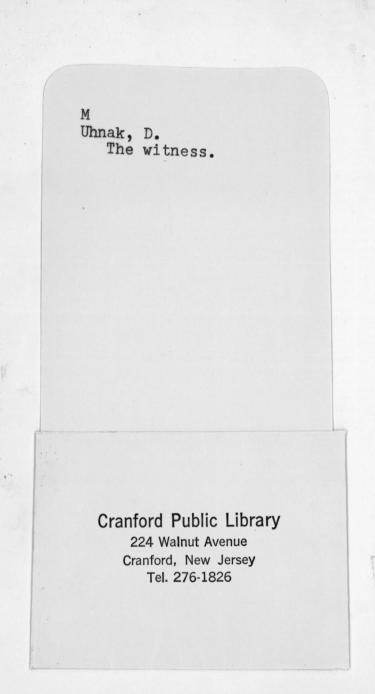

M
Uhnak, D.
    The witness.